Christmas on Jekyll

GEM OF THE GOLDEN ISLES SERIES
BOOK FIVE

BEACH HOUSE
PUBLISHING

Christmas on Jekyll

GEM OF THE GOLDEN ISLES SERIES BOOK FIVE

SANDY MALONE

BEACH HOUSE PUBLISHING

Beach House Publishing

544 Old Plantation Road

Jekyll Island, GA 31527

ISBN: 979-8-9901756-7-9 and 978-1-969221-01-9 (paperback)

ISBN: 978-1-969221-00-2 (ebook)

Cover design by: Patricia Tait, Gravitait Design

Cover photo by: Carol Ann Wages

Printed in the United States of America

Disclaimer

This is a work of fiction. Unless indicated below, all the names, characters, brides, grooms, businesses, places, events, venues, and incidents in this book are either the product of the author's imagination or used in a fictitious manner. Any resemblance to actual persons, living or dead, or actual events is purely coincidental.

Jekyll Market, At Your Service Jekyll Errand Girl, Tribuzio's Grille, Sunrise Grille, Brittney's Closet, and Beach Life Massage are all real businesses on Jekyll Island and the author wholeheartedly recommends and endorses them.

Dedication

This book is dedicated to the very first friend I made in Georgia, Emily Hendrix Slaughter.

Emily was our realtor when we bought our forever home on Jekyll Island, and she was fabulous! But she became a true friend before we even got to closing. She gave us our first Jekyll treasure ball as a housewarming present and told my husband that he'd just have to get used to her hugging him hello, because it was a southern thing. Then she helped me clear out my mom's ginormous house in Jacksonville when she moved up to St. Simons to be closer to us.

Emily, I hope the new Bill Hendrix Art Scholarship, established by the Society for the Enrichment of the Arts on Jekyll (SEAJekyll), will help to preserve your parents' art legacy for future generations. Thank you for being such a good friend. XOXO!

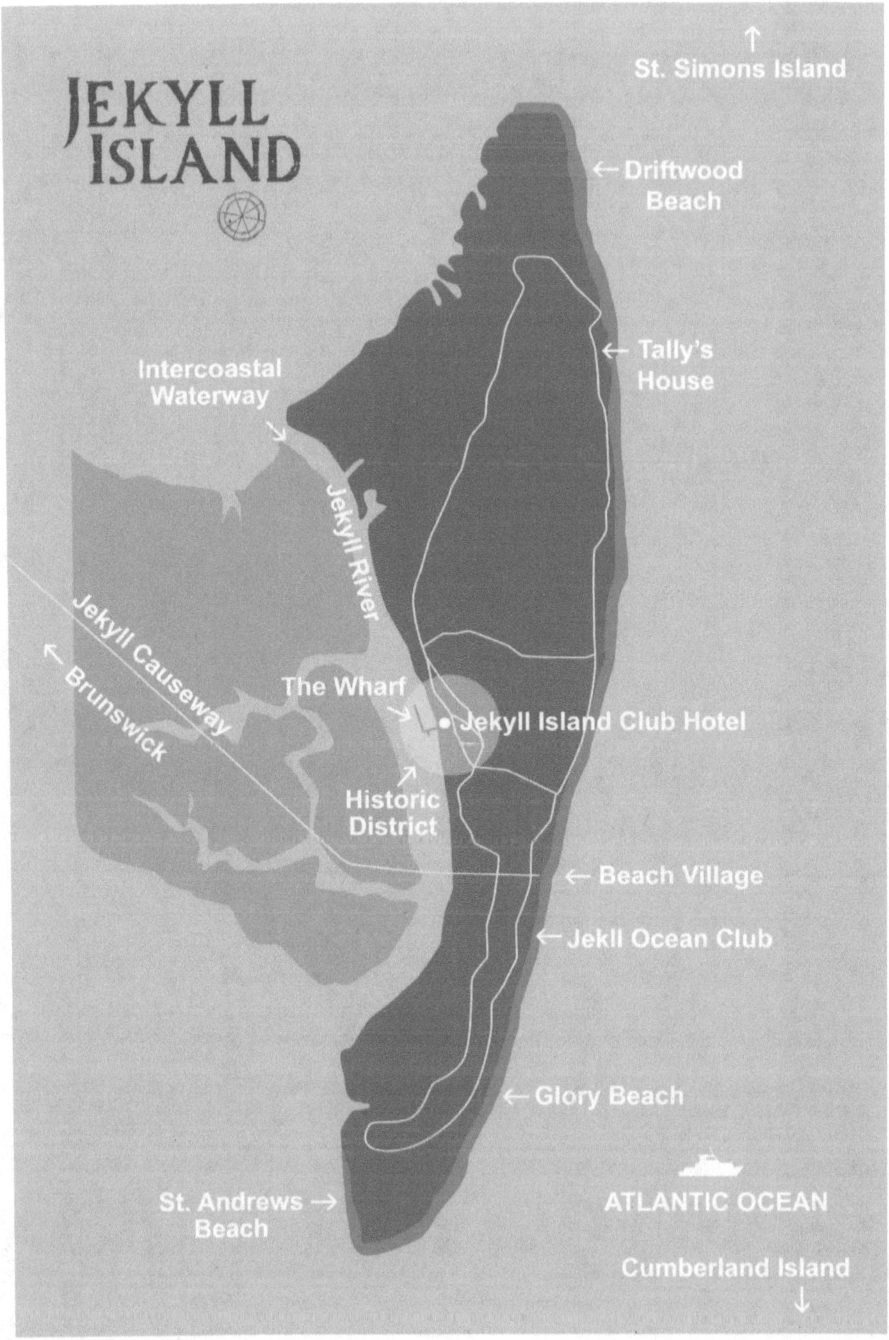

JEKYLL ISLAND
St. Simons Island
Driftwood Beach
Intercoastal Waterway
Tally's House
Jekyll River
Jekyll Causeway
Brunswick
The Wharf
Jekyll Island Club Hotel
Historic District
Beach Village
Jekll Ocean Club
Glory Beach
St. Andrews Beach
ATLANTIC OCEAN
Cumberland Island

Chapter 1

September 2023

Tally Davis stood way back, under the shade of a tree, and watched the small wedding ceremony unfold on Driftwood Beach. She wasn't being sneaky. If any of the women on her staff looked toward the dunes, they could easily see her. But her new wedding planning interns didn't notice because they were busy making a couple's wedding day perfect on the famous beach on the tiniest of the little islands off the coast of Georgia.

Tally wasn't getting too close because she didn't want to freak out the three young women who were running the ceremony. Kayla Hendrix and Kelsi Brooks, her senior account executives, were right there to help if the brand-new interns screwed something up. All three girls had arrived the previous weekend and started training at Jekyll Weddings just five days earlier.

Yesterday, the interns had assisted as Kelsi executed a flawless wedding for a sweet older couple from Alabama with 40 guests on the lawn at the historic Jekyll Island Club Hotel. Kayla had been there, too, just in case something went sideways. Kelsi could do a wedding that size with her eyes closed, but the college girls helping her were an unknown quantity.

Kayla, who'd been with Jekyll Weddings for more than five years, told her boss afterwards that she'd found herself having to poke the new girls into action at the historic hotel more than she thought she should. But she allowed that it was their first event, and the Jekyll Island Club Hotel was a bit intimidating even to her, despite having executed at least 50 weddings there, so they might just be getting comfortable. At least that's what Kayla told Tally when she reported in after the wedding was over.

Kayla and Kelsi had talked their boss into hiring interns to help them juggle the overload of wedding bookings that never seemed to let up. Tally's social media marketing efforts over the past few years had been really successful – so successful that she was turning away as many potential clients as she was booking. And that wasn't good for her reputation. Yet Tally lived in mortal fear of growing her wedding planning business too quickly and losing control of things. She could only be in one place at a time, and the idea of her company doing three weddings on three different islands on the same day was overwhelming. If they hired interns who were in their senior year of college, or who had just graduated, they could extend job offers to them at the end of their internships if they were awesome. Both account executives had been interns with other wedding planning companies before they'd come to work for Tally and they were spectacular. Kayla and Kelsi had promised the extra training effort would be worth it.

Tally was cautiously optimistic about the three girls flittering around on the beach – *wait, why was the brunette sprinkling rose petals toward the water?*

She could tell nobody else had noticed so she took a couple steps forward and waved to get Kayla's attention. They made eye contact, and she pointed to the oversized flower girl who had just literally thrown rose petals into the water and seemed to be watching them float away. Kayla started laughing and yelled something in the intern's direction. Tally watched her walk over and explain to the intern that they usually put the rose petals *down the aisle,* not from the ceremony spot into the water.

A moment later, a text popped up on Tally's phone. "Don't worry, I have extra petals," Kayla wrote, followed by an eye roll emoji. Tally responded with a laughing emoji.

Tally figured that no matter how smart the new interns were, or how enthusiastic Kayla and Kelsi were about supervising them, she would have to keep her eye on things for a while. There were a lot of moving pieces for a wedding, and if you screwed something up, there was no fixing it.

"There are no do-overs in weddings," Isabelle, her former boss and current mentor, always said. If you dropped the ball or forgot to do something on a wedding day, you couldn't undo that mistake. There was no fixing it. One shot only. If you messed up, the bride and groom would always remember that they were supposed to have had cupcakes, in addition to the brownies, at their day-after beach party. And they would never forget if their wedding planner forgot to put a certain song on the DJ's *do-not-play* list.

Tally knew she sounded dramatic when she talked about how important it was to triple-check every list and always have an extra of things on hand. But truly, all it took was one disappointed bride posting a one-star review on Wedding Wire about how the wedding planner forgot to put her dead father's picture on the first seat at her ceremony. Or writing about how her wedding planners let a random drunk guest get ahold of the microphone during toasts, after the bride and groom had given them a specific list of people who were invited to speak. It would only take a couple of pissed-off brides to completely tank Jekyll Weddings' hard-earned, five-star rating on the most important marketing website online and that was not a risk that Tally Davis was willing to take.

She watched the action from afar and eventually plopped her butt in the sand. Tally had assumed her assistance would be needed and she hadn't considered bringing a chair for watching. But Kelsi and Kayla had the routine down and they rarely needed her anymore. Which was a good thing, since 35-year-old Tally Davis ran her wedding and flower businesses on Jekyll Island in addition to being the mother of twin toddlers, Molly and Moody, and the wife of a state trooper.

Something was happening at the wedding setup down the beach, Tally noticed, and she forced herself to tune back in. She checked the time on her phone, looked at the schedule, and smiled. She watched Kayla answer her phone and spring into action.

Kayla said something to Kelsi and then started walking up the path to the parking area at Driftwood Beach with two interns hot on her heels. *The wedding couple must be arriving*, Tally thought.

As if by magic, a wedding suddenly appeared on the beach in front of her. The minister, wedding photographer, and a guitarist all took their places. The photographer trailed the wedding planners up the path to get arrival shots of the bride and groom. The minister took his place on the sand at the spot where the rose petals were supposed to end. And the guitarist started playing whatever the couple had chosen – Tally was too far away to hear it – standing where the path met the beach so that the bride could hear the music the entire walk down the aisle.

Nicely done, she thought. She had taught Kayla and Kelsi well, and they were passing it on to the interns. Maybe they were onto something with this recruiting strategy. She reminded herself to thank her account executives for coming up with the idea and executing the plan as she sat back to watch the show.

***

Kayla stopped the interns on the beach side of the road, and they waited together while the Westin hotel van pulled up to deliver the bride and groom, Lisa Howell and Alex Wilde, and their tiny flower-girl daughter, Alexandria, to Driftwood Beach to get married.

She had snuck out of the wedding that Kelsi was supervising over at the Jekyll Island Club Hotel last night to greet this couple and help get them settled at the Westin. Upon arrival, Lisa and Alex seemed like perfectly normal people and Kayla was relieved. She'd chosen them for the interns' first wedding because it was a standard elopement package with a specific list of things to provide. They hadn't added anything weird or wonderful to their wedding and so it made an excellent teaching model for the new arrivals. Everything had been planned for six months, and all the interns had to do was follow the established checklists.

Lisa and Alex were from Atlanta and Kayla knew from their conference call that they both worked in finance for different firms. They'd been engaged for more than five years but hadn't had time to plan a wedding because they were too busy building their careers. The unplanned arrival of Alexandria about 18 months earlier had changed their paths yet again, and today they were finally making it all legal.

"Wrong order, right decision," Alex joked on their call.

He was a good-looking guy. Tall and muscular, with thick, dark, curly hair that extended into a full beard that had become the style during the pandemic. Very Paul Bunyun. Kayla was not a fan, but she didn't have to kiss him, so it wasn't her problem. Lisa was adorable – she was about five feet tall with wavy, blonde hair so perfect that you would assume it was dyed, if you weren't looking at her little mini-me standing next to her with the exact same natural tresses.

They were getting married on Jekyll Island today and then boarding a month-long cruise out of Port Canaveral in Florida tomorrow afternoon. Lisa had explained that they had a full-time nanny for Alexandria at home in Atlanta, and they were terrified they were missing out on the best part of her childhood. They were able to steal this time away together as a family, so they'd given the nanny the month off and were going to share their honeymoon with their little girl and make amazing memories.

"Everybody smile," Kayla told the interns as she waved a welcome at the approaching shuttle. The interns copied her, smiling and waving. But the people inside the van weren't smiling and waving back.

She was careful to keep a happy expression on her face as she said, "That doesn't look good."

The wedding planning team could hear the screaming before the door of the shuttle van opened. The bride got out of little bus, much faster than Kayla could have moved in that big Cinderella wedding dress, carrying a sobbing little girl in her arms. Lisa ignored the wedding planners and walked away from the shuttle, over to the shade of a nearby tree. She set Alexandria down, squatted next to her, and talked softly as the little girl slowly calmed down.

Alex didn't get off the shuttle van – which was weird – so Kayla went looking for him.

"What the?" Kayla stopped short of saying what was in her mind when she caught sight of the groom. She started to laugh, but then she saw the tracks of tears on the big man's face. "Oh no." Suddenly, the situation was clear to her. She pulled out her phone to call Tally, but first she confirmed her suspicions.

"Tell me what's going on."

"I didn't have a beard when I proposed to Lisa and so I thought I'd surprise her for the wedding by shaving it off. It's been years and she isn't really a big fan of it," he explained. "I didn't think about tan lines or the fact that Alexandria wouldn't recognize me. I scared her."

The big man started to cry, and Kayla shot off a text to Tally. "Need you ASAP at shuttle. Dad shaved. Baby freaked. Need a mom fix." She wasn't sure it made that much sense, but Tally would get it when she arrived and saw the groom's face.

Alex obviously spent a lot of time outside – he'd said something about wishing he had time to golf on Jekyll so maybe that was it – but she would have never guessed that his face was *that* pale under the beard. It almost looked like he had put on white face paint where the beard had been. Or that somebody had done a really, really bad job applying bronzer. Ugh. Why hadn't they called her about this? She could have helped.

"It's going to be fine. I know it doesn't seem like it now, but this is going to make for an absolutely hilarious story in a few years. The pictures will say it all. And might I suggest that you all consider doing your first anniversary back here on Jekyll and we can retake these pictures with your face looking less like... like it does right now," Kayla tried to sound diplomatic, but she couldn't help smiling.

It made Alex laugh. Kayla passed him the small pack of Kleenex she always carried and told him to get himself cleaned up while she checked on his girls.

Outside, she found Tally holding Alexandria, rocking her a bit, and chatting with Lisa, who was trying to make her wedding dress look as though it hadn't been mangled by her flower girl. The interns were standing where she'd left them, clearly unsure whether to involve themselves. But they'd gathered the necessary ceremony items and were waiting for further instruction. *Good call, ladies,* Kayla thought.

"Just hang here while I see what's up," she told them softly, and took the basket of rose petals sitting in a box next to them. She approached Tally and Lisa slowly, not wanting to upset Alexandria now that she was smiling and calm.

"Has anybody seen a flower girl?" Kayla asked. "I only see two brides, and I was told there was a flower girl here."

Alexandria giggled, and that made Lisa smile. The little girl struggled to get down on the ground and pose next to her mother. Her dress was a teeny-tiny identical version of Lisa's wedding gown. A true mini-me. And now, both of the brides were smiling.

"So, what's our plan?" Kayla asked Tally softly.

Chapter 2

"Well, that was certainly a baptism by fire," Tally laughed, clinking her bottle of Mike's Hard Lemonade against Kelsi's. Kayla was drinking bottled water, and she held it up in the air in solidarity.

The wedding planners were sitting on lounge chairs on Tally's front porch looking at the waters of the Atlantic Ocean as the sky got dark. They weren't watching sunset because the oceanfront house faced east. But it was Tally's favorite time of day on this side of the island because there was nobody around. All the tourists were watching the fire in the western sky over the Sidney Lanier Bridge from the bar at The Wharf or Zachry's on the river side of Jekyll Island.

"For a minute there, I didn't think we were going to have a wedding," Kayla admitted.

"I was just standing down on the beach wondering what was happening up there since nobody bothered to update me," Kelsi joked in a snippy voice. "I just stood there with Liz – that's the brunette's name, by the way – and made conversation while we patiently waited for you guys to send Lisa down the aisle 20 minutes late.

"I think it was probably good – I told her at least 10 times that sometimes you just have to stand and wait til whatever is happening that you can't see gets resolved and things start moving again. And I led by example," she added.

"Yeah, I'm sorry – we should have used the radios, and I should have kept you in the loop," Kayla admitted.

"I'm just giving you a hard time," Kelsi quickly replied. "We never use radios for elopements unless there's something unusual planned."

"Maybe we should," Tally suggested. "Now that we have all these new girls training. I didn't overhear anybody saying anything stupid, but we do need them to learn how to work their radios and use them to communicate at big venues. Today would have been excellent practice time."

"Valid," Kayla agreed. "We'll put it on the supply list."

"We are all learning right now," Tally said. "So, what did you think of their performances today?"

It hadn't gone as planned, obviously, because nobody had anticipated that the flower girl would not recognize her daddy after he shaved – or rather, nobody had advised them of his plan to shave it so the professionals could tell him it was a bad idea. While the plan had called for the interns to run things, Tally had jumped in to help, and Kayla never really handed them the reins. Once things went sideways for the clients, there was no chance they were going to put the rest of the ceremony into the newbies' hands. That said, if they were paying attention, all three interns would have learned some important lessons today.

Once the flower girl was calm, Tally led Alexandria over to the shuttle van and had her stand on the steps where she couldn't see into the vehicle. She told the little girl to call for her daddy and see if he was inside. She did and Alex responded, and she recognized his voice. She poked her head into the van to look for her daddy, saw the beardless Alex, and started freaking out again. But she stayed put, holding Tally's hand, while Alex talked to her in a soothing voice and after a few minutes, she stopped trying to run away from him.

Tally negotiated with her. Alexandria was willing to walk down the aisle with her mommy holding her hand, as long as she didn't have to get too close to that man who said he was her daddy.

"It's fine," Alex laughed when the process was explained. "I've got another 75 years to tease her about this. I wish we'd paid for a video."

"I'll have an intern film everything if you want," Tally offered. "It won't be fancy, but it will still be hilarious."

"Thanks. That would be great."

"I need you to get off this shuttle bus now and follow the path to the beach and find the minister who has been patiently waiting for you. He'll be the sweaty guy wearing shoes and khakis beside a circle of rose petals," she winked at the groom. "Smile as you go because the minute you step off the shuttle, you'll be in pictures!" Her tone had changed to upbeat and perky in an effort to spread the wedding joy.

Alex read her vibe and smiled. Then he followed her instructions perfectly and went to get married. He proceeded carefully, giving a wide berth to the little flower girl who was still eyeing him suspiciously. But Lisa mouthed "I love you" at him as he walked by and the wedding planners could see him stepping more lightly.

As anticipated, Alexandria stole the show. She'd been training for weeks for this day, having had her mommy repeatedly read her all the available books about being a flower girl at bedtime. She knew that she was supposed to put the petals down in front of the bride, but she wanted to hold her mommy's hand. The earlier plan had called for her to sprinkle her way down the aisle to her daddy and wait for her mommy there. That wasn't going to happen today.

Alexandria solved the problem herself by making the bride stop every 10 yards or so to wait while she ran ahead to scatter rose petals. Then she'd tear back to Lisa, take her hand, and drag the bride as far as the end of the petals before starting the process all over again. It took a long time to get them to the ceremony spot, but the pictures and video would be priceless.

The Westin's shuttle driver had hung around for the ceremony because by then, he was so invested in the drama that had unfolded in front of him, there was no way he wasn't staying to see if they ever got to the "I do" part of the day. That meant he was still there after the ceremony when Alexandria started acting scared of Alex again.

The wedding team saw them off and then called the Westin to warn them the bride and groom were headed back their way a little earlier than planned. Fortunately, they'd arranged a special wedding dinner on a private terrace that would give the three of them a chance to recover. When they returned to their room, they'd find a bottle of champagne, and a few different flavors of Capri Sun, waiting with a card signed by the Jekyll Weddings team.

"I thought your interns handled it all pretty well," Tally told Kayla and Kelsi. "I'm glad they stayed quiet and watched because the whole scene was already feeling chaotic. We didn't expect them to know how to handle that one. I wasn't entirely sure what I was doing.

"It's happened a couple of times with our twins because Mitch has had to grow a beard for undercover stuff on the task force. And one time, he came into the house in camo face paint when the twins were still up," she shook her head at the memory. "Bet he won't do that again," she joked, her blond curls bouncing. She looked much younger than her 35 years and could be easily mistaken for one of her young employees.

"I'm just glad you were there," Kayla said, and Kelsi nodded her head vigorously in agreement.

"I would have told you I was coming but I wasn't sure that I would make it in time. My conference call with that historic wedding planner lady ran a lot longer than I planned," Tally explained. "What she wants to do with us is pretty cool, but I need to read through everything she emailed to me and think about it before I loop you two in."

"That's fine, because I have enough stuff on my to-do list right now. I had no idea that living with the interns would be such a time suck," Kelsi made a face and then took a big gulp of her spiked lemonade.

Tally and Kayla burst out laughing. Living with the interns they hired had been Kelsi's idea and they tried to talk her out of it. Kelsi had politely reminded them that Tally had put her in charge of figuring out the girls' accommodations for the next 12 months. She was determined to keep them on Jekyll so she wouldn't have to figure out transportation to the office for them. She considered the fact that she could save some money by rooming with them a bonus for her efforts.

So, Tally and Kayla kept their mouths closed and did a lot of eyerolling while Kelsi found a long-term rental for all of them on Old Plantation Road.

***

It was a two-story, free-standing guest house with a full bathroom and a tiny kitchenette that consisted of a fridge, microwave, and coffee maker. It was located in the backyard of the house across the street from Susan McLemore and it wasn't for rent when Kelsi found out about it.

The main house was kept as a rental property. The owners were elderly and lived in New England and the house had been rented out 12 months a year for as long as anyone could remember. But the guest house wasn't included in the rental. It was locked up tight and filled with items the family didn't want the renters to use. According to Susan, the owners had never been interested in renting out the guest house. But Kelsi hoped that might have changed. Susan gave her a phone number for the owners and wished her luck.

At that point, Kelsi enlisted the help of Tally's Aunt Etah, who it turned out knew the family who owned the house. It wasn't a surprise. Etah Davis knew everybody on Jekyll Island, and everybody knew her. If she hadn't personally known the Lynches, Mitch's grandmother, Bonnie, probably would have. Etah and Bonnie had lived across the street from each other on Jekyll Island forever and had been some of the first "commoners" allowed to build private homes after Jekyll became a state park.

Etah, newly retired from her life as a political journalist, had ambitiously jumped in to help Kelsi get in touch with the Lynch's oldest son, who was managing his parents' property now that they were both in assisted living. By the time Tally heard about Aunt Etah's involvement in securing a lease on the guest house, the deal was pretty much done. And Kelsi had brought it in way under budget.

"None of us have been there in 10 years," Brian Lynch admitted to Etah, whom he remembered from childhood. "I don't even know what's in the guest house. I probably should come down and clean it out, but I haven't had time. From what I remember, it's mostly bikes and stuff like that. Your girls are welcome to use it or toss the stuff that's gotten too old."

Etah knew Brian had three children and saw his parents several times a week, and she understood his conundrum. By the time they hung up the phone, Etah had talked him into letting Jekyll Weddings rent the guest cottage for at least one year, with an option to extend, and promised that she and Kelsi would box up anything family-related that should be with them in New England.

He told her they could throw out whatever they wanted to get rid of and paint the interior at his expense (he'd buy the paint if Kelsi wanted to do the work) and they'd agreed on a rental price that included everything except the electric. He was going to have a separate meter put on the guest house so they could pay exactly what they used, rather than trying to split the cost of their window units with what it was costing them to cool the big house for renters.

Tally could only smile and approve the plan when it was presented to her – Kelsi had double-checked every detail.

"I went over and got the keys to the guest house from Jekyll Realty," Kelsi explained. "And I checked it all out and made a video for you guys to see," she pulled out her phone.

"It was crazy hot inside, so I turned all on all air conditioners – I think nobody has been in there in 10 years for real – but the AC works, even if the one upstairs is kinda loud. But that's okay because I have an idea about that. It's going to be my room, and I sort of like the idea of a sound buffer since there's no door."

"No door?" Tally asked. "This sounds like a horrible plan."

"No wait," Kelsi stopped her. "It's a great plan. And as for no door – think of a loft in New York City."

"Okay," Tally smiled and tried to look enthusiastic, but she wasn't sure she succeeded. She was just glad she didn't have to live there with them in a house with no doors.

"Right now, there's a queen bed downstairs and two sets of bunk beds upstairs," Kelsi explained. "I'm going to flip it, so I basically have a studio apartment upstairs, and the interns live downstairs."

"Isn't that going to be crowded?" Kayla asked. She wasn't going to poopoo Kelsi's plan. She had recently moved in with her fiancé, Kelsi's younger brother, Jake. And Kelsi lived there, too. She was close with her veterinarian brother, and they were good roommates. Until he asked her best friend to marry him and Kayla sort of stole her spot. At least that was how Kayla saw it.

Kelsi didn't agree with that assessment at all. She was thrilled Jake and Kayla were engaged. She said she didn't want to live with them, but she would continue to claim pool privileges at her brother's house forever.

"I thought about that, but I think it will work," Kelsi said. "Remember, the plan is to keep the girls on for a year, but we know that won't happen with all of them. Some will quit, or not be good enough to be extended for the winter and spring weddings, so we'll replace them. By providing their housing as part of the compensation package, nobody has to find a place to live to work for us. And we won't feel as badly if we have to send them home because they won't have signed leases."

"Good point," Kayla added. "It's actually a good deal for them, crowded or not. They get a monthly stipend, plus housing. They get fed constantly at the office and wedding events. They'll literally never be home except to shower or sleep. You guys are going to have to figure out a morning schedule that works with four women and only one bathroom though," she still sounded a little skeptical.

"Nah, it'll be fine. I always shower at night, and I'll get in and out of the bathroom fast in the mornings. It'll just be the three of them fighting over it while I get ready upstairs. I'm going to get a big armoire with a mirror on it to give them extra closet space, and then they'll have more than one place to put on makeup or do hair. It'll be like a dorm room," Kelsi said. "And I'm the house mom."

***

Jake, Kayla, and Kelsi spent a lot of free time working on the little guest cottage before Kelsi moved in, and the house was adorable by the time Tally and her husband were invited for a tour, the week before the interns arrived.

They stopped to read a sign on the cottage's sliding windows that faced the main house. "This is a private property occupied by full-time residents. Please do not trespass," it read.

"Smart," Tally's husband, Georgia State Patrol Trooper Mitch Durham, observed. "People are nosy. They should keep the curtains pulled anytime they're gone, or all the time if there are renters in that main house."

"They'll rarely be home in the daytime, Mitch," Tally laughed. "Think about my wedding schedule and make theirs 10 times worse." She led him across a path of steppingstones to the side of the little guest house.

There was a small bike rack mounted against a tree by the side door with three brand-newish looking bikes parked in it. Tally smiled as she figured out how Kelsi had solved the transportation problem. There were plenty of vehicles to go around on event days but letting the girls take a work vehicle home was a liability.

She'd granted a delivery driver take-home privileges last year and he'd used the Jekyll Flowers van to help sex-traffickers ferry women after they'd been snuck into the country via the nearby Port of Brunswick. She wasn't going to do that again. While it was unlikely any of her college-aged interns would be running drugs or women, she wasn't willing to risk having them drink and drive, or do anything else irresponsible, after hours in her business vehicles.

Therefore, Tally thought the bikes were an excellent plan for commuting on the one-mile by seven-mile island. Most of the places they'd need to get to on bikes were within a couple of miles, and the entire island was ringed with a beautiful bike path. She noticed that all of the bicycles had baskets on the front and some sort of carrier bag attached under their seats. It occurred to her that they should order Jekyll Weddings backpacks for the interns to make life a little easier. It would also be good advertising.

Mitch police-knocked on door on the far side of the little house and Kelsi answered it immediately.

"Come in!" Kelsi greeted them with a smile and swung the door wide.

There was a narrow staircase to the upstairs directly in front of them, and a sizeable room to the right. Almost one entire wall was a big glass window with a slider. It was covered by what Tally assumed were new curtains. Kelsi pulled them open to show off the view.

"It's got lots of light but if they want to sleep through on a down day, it's pretty dark with all the curtains pulled," she demonstrated.

"I thought about debunking one of the beds, but then I figured that all of them would have a friend visit at some point so having an extra bed was probably a good idea. I bought this crazy pillow that converts that bottom bunk into a sofa for them to hang out on when it's unoccupied," she flopped on the makeshift couch to demonstrate and pointed to the TV on the opposite wall. "The Wi-Fi is all set up on this TV, and I have a TV upstairs, too."

The white wooden bunk beds were situated perpendicular to each other on adjacent walls. They both had drawers underneath them. Kelsi had chosen the linens and décor well and it looked like an awesome beach cottage to vacation in. There was an armoire on one wall and a small round table in the center of the room with chairs around it. There were lights wired beside the beds for reading, and a fun chandelier hung over the table in the middle. Underneath the TV, which was mounted close to the ceiling in a corner, was a tiny kitchenette that had everything the interns might need. There was a half-size fridge, a microwave, and a coffee maker.

"I have a small fridge upstairs, too. But I figured that was enough load on the breaker box without accidentally trying to use two microwaves at the same time. I have a feeling we're going to knock out the lights a few times with our hairdryers and curling irons," Kelsi explained. Tally laughed at the prospect while Mitch nodded in agreement with her assessment.

She showed them the tiny bathroom, decorated in a rubber ducky theme, and explained that they had their own hot water heater, separate from the main house.

"That's good. You don't need to share hot water with a houseful of renters after a long day," Tally pointed out.

"And whenever there's nobody in the main house, we can use that awesome outdoor shower on the patio," Kelsi pointed out the window to a wooden structure on the back of the main house.

"We can get in and out through the garage or by using the side gate – whatever's easier depending on whether you're on a bike you need to pull into the backyard," she explained. "Do you want to see my apartment now?" The younger woman grinned at her boss and bounded up the stairs, two at a time.

"Her apartment?" Mitch mouthed at Tally, amused.

"Shhhh," Tally held a finger to her lips. "Don't ruin the illusion." They followed Kelsi up the stairs.

Her "loft," as Kelsi also called it, was adorable. She had downsized from a queen bed to a double and boosted it up to give herself more storage underneath, the same way Tally had in her dormitory at Georgetown. Her TV was also mounted on a wall, and a variety of refinished old dressers and an armoire completed the shabby chic look. She had a loveseat with a throw blanket over it and a coffee table made from a fallen live oak tree branch that Tally knew Kelsi had picked up for free in a neighbor's giveaway pile. All of the fabrics in the room were Lilly Pulitzer, or something close enough that you wouldn't know otherwise, and it was a cheerful space for a young woman to occupy.

"I love it," Tally declared.

"So do I."

"Good, because you're stuck with it for at least a year. I signed the lease," Tally reminded her young protégé.

***

Tally put an end to the party on her deck an hour later, after Kelsi's stories of her first week living with the interns made Kayla and her laugh so hard that it hurt. On the plus side, she'd learned the interns' names and a little bit more about each of them. At least, she thought she had them straight now. Although she'd have to resist the urge to use the nicknames Kelsi had given them.

Liz Harley was from Columbus, Ohio. She was a short, chubby brunette who got all excited when she found out that Kelsi's brother, Jake, was a Buckeye, too. Liz had just graduated from an event planning program at THE Ohio State University (yes, that's exactly how she wrote it on her resume) and came highly recommended by an event planner she'd worked for last summer. Kelsi called her "Baby Buckeye" and found her eternal optimism and perk seriously annoying at both 8 a.m. and 10 p.m.

"Little Miss Maidenhead" was what Kelsi called Tori Maidenhead of Savannah, Georgia. Tori was a budding senior in the Hospitality and Tourism Management School at College of Charleston. She needed this internship to be a success in order to receive enough credits to graduate in May, and her stress level showed it. But she'd gotten off to a rough start with both Kelsi and Kayla – separately, they'd both caught Tori surfing social media when she should have been paying attention to what was happening right in front of her. When Kelsi tried to talk to her about it, she'd become defensive and explained she was missing fall rush at her sorority and was questioning her decision to intern so far away from school. Kelsi told Kayla and Tally that if anybody was going to wash out, she'd put her money on "Little Miss Maidenhead Pain-in-the-Ass." She looked like a sorority girl and wore her obviously-dyed, platinum hair in a ponytail with a bow most of the time.

Tally had learned the most about Katy Caldwell, a New Yorker who had just graduated from the University of Florida in Gainesville with her degree in event management. She didn't chatter as much as the other two and Kelsi had instantly bonded with her. Unfortunately, so far, Katy had proven to have a real problem arriving anywhere on time when she had to do it under her own steam.

Kelsi had told the girls the day they arrived that she was happy to give them a ride to and from work if they were ready to go when she was, but that she wouldn't wait around for anybody when it would take them less than 10 minutes to ride a bike over to the Jekyll Weddings office, which was located next door to the Jekyll Market in Beach Village.

Kelsi was, admittedly, not a fan of mornings, and she didn't want to make conversation with anybody before she'd had her morning coffee. She usually waited to do that at the office, where she could take advantage of the Nespresso machine and Yaya's fancy coffee creamers. Therefore, when she was ready to leave for the office, she was trying to get to her first cup of coffee. No pokey intern was going to stand in the way of that.

Despite the warning, Liz and Tori had been horrified when Kelsi left Katy behind on her very first Monday at Jekyll Weddings. Kelsi wasn't thrilled she'd had to do it, but she'd warned them the night before that she would be rolling out at 8 a.m., with or without them. The interns didn't *have to* be at the office until 9 a.m., so they could wait and leave 45 minutes later and ride a bike over in plenty of time. Kelsi always went in earlier than she had to be there – especially on a Monday - because that way, she was certain to have had coffee before the unpleasant stuff hit the fan.

If Katy had been almost-ready, Kelsi would have waited a few minutes for her that first day. But Liz and Tori reported that Katy had just stepped into the shower when the clock struck 8. Being *that late* made riding to work her first day her own fault. Kelsi called her "Late Kate."

"We've gotta stop," Tally told them for at least the third time, wiping tears from her eyes. "I need to get the kids to bed and make some dinner before Mitch gets home. We're supposed to be having a stay-in date night."

"You'd better shower then," Kayla told her, matter-of-factly.

"Thanks girlfriend," Tally snarked. "I planned to do that after I put Molly and Moody to bed."

The girls stopped to say goodbye to the twins, who'd remained curled up on the sofa watching cartoons throughout Kayla and Kelsi's visit. The two women were in and out of their house so much, Tally's kids thought they both belonged to them and called them Aunt Kayla and Aunt Kelsi. She didn't know who had started that, but she and Mitch were perfectly okay with it.

"Anybody want to place a bet on whether Late Kate rides to work with me on Monday?" Kelsi asked as they were leaving.

Kayla, the more serious of the two, rolled her eyes and sighed. "It's like she's cheering for one of them to wash out."

"Sort of," Tally agreed.

"No, I'm not," Kelsi whirled around to defend herself. "It's just that statistically, with this sort of internship program – long hours, shitty pay, remote location, etc. – one of the three of them will opt out within the first two weeks."

"Stop playing with AI and give the kid a chance," Kayla scolded her. "You're not a great morning person yourself."

"Yeah, but I've never made you late to anything, ever."

"Touche," her best friend agreed.

Chapter 3

Tally dreaded the month of September every year. As a wedding planner on a barrier island off the coast of Georgia, she spent the entire month watching the National Hurricane Center app and stalking "Mike's Weather Page" on Facebook, because he was right more often than the Weather Channel.

The good news was that Jekyll Island's location, so far south in Georgia that it was almost in Florida, had proven lucky for the tiny island. Most of the storms that came up the East Coast seemed to bounce off Florida, and go around the Golden Isles, as Jekyll, St. Simons, and Sea Island were known. And luckily, most of the storms that came off the Gulf of Mexico ran out of steam crossing Florida or swung north before hitting the coast of southeastern Georgia.

Oh, they still got several hurricane watches and warnings on Jekyll every fall – usually in September or October – but Georgia's Golden Isles hadn't taken a devastating direct hit since 1898. At least that was what her husband, Mitch, reminded her when he caught her pacing and watching hurricane news on her phone on Sunday night.

"You're paranoid," he accused her.

"Am not. I want to be informed."

"You have a problem," he said with a chuckle. "It's like you're almost cheering for the storm." She was watching something that had formed overnight in the Gulf that had the potential to bring them lousy weather the following week.

"I am certainly not cheering for the storm," she argued. "I am watching it because if I watch it, and if we prepare, and if we have a Plan B for every event that needs one in inclement weather, we won't need any of it. But if we don't pay attention and we don't prep every time there's a chance of a hurricane, we will get slammed. That's how it works. Plain and simple."

"You're nuts," Mitch said.

"No, I'm superstitious. There's a difference."

Tally also firmly believed that if you put up a tent for a wedding, regardless of the forecast, the vast majority of the time it would not rain. However, if the bride and groom refused to spend the money to put up a tent just in case, that would be the day it would rain torrentially. That was just how it worked.

In all fairness, she probably still had some PTSD from Hurricane Maria. That nasty, Category 5, monster storm struck Vieques Island, Puerto Rico, in the middle of the night and took out the power for 17 months afterwards. The house where she'd lived with her boyfriend had been destroyed. The wedding planning company that she'd worked for had closed permanently. And her then-boyfriend, Eduardo, opted to stay behind on Vieques when she was evacuated stateside. So, Tally had started over on Jekyll Island, the place she considered home.

Tally also believed in the adage, "When God shuts a door, he opens a window." She'd thought she'd lost everything in Hurricane Maria, but going home to Jekyll took her career to the next level and brought her together with the love of her life. She'd grown up with Mitch Durham on

Jekyll but hadn't seen him in more than 10 years when she returned to the island and ran into him in his Georgia State Patrol uniform. It seemed like all of that happened forever ago, but really, they'd only been married for a few years.

Jekyll Weddings was about to celebrate its seventh year in business and Jekyll Flowers would be celebrating six. Their twins, Molly and Moody, were turning two in January. Considering how much they both had on their plates, Tally thought she and Mitch were doing a pretty good job holding it all together.

Of course, they couldn't get through a week without help from Tally's Aunt Etah and her best friend, Bonnie, who was Mitch's grandmother and lived across the street from them. Etah lived on the other side of the island in a new condominium at The Moorings, next to the Jekyll marina. She'd given the waterfront house on Tallu Fish Lane, where Tally had grown up, to Tally and Mitch as a wedding gift.

Mitch's mom, Roberta, spent just as much time with the twins as the others, even though she and his dad, Tom, lived across the causeway in Brunswick. Tom Durham was a state trooper, too, and he had been assigned to Jekyll Island for as long as Tally could remember. It was because of Roberta, Bonnie, and Etah that Tally could keep running her businesses while Mitch was frequently gone on missions with his task force. The twins loved all of the older women, who spoiled them rotten in an effort to outdo one another.

Tally's best friend, Yaya, had moved from Vieques to Jekyll a year after Tally to run the flower shop she opened to service her weddings and supply flowers to homes and businesses on Jekyll. And that was who Tally was thinking about when Mitch caught her pacing. Like Tally, Yaya had also met the man of her dreams in Georgia.

Yaya's *Señor Right* was a Glynn County sheriff's deputy named Matt Baker, and they'd eloped to Puerto Rico a few days earlier. They got married with her family as witnesses on Luquillo Beach, and then she'd taken Matt over to Vieques for a mini-moon. Tally and Mitch had treated the newlyweds to a beautiful room at Hacienda Tamarindo, the prettiest hotel on the island, as a wedding gift. Yaya had confided to Tally that she felt strange going *home* and staying in a hotel. She'd never stayed in a hotel on Vieques before.

"You're in Room 5 – my most favorite room in that hotel. It was where the clients always wanted to stay for their weddings," Tally told her. "Just enjoy it and show Matt all the most amazing places on Vieques. Take him to the biobay and the beaches, and don't let him get too sunburned."

"Girl, you know I'm Puerto Rican. We sit under the trees."

Tally laughed because she knew it was true. Whenever she and Yaya met up at Sun Bay, it was a race to see who got there first to choose the spot. Yaya would always choose to be under the shade of the palm trees, and Tally would park their beach chairs as close to the water as possible. Only the gringos did that, and Yaya teased her about it.

Yaya had been worried that Tally's feelings would be hurt when she told her that they were going to elope, but that hadn't been her friend's reaction at all.

"That's awesome. How can I help? I'm sort of jealous," Tally said. "Our wedding was a lot of fun, but I don't think that I even talked to everybody who was there – it was so much activity with so many people – even though it's what I do for a living, I was overwhelmed."

"I remember," Yaya rolled her eyes. "I was there."

"Shuddup."

"But seriously, this is what we both wanted to do. He doesn't really have any family left, and my parents won't travel anymore. I want him to meet them, and it's been too long since I've been home," Yaya said.

"That's your own fault. You're the one who won't take time off," Tally interrupted.

"I know, I know," she agreed. "But this isn't about that… I'M GET-TING MARRIED!"

Tally squealed with Yaya, and they both jumped around celebrating and being ridiculous for a moment. The next morning, she'd surprised Yaya with an engagement card that told her about the gift of Hacienda Tamarindo for their mini-moon.

Here she was, a month later, watching the Weather Channel and praying that Tropical Storm whoever-it-was would dissipate and not ruin Yaya's special time on Vieques with Matt. She also didn't want it to ruin the weddings that were about to be underway on Jekyll Island for the next weekend. She turned off her weather app and looked at her husband.

"I hate it."

"I know, babe. But watching it won't make it go away. Just like ignoring it won't make it come any faster," Mitch said.

"You don't know that. Putting up a tent keeps the rain away," Tally insisted.

"So put up a tent."

"I said it keeps the rain away. It does nothing to deter a hurricane." She gave her husband a "duh" look and stomped out of the bedroom to make her point.

Mitch watched her go and laughed. Being married to a wedding planner was like being married to a full-time Bridezilla some days, but she was advocating for other women and their weddings, not her own. And that's why he let Tally get away with it.

Chapter 4

Blessedly, the storms that had Tally worried became big nothingburgers before the end of the week, when Jekyll Weddings had to execute three beach weddings flawlessly. Kayla and Kelsi met Tally for breakfast at the Sunrise Grille early on Friday morning to figure out the best way to deploy the interns for the wedding weekend.

Late Kate was still having trouble getting places on time. She hadn't been late for any wedding events, yet. But she'd missed her ride to the office several days in a row and on one occasion, hadn't bothered to thank Kelsi after her boss gave her a 20-minute grace period on a rainy day. It was the bad manners that really aggravated Kelsi, who considered herself an excellent judge of character and had hand-picked Katy from the resume pile. She wasn't going to be trusted with anything on her own yet.

Katy's tardiness wasn't nearly as annoying as the food habits of one Miss Pain-in-the-Ass (Kelsi had shortened Tori's nickname already). Tori didn't seem to know how to feed herself, Kelsi reported. At least that was how Kelsi described the problem to Tally and Kayla.

"I took them all to the Publix grocery store the day after they arrived and told them to shop. I told them we'd pick a weekly day to do a grocery trip together, or they could take a work vehicle during the day when they had downtime."

"Sounds like a good plan."

"You'd think? Right? Well, it's fine for Liz and Katy – Late Kate is always there on time when it involves food – but Miss Pain-in-the-Ass claims she's never been grocery shopping before. Says their housekeeper cooks or her mommy orders from a delivery service, and that she lived in the sorority house and their meals were prepared for them. The idea of grabbing some basics she can use for sandwiches or to make a quick salad is completely beyond her. She was totally flummoxed," Kelsi complained.

"Did you help her?" Kayla asked.

"I tried. Seriously, I tried. But she bought a head of lettuce and a loaf of bread and said she had everything she needed."

"Weird. I wonder what she plans to do with that." Kayla frowned in concentration.

"She'd better not be planning to eat it with the shaved deli turkey I bought when she wasn't shopping," Kelsi declared. "I don't get it. She's super book-smart and comes off as fairly worldly but figuring out how to feed yourself is a basic life skill."

"One that Tori never had to tackle before she got here. Remember, she's an undergrad and a sorority girl. Lower your expectations a little bit. Not everybody picks things up as fast as you and I do."

"Fine. I'll cut her some slack," Kelsi agreed. "But in the future, we need to ask our applicants how they'd rate their ability to seek food and feed themselves on a 1-to-10 scale. *Please rate your ability to survive somewhere with no food delivery after 8 pm*, okay? Maybe we need to ask them about their ability to clothe and bathe themselves, too. Sheesh!"

"Probably," Kayla agreed sympathetically. "But let's find a way to ask that isn't insulting."

"Fine, you write up the application next time." Kelsi's tone was joking but Kayla and Tally could tell she was starting to get tired of intern shenanigans.

"Okay, okay," Tally interrupted. "I get that they're not the best roommates. How are they doing with wedding planning?"

"Not too bad," Kelsi answered honestly, her tone more optimistic. She sat up in her seat and put a professional face on.

"It's interesting how different they all are," Kayla added. "Liz and Tori can talk to a wall which, as you know, is a good skill to have at wedding events. But they've really just been shadowing us with the planning so far. This weekend, each of them is assigned to a different wedding. They each have to work two weddings – one as the primary in charge, one as a helper – and they can each sit one out, or volunteer to come and be part of it if they so choose."

"Huh," Tally grunted. "That'll be interesting. Let me know who does what."

"Seriously, I'd never have skipped a wedding that early in an internship," Kelsi exclaimed. "I wanted to be at everything back then. Also, I wanted to eat all the wedding food."

"You haven't changed much, have you?" Kayla laughed.

"Don't even start, you two," Tally warned, but she had a smile in her voice. The two women sitting in front of her eating pancakes were the reason she hadn't lost her mind trying to run weddings after she became a mom. Kayla and Kelsi were goofy at times and easily distracted – *squirrel!* – but when it came to making beautiful weddings happen, they were the absolute best. That's why she'd allowed them to try out this hairbrained intern plan. It remained to be seen whether Tally would end up regretting the decision.

"No, but seriously, things are going fine with all of them," Kayla said. "I'm sort of interested to get Yaya's read on them when she gets back to town. She always seems to peg the bad ones right off the bat."

"Don't be so optimistic," Tally joked.

"You know what I mean. It's hard to get one past Yaya," Kayla said.

"Indeed, it is. We'll have to do this breakfast thing again after she's had a few days to figure them all out," Tally agreed. "But in the meantime, who is doing what? I'm covering for Yaya at Jekyll Flowers this week so that all of your brides get exactly what they ordered. That means that I won't be at the wedding events unless you run into a problem and need me."

"Nothing is too huge or unmanageable, so we shouldn't have a problem on our own," Kayla told her. "The biggest wedding is about 60 people, and that one's at the Holiday Inn. They always handle our weddings beautifully. I've got that one," she added.

"Kelsi is running the elopement on Driftwood Beach and the 30-person ceremony on Glory Beach with the reception afterwards upstairs at Tribuzio's Grille. It's all stuff we've done before. This is the test to see if these interns make our lives easier or harder," Kayla explained.

"I can already answer that," Kelsi volunteered.

"Shut up. We told you not to live with them. You have to base all assessments on their work performance, not whether they rinse out the bathroom sink properly," Kayla told her.

"So you say," Kelsi said in a snotty voice. Kelsi replied by sticking her tongue out at her best friend.

"Ladies, let's remember to be charming and attractive," Tally reminded them, quoting her high school headmistress, Mrs. Donna Doll Day Diamond. Mrs. D had reminded all her girls to be "charming and attractive" whenever she let them off campus for a field trip or social activity. Tally was certain she wasn't the only St. Margaret's alumnus who quoted that line on a regular basis.

Chapter 5

Everything was going to be perfect for Chris and Shari's wedding ceremony on the beach in front of the Holiday Inn. The Jekyll Island Authority had *finally* replaced the walkway over the dunes that had washed away during a nasty winter storm, and both sides of the steps to the beach were wrapped with stunning blue dendrobium orchids that Tally and the interns had spent an hour attaching to the wooden railings. Tally would have asked Aunt Etah to help, too. But she was gone on a month-long Mediterranean cruise with some of her reporter friends.

The bride and groom were both doctors from Arizona who'd found Jekyll Island while attending a medical convention on Amelia Island in Florida. They'd been engaged for about a year before the trip, but they really hadn't discussed too many wedding plans because they had such busy careers. When they had a few moments of downtime together, the last thing they wanted to bicker about was where to get married – he wanted Mexico and she wanted a vineyard in Massachusetts. The one detail they could agree on was that they weren't getting married in Arizona, or in either of their midwestern hometowns. Their families were too complicated.

Shari had added a few vacation days onto the end of their Florida business trip, and they'd driven up to Jekyll Island, just over the Georgia state line, before spending a few nights in Savannah. Shari had been intrigued by the beautiful historic hotel and the empty beaches, and she had an idea.

The last morning of their trip, she woke Chris up earlier than planned and proposed that they stop on Jekyll Island, again, on their way back to the airport. The first time there, they'd driven around and looked at the pretty historic district from their car and then gotten out to go for a walk at the famous Driftwood Beach. Shari told Chris she wanted to go back and see what else was there and maybe stop in the shopping district. They could have lunch if they had time. He was all in.

Shari did the driving, and she took them on a tour of Jekyll based on a map she'd found online the night before. In the process, they saw the outsides of all the hotels – big and small – on the seven-mile by one-mile island. After they'd finished their lap, she pulled into Beach Village and found a parking spot in front of the Jekyll Market.

"Are we shopping?" Chris asked, eyeing a sunglass store on the opposite corner.

"Sort of," Shari replied as she got out of the car.

Chris followed her into a flower shop he hadn't noticed, next door to the much-bigger Jekyll Market. He stopped dead in the threshold when he heard her asking for information about planning weddings on Jekyll Island.

***

Eighteen months later and they were about to get married on the beach and have their reception at 24 Coastal Grille, the waterfront restaurant where they'd eaten lunch after visiting the flower shop.

"Are you ready?" Kayla asked Shari. She'd noticed the bride's face looking very serious as her maid of honor attached her veil.

"Oh, I am," Shari smiled. "I was just thinking about something my dad said last night, and I'm hoping that he was joking."

"What did he say?" her wedding planner asked, looking concerned.

Shari grinned at Kayla. "If he does it, you'll know. I'm not going to jinx myself by talking about it."

"Will I need to do something if this happens?" Kayla asked, her anxiety suddenly through the roof. She'd worked on this wedding for 18 months and she really hated surprises.

"There won't be anything you can do about it, I suspect," the bride seemed amused, and that made Kayla breathe a little easier. "It'll make for *interesting* wedding photos though. And Chris will be so mad."

Chris was definitely more strait-laced than his bride and Kayla understood what Shari meant. The bride could appreciate a prank on their wedding day more than her future husband.

"You need me to talk to your dad?" Kayla asked.

"Don't bother. He was probably kidding. And if he wasn't, well... you'll see." The bride shook her head and then turned around at the photographer's instruction to take some more pictures with her girlfriends.

Chapter 6

It was a long walk down the aisle to the beach for the members of the wedding party. When Tori radioed Kayla and told her that the guests were seated and the groom and his groomsmen were in place, Kayla started sending Shari's bridesmaids out the sliding doors of the big suite where they'd been dressing. They walked across the pool deck to the path that led to the beach walkway. They'd timed it out so that the next bridesmaid would appear at the top of the staircase right after the previous one had taken her place up front. It wouldn't be perfect, but more often than not, it kept them from getting a logjam in the aisle.

Shari's father was supposed to meet the bride in her suite, but he wasn't there when it was time. Kayla radioed Tori to find him.

"He's right here," Tori told her. "I think he got confused. He said he was supposed to meet her at the end of the aisle. Want me to send him to you or keep him here?" Tori was posted at the start of the walkway where nobody on the beach could see her.

"Hold onto him, I'll send Shari to you. Just tell me when."

The radio crackled again about two minutes later and Kayla heard Tori say "now."

Kayla wouldn't usually escort a bride out of the suite because it would put her in pictures, a serious wedding planner no-no that her boss, Tally Davis, would surely comment on when she saw the professional photos. But Shari's dress was ginormous – a real Cinderella ball gown with a massive skirt and train. The teeny-tiny bride was wearing stiletto heels that she refused to remove – she'd actually practiced walking in the sand with them – but she wasn't terribly stable in the huge dress and cathedral length veil on solid ground. So, Kayla extended her arm and walked Shari out to the aisle to get married.

When they got close enough to see Tori and Jim, the father of the bride, Kayla stopped in her tracks. Shari started laughing.

"He really did it," she giggled.

Her dad was wearing khaki shorts with an obnoxious Hawaiian shirt that definitely didn't fit into the wedding party motif. But the best part was the giant fake parrot that was mounted to his shoulder.

The father of the bride smiled and extended his arm to his only daughter as if there was nothing unusual about his appearance.

"I suppose I should be happy you're not wearing an eye patch or a hook," Shari sighed as her father kissed her cheek.

"Don't worry," he said. "I have an eyepatch in my pocket for the reception."

Tori gave Kayla a panicked look as the bride's father led his daughter down the staircase to the beach.

"Do you think he was serious?" the intern asked.

"Probably," Kayla sighed. "But Shari knows and she just laughed, so that means it's not our problem."

"She's a really beautiful bride. I hope I look that much like a princess when I get married," Tori said with a hopeful sigh.

"You should tell her that."

"I will," Tori nodded.

"Maybe she'll let you borrow the parrot for your dad," Kayla suggested with a smile.

"Nah, that's okay," Tori said. "My dad has his own."

Chapter 7

"No, he didn't," Tally couldn't stop laughing as Kayla told her and Kelsi the story late that night. They were drinking spiked seltzers and watching the moonlight dance on the Atlantic Ocean.

Kayla had texted her boss as the reception was wrapping up and included a picture of the bride being walked down the aisle by her father and his parrot.

Tally had replied with a string of various laughing emojis and said that she needed more details. "If you girls aren't too tired, stop over here and tell me all about it. Mitch is at work and I'm jealous that I wasn't there with you."

Kayla quickly agreed and promised they'd come over. She texted Kelsi, who was finishing up the reception at Tribuzio's Grille with Katy and Liz, and asked her to join them.

"Gotta drop off the interns at home first and then I'll be there," Kelsi replied with an eye-roll emoji.

Tally and Mitch's oceanfront beach house, where Tally had grown up after her parents died in a plane crash when she was 12, was just a few minutes down the road from the Holiday Inn wedding venue. She frequently claimed it was the proximity of their home to her work that made it possible for her to juggle everything, most of the time. But it also made her front deck their office social club, and she loved that, too.

"I guess the pirate thing was an inside family joke because everybody cracked up when they saw Jim and Shari on the stairs," Kayla explained. "Everybody except the mother of the bride. She was totally *not* laughing. She was pissed."

"Oh no," Tally groaned.

"Oh yes. And she was even more mad when he put on an eye patch before he gave his toast," Kayla explained. "He started the toast with, 'Argh!'"

Tally and Kelsi burst out laughing.

"Yes, it was hilarious. Cuz it wasn't my wedding," Kayla said.

When they stopped giggling about the father of the bride's antics, Tally asked about the reception.

"Oh, everything went great and the couple was really happy. They rode off in a horsedrawn carriage to the Jekyll Island Club Hotel where there is a fancy suite full of goodies awaiting them. Shari thanked us a billion times and I think Chris relaxed enough to have fun, too. He loved the 'Rock Chalk, Jayhawk' groom's cake, too."

"I'm glad. That was a pain in the butt," Kayla commented.

"Anything for the clients," Tally reminded her.

"I know. I just wish she'd had the idea for the groom's cake more than 24 hours before the wedding reception," Kayla complained.

"But you got it, didn't you? And now Shari thinks you are magic. You made it happen. Good for you. Don't forget to send thank you flowers to the cake lady, please," Tally said.

Owning a flower shop made it simple to send thank you gifts to the vendors who made their jobs easier. Tally made a habit of it and as a result, she always had somebody she could call in an emergency.

There was a gentle knock on the doors behind them and then they opened, and Tally's husband greeted them.

"I didn't want to startle you ladies," Mitch said. He kissed his wife and sat down in an empty chair on the deck.

"You're home early," Tally smiled.

"I know," he grinned back at her.

"That's our cue," Kayla said and stood up.

"No wait," Tally stopped her. "Let's talk about Monday real quick. Will everybody be at the staff meeting?"

It was a must-attend weekly meeting that sometimes had to be shifted if there were clients on the island.

"I'm good," Kelsi said.

"Me too," Kayla added.

"I have a meeting with a potential client tomorrow afternoon. If she's going to be here on Monday, too, I may have to shift things. In which case, I'll text everybody. I'm not entirely sure what kind of consultation it is – she was a little cryptic," Tally explained.

"Huh. Interesting," Kayla commented as she gathered her belongings. "Keep us posted."

"Drive carefully," Tally told them.

Mitch walked his wife's employees to their front door and whispered goodbye to them. The twins' bedroom was located next to the front porch, and it wouldn't take much to wake them up. Kayla and Kelsi spent so much time at Tally's house that they were used to the tippy-toe protocol coming and going.

***

Mitch and Tally chatted on the back deck after the Kayla and Kelsi had gone.

"I didn't mean to run them out," Mitch apologized.

"You didn't. They'd both been working all day and I asked them to come by. It's better they get out of here and go home or whatever. I think on late-late nights, they both usually go back to Jake's house."

The wedding planning team had first met Jake, who was a local vet, when a miniature dachshund best man swallowed the wedding rings at a wedding rehearsal about a year ago. That was how Kayla met Jake's older sister, Kelsi, who ultimately ended up being her wing-woman at Jekyll Weddings and her best friend.

So far, everybody seemed to be getting along just fine. Tally had worried that her entire staff could end up at odds if things went south between Kayla and Jake. But things had been smooth – probably because both Kayla and Kelsi were easygoing women – and if anything, the quality of their work together for Jekyll Weddings had improved.

Tally knew that Kayla's ultimate goal was to help her launch another wedding planning location over on St. Simons Island next door. Jekyll Weddings already did a few weddings every year on the island that locals referred to as "SSI." But Tally had never marketed to potential St. Simons brides because they were already stretched to their staffing limit over on Jekyll Island. A few wedding weekends a year that required a million trips over the causeways and bridges to and from all of the events on St. Simons had convinced her that she had plenty of work over there already. She'd admit there were some gorgeous wedding venues that she'd love to decorate on their bigger sister island to the north, but she simply didn't have the bandwidth to cover it yet.

Kayla had been persistent about the expansion and felt strongly that she could make a big success of St. Simons Weddings – that's what she'd proposed calling it – and she really wanted to be the one to build it for Tally.

It was a conundrum for the young business owner, and she'd been struggling with what to do about it for months. Tally agreed that Kayla's business instincts were sound, and that strategically, expanding her little business to St. Simons was a good idea. But she also believed in proceeding cautiously. The only thing keeping her sane was having both Kelsi and Kayla in the Jekyll Weddings location to deal with clients and weddings so that she could spend time with her twins. When Kayla moved over to working SSI full time, things would have to change. Which was why they needed to find another Kayla for Jekyll before the original Kayla could leave. That led to the girls' request to hire interns that might turn into real employees.

Tally and Mitch cuddled on their favorite bench and talked about her company's future and her goals. He listened, asking a few questions here and there, but didn't offer many opinions. He realized he was more of a sounding board than an advisor in this conversation.

After Tally had talked it out, Mitch filled her in on the task force work he'd been doing earlier that evening. He and his partner, Camden County Sheriff's Deputy Joe Moody, had been "sitting on" a potential stash house for human trafficking victims. The big Port of Brunswick, located between Jekyll and St. Simons, opened the door to all sorts of smuggling, from drugs to young girls from foreign countries who had either been kidnapped or promised a better life in America. They were assigned to a multijurisdictional task force run by the feds that had been instrumental in shutting down some of the bigger trafficking operations using the Georgia port over the past 12 months.

"But we got some news tonight," he said, sounding more enthusiastic than usual. "Joe and I are getting transferred to another task force for a few months."

Tally sat up abruptly and looked at him. Change made her nervous. The first year he was on the task force, he'd been shot in the head while trying to stop a drug dealer. Knowing he was mostly just babysitting cargo ships for the past year had made her life less stressful because she didn't worry as much.

"What kind of task force is it? It is nearby?" she asked, fearing the answer. Mitch was a state patrol trooper and as such, could be relocated anywhere in the state at any time. So far, they'd been lucky because he'd been assigned to a task force working in their region.

"I don't have much info yet. We're both off tomorrow and then I've got that swearing in ceremony in Atlanta Monday morning. Afterwards, we'll check in with the new bosses and find out what's up. I know it's another state/federal collaboration, and it's probably in this area, or they wouldn't be sending Joe with me," he explained.

Joe Moody, was a Camden County sheriff's deputy who Mitch had worked with since he first joined the task force. They'd ended up best friends after they got shot together on their first assignment. And then he and Tally had named one of their twins after Joe.

"Will you be gone long?" she asked.

"At least one night," he said. "But hopefully we'll be back on Tuesday evening. I'll let you know as soon as I know what's going on. I need to call Tommy and Frank and see if we can crash with them."

"Won't GSP pay for a hotel?"

"Of course they will," Mitch laughed. "But then I have to pay for an Uber to get our drunk asses home after we hang out with my brothers. It's easier to cut out the middleman and just stay with them."

"Alrighty then," Tally laughed and shook her head. He didn't go out and get rowdy with the boys often enough for her to have any objection to debauchery with his older brothers, who were also both state troopers. "Just stay out of trouble. Try not to embarrass yourselves."

"But that's half the fun," Mitch joked. "I'm looking forward to seeing them and catching up."

"We haven't seen much of either of them on Jekyll lately," Tally observed. "I thought maybe we'd see more of Frank after he met Kelsi this summer, but he hasn't been back since that beach day."

"You never know what's going on with him," Mitch said. "I'll see what I can find out when I see them."

They talked a bit longer about the upcoming holiday season and how much fun it would be now that the twins were a little bit older.

"I've got to call Stephanie Conti and get on her schedule for our Christmas card pictures," Tally said suddenly, and reached for her phone to email herself a reminder.

"We take professional Christmas card pictures now?" he asked with humor in his voice.

"We have almost-two-year-old twins. Of course, we are expected to send out a cute picture of our family for everybody to put on their refrigerators," she said and then stopped. She looked at her husband and started laughing.

"Oh my God, did I just say that?"

"You did." Mitch smiled.

"Okay, fine, but I do think it's a fun idea and I'd like to have a special Christmas picture to frame every year," Tally explained, but sounding much less aggressive than before.

"I can't argue with that. Let me get my schedule sorted out and you can call the photographer," he said. "Are you going to make us all wear something stupid? Like matching pajamas?"

"I wasn't planning on it, but that's not such a bad idea," Tally said. Mitch groaned and that made her laugh.

When Tally started falling asleep mid-conversation, Mitch led her to their bedroom and tucked her in. Then he checked on the twins and moved Moody over to his own crib – they'd been trying to get them to sleep separately for months and although they didn't scream anymore when they were put to bed apart, it wasn't unusual to find that one of them had Mission-Impossibled from their own crib to their twin's. He made sure all the doors were locked and turned off the lights all over the house before he joined his sleeping wife.

Chapter 8

Sunday had been a fun, lazy day on the island and the weather had been perfect for an afternoon on the beach building drip sandcastles. It was rare that Tally and Mitch had an entire 24-hours together, uninterrupted by client or police demands. They'd shared a bottle of wine over dinner and gone to bed much earlier than usual because both of them were pooped from a day in the sun supervising toddlers. Tally slept like a rock because all was right in her world.

Monday morning, on the other hand, was nothing short of pure chaos in the Davis-Durham household on Tallu Fish Lane. Mitch had to leave for a Georgia State Patrol induction ceremony in Atlanta by 6 a.m. and he woke Tally up at 5:30 after a failed frantic search for part of his uniform.

"I'm sorry to wake you up," he said, not sounding sorry at all.

Tally looked at her handsome husband, fresh from the shower, smelling great, and holding up the pants to his dress uniform.

"No problem. What can't you find?"

"My belt for my Class A uniform – I've looked everywhere that makes sense. Why do you hide things from me?" he joked, but he was being partly serious. Mitch tended to leave a trail behind him everywhere he went in the house. Tally had given up on retraining him – she blamed his mother, Roberta, and told her so on a regular basis – and now she just followed behind him picking things up and putting them away.

When Mitch needed something, he'd usually go look for that item where he remembered dropping it, no matter how long ago that might have been. When he didn't find the item on the couch, or the counter, or the living room floor where he'd left it, he accused Tally of hiding things from him.

"Putting things away is not hiding them," she told him every time he complained.

Today was no different. Tally got out of bed, led him down the hall into his Armory, and pointed to the closet shelf where were all of his uniform belts and holsters were stored. It was labeled, but that hadn't tipped him off.

"Anything else you can't find?" she asked sweetly.

"Did you hide anything else from me?" he asked with a grin.

Tally shook her head and left the Armory on a mission to engage with her Nespresso machine before the twins heard Mitch making noise from their bedroom next door and decided to end her quiet morning.

The curtains were pulled across the big glass windows on the oceanfront side of the house, but the bright beams of sunrise still lit up the entire inside of the house. Tally sighed contentedly and reached for her coffee mug. She noticed the coffee machine was exactly as she left it the night before and realized that Mitch hadn't had any caffeine yet. *That explains his inability to dress himself,* she thought. Tally grabbed his favorite travel coffee mug from the cabinet and set about making his drink first.

Any minute now, her handsome husband would rush in to kiss her goodbye, and she would have a fancy coffee ready to give him. As the milk frother whirled, she put an apple and a granola bar in a small shopping bag from her most recent splurge at the Golden Isles Olive Oil Culinary Center on St. Simons. She added a baggie of chocolate chip cookies, and at the last minute, she tossed in two of the toddlers' apple juice boxes.

Tally would never be the kind of perfect cop wife that Mitch's grandmother had been and that his mother was – Roberta brought fresh baked goods into the post where his dad worked at least once a week. And when rookies or transfers arrived to serve time at the Georgia State Patrol barracks on Jekyll Island, she welcomed them with donuts and invited them to dinner at their home.

Fortunately, Roberta and Bonnie lived close enough by to pick up the slack left by Tally's insane working schedule. If she wasn't planning a wedding, she was talking to potential clients or helping assemble flower arrangements. She was a multi-tasking wonder, but she was only human. Running a wedding and floral business on a tiny island where she also lived was a 24/7, 365-day-a-year challenge. So was being the mother of twins who would turn two in January. She couldn't imagine what the Terrible Twos would be like in their house, but she suspected that Molly would be the ringleader and Moody would back her up. It was terrifying to think about before coffee.

She put a lid on Mitch's coffee and started making her own, the way she liked it with heavy cream and a splash of cinnamon coffee milk with four double shots of espresso. Tally rarely had more than two coffees a day unless she had to leave the island and happened to pass a Starbucks. The Jekyll Island Authority had been promising residents a real coffee shop for years, but it hadn't materialized yet. She refused to give up hope.

"You made me coffee?" Mitch swept into the kitchen with both hands full to say goodbye to her. He sent down several pieces of equipment on the counter and finished assembling them, including popping a magazine of ammunition into a Glock 26.

"My department-issued gun has never fit this damned dress holster properly," he griped. "I doubt anybody will notice I'm wearing my own." He said it in a way that told Tally he was trying to convince himself that nobody would notice the slightly-smaller weapon that fired the same 9mm rounds as the Glock 17 he'd been issued. They were moving all the troopers over to Glock 45 Gen 5 guns in a few months, and those were a little more forgiving in the holster and had more grip options for different-sized hands. Some of the higher-ranking officials were already carrying them, or so he'd heard.

"You look fantastic, babe," Tally told him and then took a long first slug of her own fancied-up coffee. She couldn't help making an "mmmm" sound and Mitch rolled his eyes at her.

"Don't mess with me," she warned him. "I found your belt, and I can lose it again."

"You know you're going to hide it again so don't bother trying to threaten me. I just assume it's going to happen," Mitch laughed.

"I don't hide anything from you, I just put things away," Tally started to rant.

"Oops, gotta go," Mitch bent over and planted a kiss on Tally's lips. "Have a great day and I'll let you know what's going on and when I'll be back after my meeting."

"Stay safe," she called to his back as he rushed for the front door, stopping to pick up a gear bag he'd left at the threshold. Tally told him the same thing every time he left the house. She'd picked it up from the other Durham women and it would never occur to her to let Mitch, her childhood best friend and now, lifelong partner, face the scary world of law enforcement without telling him to be careful. It was just a cop wife thing. Sort of like loving the sounds of Velcro in the middle of the night because it meant your law enforcement officer husband was home safe and sound and taking off his equipment.

Chapter 9

Things had been quiet in the house for about an hour after Mitch left for Atlanta. Tally drank her coffee, posted to her wedding blog, and started answering emails from potential clients who'd reached out to request a free consultation at some point over the weekend. It was important to respond to those requests as fast as possible because it was the first impression they'd have of Jekyll Weddings.

She saw an email from a wedding planner she'd met with a couple of weeks ago and clicked on it, curious what the other woman had to say.

Clementine Daisy was a destination wedding planner from the Washington, DC, area who only planned "historic" weddings. She'd defined that as being weddings at historic locations all over the United States. Clementine had explained that most of her clients wanted a nice, normal, contemporary wedding at a cool historic venue, but that some of her brides and grooms actually carried a historic theme through their wedding weekend, or at least at some of the events.

Clementine said she had reached out to Tally because she'd had a few requests for weddings in the Golden Isles, and the way that her business model worked, she needed to establish a relationship with a wedding company located at her destination in order to gain access to the best vendors. It simply wasn't possible for her to know the best people to work with everywhere, she'd said. So, she had to rely on the best local vendors she could find and form business relationships with them.

"I'm not trying to compete with you," she assured Tally. "I have my own clients who come to me specifically and I need help with their weddings. I'm willing to compensate you well for your time."

She told Tally that she was based out of DC, but that she was on the road more than 45 weeks of the year. If she wasn't planning a wedding with a couple at Thomas Jefferson's favorite getaway, The Homestead in Hot Springs, Virginia, she was probably supervising the décor at a wedding on a mountaintop in New Hampshire at the Omni Mount Washington. Clementine explained that she spent the first few days of every week planning with brides and the last few days of every week executing weddings. She didn't want to be Tally's competition – she just wanted to hire her for her help with clients who had already hired her for historic wedding planning.

It was a sweet little setup, Tally told Mitch when she explained the other wedding planner's proposal. Clem, as she said to call her, told Tally that she was willing to hire Jekyll Weddings to help her on an hourly basis, or come up with a split-fee model that would incentivize Tally to make her clients a priority and help boost their spending. But those clients wouldn't be her clients, they'd be Clem's and Tally wouldn't be able to use their pictures for marketing purposes or plan on getting good Wedding Wire reviews out of them. She'd said she had to think about it before she made any decisions.

But Clem wasn't letting any grass grow under her feet.

"Hi Tally," she'd written in the email. "Have you thought any more about my proposal to work together on some weddings? One of them wants to book just six months out and there's no way I'll accept their wedding unless I know I have a wing-woman down there. Let me know what I need to do to help you make up your mind."

Interesting, Tally thought. She's being pushy without seeming too aggressive and let's face it, Clem's approach was working. She was seriously considering the other wedding planner's proposition.

A text popped up and distracted her. It was from Aunt Etah and Tally opened it quickly, excited to hear from her world-traveling aunt. It hadn't surprised her when Etah announced she was going on a month-long cruise with one of her old friends. Tally had expected Etah to get bored with retirement pretty quickly on Jekyll Island. But Tally had come to rely on her aunt to help with her twins, more than she'd even realized, until Aunt Etah was gone for a whole month.

Etah wrote that her trip was going well and the Greek Isles by cruise ship were everything she'd been promised. She said she'd made friends with some of the other "single" travelers on the trip and had been enjoying excursions with her new friends.

"That's great. We miss you so much," Tally texted back. "I hate you being gone so long. I got used to having you here." She felt guilty for a moment because she didn't want Etah to feel bad about taking a vacation. But Etah's fast reply allayed her fears.

"It's been a good break, but I miss Molly and Moody so much. Tell them I've gotten them presents from almost every port."

"Of course you did," Tally replied. "I miss you. Have fun and stay safe!"

Her attention was pulled away suddenly by a scream through the baby monitor that echoed all over the house. That scream was followed by a wail, and that was followed by both twins screaming "Mommy Mommy Mommy" at the top of their lungs. *So much for quiet time,* she thought as she headed for Molly and Moody's room to get them up for the day.

Chapter 10

The Brubaker/Sherman wedding was an all-hands-on deck-situation for the team at Jekyll Weddings. The clients had 200 guests and four days of wedding activities. They'd bought out the entire Jekyll Ocean Club, the beachside half of the historic Jekyll Island Club Resort, so they could have their wedding reception in the restaurant, Eighty Ocean.

Kortney Brubaker was an advertising executive from Chicago, and her fiancé was a venture capitalist. They'd been together since college at Northwestern, and from the sound of things, the bride and her mom had been planning this wedding in their imaginations for years.

Her mother, who was originally from Georgia, participated in every planning call and had accompanied her daughter to Jekyll Island to choose her wedding venue, without her future son-in-law. She knew exactly what she wanted, and but her daughter was not in lockstep with some of her ideas.

The groom, Mike Sherman, hadn't participated in many of their wedding planning conference calls, having told his bride-to-be to just let him know when to show up and what to wear. All of the important decisions had been left up to her. And that was just how Kortney liked it.

By the time the Brubaker/Sherman wedding rolled around, the interns had survived several weddings each that they'd been in charge of prepping, and nobody had been sent home for screwing up, yet. Kelsi still griped about living with college girls, but the complaints were all roommate-related and had nothing to do with work. In fact, Kelsi had even stopped referring to Katy as "Late Kate" after the intern woke her up when her alarm didn't go off for an early setup on a wedding day.

Liz was clearly the most organized of the three girls, and Tori was probably the most fun after work. But together, they were becoming an unbeatable threesome. Kayla had suggested letting them execute a wedding themselves with somebody higher up on site to triage if there was a problem and Tally was giving the idea some thought.

It seemed irresponsible to let the bride and groom become her interns' experiment, even though she knew darned well that was how she and Kayla and Kelsi had gotten their starts. Tally planned to call Isabelle, her boss at Vieques Weddings, and get her advice on it. Isabelle had run an intern program for a number of years before Tally arrived in Puerto Rico. By that time, Isabelle's company was big enough to afford more employees, and she'd given herself a break from teaching college girls her tricks. Tally was starting to understand why her mentor had gotten sick of it.

Kortney and Mike's wedding was a good opportunity to give all of the interns a bigger piece of responsibility, simply because the guest list and number of events was a tremendous challenge. Everything was all planned and ready to go. The clients had paid their final balances. All the interns would have to do is prep properly and stick to the schedule of events that Kelsi had already written up and had blessed by the bride.

Kelsi was technically the senior account executive for the Brubaker/Sherman wedding weekend, but Kayla had known from the get-go that she'd need to be a second set of experienced hands for that wedding weekend. Kortney would want somebody within shouting distance at all times, and Kelsi needed to be free to supervise the expensive décor plan the bride had chosen.

Tally was going to deal with the flowers for the Brubaker/Sherman affair because Yaya had four weddings to do on St. Simons Island that Saturday and Sunday, and she would need to be over there all weekend. Technically speaking, the Brubaker/Sherman wedding on Jekyll was staffed with too many chiefs and not enough Indians. But it was better to have too many hands than not enough, especially with some of the things this couple had wanted.

"I'm dragging all of my friends and business associates here, all the way from Chicago," Kortney had said at their first consultation. "It has to be worth their time and effort to come to Georgia." She said the word "Georgia" as if inviting her guests to beautiful Jekyll Island was akin to asking them to come to Versailles, Kentucky, for a wedding in that cheesy castle in the middle of a cornfield where Brittany Cartwright married Jax Taylor on "Vanderpump Rules." But Tally kept her face neutral and listened.

"Stop it," Vera Brubaker told her daughter. "You and I have been planning your wedding down here for your entire life," she turned to Tally and continued, "I grew up in Savannah and spent my summers here. We used to come watch the musicals that the college students performed in the amphitheater in the summers. I understand that's not here anymore?"

"No ma'am," Tally said. "It's been gone a long time."

"Such a shame. It was a wonderful program. College students from Valdosta State, the University of Florida, and several other schools used to come stay all summer and do these wonderful performances," Vera recalled. Then she made a face. "I do remember it being rather buggy. I'd have to argue with my mother if I wanted to look cute for the college boys instead of wearing long pants and long sleeves and being doused in bug repellant before leaving the house." The mother of the bride looked wistful, remembering happy childhood memories in this place.

Jekyll Island had been an early haven for the arts in southeast Georgia and hosted a lot of community events that longtime residents talked about fondly. Some of those events had been taken over by the Jekyll Island Authority when that entity started finding a way to make money on everything that happened on the tiny island that was actually a state park. Over time, they cancelled some things, citing a lack of interest from the community. The pandemic was the final nail in the coffin, according to most people. Any of the events that were left had to be cancelled, and most of them never returned, even after people stopped wearing masks. The amphitheater had been gone long before that, but the fact it had ever existed spoke to the rich cultural history of the arts on Jekyll Island.

"My Aunt Etah remembers it the same way you do," Tally assured her. "Fantastic shows and mosquitos the size of bats. I remember going to a few performances there when I was really tiny, but I don't remember many details."

"Can we take a detour from Memory Lane?" Kortney interrupted them in an annoyed voice. "We're here to talk about MY wedding."

So that's what kind of bride you are, Tally thought. But she kept a smile on her face.

"Absolutely," Tally said. "Why don't Kelsi and I help you outline what you have in mind, and then we can take you to look at appropriate venues for everything?"

"That sounds good," Vera agreed.

"Tell us what kind of wedding you've always imagined," Kelsi said, directing the question to Kortney specifically.

"I want everyone to be treated like royalty," the bride began in a tone that brooked no argument.

Kelsi and Tally made eye contact and had to look away from each other, so they didn't laugh. Tori, the intern that had tagged along to this meeting, was staring at the bride with stars in her eyes like she knew exactly what the woman was talking about.

"Have you seen 'The Gilded Age?'" Kortney asked.

"Yes. I totally binged watched it," Tori confessed. Kelsi nodded in a way that said she'd seen the show but hadn't watched enough to really comment.

"I've read about it, but I have toddlers, so I don't get to watch anything that's not animated at home," Tally explained. "It's supposed to be fantastic. There's a lot of speculation that a future season of the show might be filmed here on Jekyll Island. Most of the main characters had a connection with the Jekyll Club."

"Really?" Tori squealed, forgetting herself. Kelsi shot her a look while Tally continued as if the intern hadn't spoken.

"Tell us more about your vision for your wedding, Kortney. Do you want to do any part of it in period costumes? Or are we just playing off the theme of The Gilded Age?" she asked.

"I'd like our rehearsal dinner to be a costumed event on the historic side of the resort, but I don't want people to wear costumes on my Big Day. The only person who should get stared at here on October 19th is me," the bride said in a tone that dared anybody to challenge her.

"Absolutely," Kelsi agreed.

"I'm a Tri Delt and I'm going to use my sorority colors for our wedding. Silver, gold, and cerulean. That's a shade of blue," Kortney informed them, and then grabbed her phone and started tapping away. She handed it to Tally to show her the inspiration board she'd created on Pinterest. Tally passed the phone around to Kelsi and Tori.

"I'm a Tri Delt sister, too. I'm a senior at College of Charleston," Tori piped up, obviously thrilled to have found common ground with this bride she appeared to adore. "Kelsi, you *have to* assign me to this wedding. Kortney and I are sisters! I can totally give her a Tri Delt wedding color theme."

Tally cringed but kept going. Kelsi waited until Kortney and Vera were glaring at each other again to give Tori a sharp look and run her fingers across her lips in a "keep it zipped" gesture to the younger girl. They brought interns along on new client consultations to listen and learn, not fangirl the bride and make promises they couldn't keep.

"I love those dresses. Your bridesmaids are going to look amazing," Tally told Kortney, getting things back on track."

"I know. I didn't want to argue with anybody about the choices or the cost, so I just bought all the dresses," the bride said.

"That was generous of you," Kelsi said. "Destination weddings can get pricey for the wedding party. I'm sure they appreciated your help."

"You'd think," Kortney replied but didn't elaborate. Tally made a note on her paper. *Bridesmaid issues?*

"Are you thinking three days of events?" Tally asked, trying to keep things on track. "A welcome party, rehearsal dinner, and then the wedding? Or did you also want a farewell brunch the day after? And were there any other events you wanted, like a ladies' luncheon on the wedding day?"

"We have to feed them breakfast before they leave," Vera cut in, letting her southern roots show. Southerners were always trying to feed people.

"So, we're doing four days of activities. What kind of welcome party did you have in mind? Something casual like Tortuga Jack's Tiki Bar or something more upscale?" Kelsi asked.

"Not a tiki bar," Vera said dismissively. "I think something on the historic side of the island would be nice. Don't you?" she asked her daughter.

"I honestly don't care, Mother. I just want to make sure there's plenty of top-shelf liquor for everybody. My friends aren't southern. They just want cocktails. The food is incidental."

Vera sniffed in a way that said this was not the first time she'd had this conversation with her extremely opinionated daughter.

"Food is not incidental to anyone above the age of 25," Vera corrected her. "We cannot ask people to fly all the way here and not greet them with food. That's just rude. And we don't need the wedding party getting sloppy the first night because nobody fed them. That's a bad look."

"You're paying for it then," her daughter replied quickly.

"I'm paying for all of it anyway, aren't I?" Vera shot back. "The only things you've suggested that you and Mike would cover were the things I said absolutely no to," she turned to Tally and Kelsi. "She wanted to have alpacas at the wedding reception after she read an article about it, for God's sake."

So this is how it's going to be, Tally thought. She smiled but kept it together for Vera's sake.

Kelsi burst out laughing, she couldn't help herself. Tally cut her off.

"Well, unfortunately, Jekyll Island a state park and we're not allowed to bring in non-native animals for events," she explained, not actually knowing if there was an alpaca exception but winging it. "Dogs are fine if they're pets and they're in the wedding, but not on the beaches that prohibit dogs. Once you involve animals in a wedding, things get a little bit trickier," she warned.

"We're not going to have any animals," Vera agreed.

"Right. Because it's your wedding, Mother," Kortney snapped in a tone that made everybody uncomfortable.

Chapter 11

While that first consultation had been pretty unbearable, Kortney and her mother weren't difficult to work with once they'd signed the contract and agreed on a venue. Kortney made decisions quickly and paid her bills on time and that was all that really mattered to the wedding planners. They didn't have a lot of lead time like they usually would for a wedding this size, and everything had to move very quickly once the venue contract was signed with the Jekyll Ocean Club. Kortney had been lucky she wanted a date they had available only because another couple had cancelled.

Kelsi liked Kortney, although she wouldn't want to have her as a friend. She found her client's wicked sense of humor to be absolutely hilarious. She was probably the snarkiest bride that Kelsi had ever encountered. But after a couple of months of working with her, Kelsi started to worry that Kortney's sharp wit and tongue might be the reason none of the bridesmaids had participated in the planning visit, or the food tastings they'd come back to do last month. Usually, when the groom wasn't involved, the bride would bring her girls along to provide a buffer with her mother. Bridesmaids could be relied on to back up the bride in disagreements with the mother of the bride. Kortney had proven to be a bit of a lone wolf, so far.

So, when Kelsi opened up an angry email from a bridesmaid a few weeks before the wedding, she wasn't entirely surprised to read that there were problems in Chicago.

"Hi Kelsi, I'm Julie Musitano, one of Kortney Brubaker's bridesmaids. I'm not going to be able to make it to Jekyll Island for her wedding because there's no way I'm wearing this dress that just arrived in the mail. I'm a size 14, not a size 8. Please let Kortney know," the message read.

This is a first, Kelsi thought. She'd never received a written resignation from a bridesmaid before, and she wasn't quite sure how to respond. The whole dress-size thing was another Pandora's Box that she wasn't about to open right away. It had to be a mistake, right? She pictured Kortney's face at their initial consultation when she told them her bridesmaids weren't *that* excited she'd bought their dresses. Kelsi wondered if she was about to receive six more resignations – Kortney had asked seven women to be in her wedding party.

Kelsi opened up her Brubaker/Sherman file and pulled out the latest copy of the master info form, the document that held the keys to the kingdom for every Jekyll Weddings event. The wedding party section had a lot less detail than usual, she noticed. But she did find the critical information she'd been looking for - Julie Musitano wasn't just a bridesmaid, she was also the bride's first cousin. Kelsi knew the name had looked familiar. There were about 20 people with that last name on the guest list. This wasn't something she could ignore, unfortunately. She was going to have to reach out to Kortney and Vera and tell them, so they didn't find out on the wedding weekend. Because Julie obviously had no intention of telling them herself from the way the email was worded.

This was a question for Tally, Kelsi decided. She forwarded the email to her boss with the heading "WTF???" and some appropriate emojis. She copied Kayla and Yaya because this was one of those shit-you-can't-make-up kind of moments and she didn't want anybody on the team to miss it.

Chapter 12

Tally was waiting at the Jacksonville airport for Etah when her aunt's plane landed the first week of October. Etah usually made arrangements with Jamie Sanders, the owner of Jekyll Island Errand Girl, to get to and from the airport. But this time, Tally asked her not to do that because she wanted to pick Etah up. She'd missed her more than she'd realized she would, and the hour or so she'd have to catch up with her aunt while they drove home would be worth her effort.

The twins were both sound asleep in their car seats in the back of her blue Jeep Grand Cherokee and she'd been doing lazy circles around the airport to keep them that way while she waited for her aunt. They were all having dinner at Bonnie's tonight because everybody wanted to hear about Etah's first vacation since she started retirement. She hadn't been able to convince Bonnie to take the trip with her, but Tally suspected that Mitch's grandmother might tag along with Etah next time. She'd been asking a lot of questions and Mitch let it slip that his grandmother had mentioned renewing her passport.

Tally also needed to coordinate the October/November babysitting schedule with Etah and Mitch's mom and grandmother. Aunt Etah had signed up to do some volunteer work on Wednesdays – which was usually her day with the twins – and so Roberta was going to take Molly and Moody to their tumbling class at the YMCA in Brunswick for the rest of the fall. She'd been covering for Etah while she was gone on the cruise, and she didn't mind keeping up with it. Roberta complained all the time that she got the short straw on time with her grandchildren because she and Mitch's dad, Tom, lived over the causeway in Brunswick. She didn't mind coming to Jekyll to babysit but Tally felt like that was a lot to ask for on a regular basis. Usually, if Roberta was taking the kids for the day, she or Mitch dropped them off with their grandmother and Roberta brought them home.

They had figured it all out in text messages, but Tally preferred to give each woman her own printout of the month's calendar to review so that nobody was confused. They teased her about being OCD, but she knew it came in handy for them.

***

Aunt Etah looked exhausted but was smiling brightly when she spotted Tally's Jeep on the curb at arrivals.

"Thank you again for coming, honey. You really didn't have to. I know you're way too busy to waste three hours in the car for an old lady," she said as she leaned in the back window to plant a kiss on Molly, who was snoozing with her head on the car door closest to the sidewalk.

"Hello there, Moody," she greeted her great-great nephew after she sat down in the car. Moody didn't twitch so she patted his hand and turned around to buckle her seatbelt.

"You know how they are with car rides. It's been blessedly quiet," Tally giggled. "I'm so bad. I would never let them sleep this long if I had to deal with them by myself tonight. But all of you are going to be at Bonnie's and nobody is going to let me near them anyway. So, you ladies can chase them until they run out of steam."

"You sound as tired as I am," Etah remarked with a chuckle.

"I'm fine," Tally smiled and reached over to squeeze her aunt's hand. "I just like to complain. You know me. Now, tell me all about your trip."

"I met a man."

"What?" Tally almost hit the car next to them because she accidentally jerked the wheel when Etah made her announcement. "A man? What kind of man? Is he old? Is he single?"

Etah had been her guardian since her parents' deaths when she was 12. She'd been spending the week on Jekyll with Aunt Etah, and her parents were supposed to fly in to pick her up. But they'd never arrived on the island because their plane crashed near Fernandina Beach, a few islands south of Jekyll. To the best of Tally's knowledge, Etah had never dated in the time since she'd stepped in to raise her great niece. This news shook Tally a bit.

Etah started laughing and then Tally, realizing how ridiculous she'd sounded grilling her octogenarian aunt, joined her.

"Okay fine, you know what I mean. Did you come home from the Med with a boyfriend?" she teased.

"Maybe."

Tally took a deep breath. "If you're funning me, you should fess up right now," she told Etah meaningfully. That had been her aunt's line to her when Tally was growing up. It was Etah's way of giving Tally permission to admit she'd done something wrong and blame any lies on the joke.

"I'm not funning you," Etah told her sincerely. "I met a man. He's from Atlanta and he's quite handsome. He used to be a band director for a high school, and he can play just about anything. I think I saw him play five different instruments on the ship. His piano playing is my favorite though," Etah bragged, sounding a bit like a teenager trying to convince her parents to let her go out with a new boy. "He's younger than me," she revealed in a whisper.

"How much younger?"

"About five years, I think."

"Does he look younger?"

"I don't think so."

"Is he retired?" Tally asked.

"Yes. He's been retired a lot longer than me."

"Good, that means he's available to travel with you if that's what you want to do," Tally said.

"I do. Not all the time, and maybe not such long trips," she said, looking into the backseat. "I really missed those munchkins. What happened in the four weeks I was gone?"

"Moody applied to law school and Molly got arrested," Tally joked.

"It wouldn't surprise me," Etah agreed. "But seriously, is Moody talking any more than he was when I left."

"No, but at least we know why now. We had a long talk with their pediatrician and apparently, it's totally normal for twins to communicate in their own language, or with looks the rest of us don't see. Moody can talk. He just chooses not to at this point. The doctor said he doesn't have to because his sister does the talking for him," Tally said.

"Tell me something I didn't know," Etah said.

"I know, I know. But the doctor said it's not a problem unless he doesn't start talking for himself by pre-school. That's when we'd have to consider putting them in different schools, or at least separate classes so that Moody would have to use his own voice."

"Well, I hate that for them. Nobody should separate twins," Etah said.

"I agree with you so let's hope it's not a problem by the time they're ready for school. We have to get them potty trained for that, first. I'm not going to borrow trouble by worrying about whether Moody will still be letting his sister talk for him when he gets married," she joked. Honestly, she was more worried about the potty training.

"Will Mitch be joining us for dinner tonight?" Etah asked.

"Probably not. He's been transferred to a different task force, and he has been in meetings all week about it and getting home late. I'm not sure what they're working on, to be honest. I haven't had enough time for him to download it all to me. Which sounds really bad when I say it out loud to you," she admitted.

"No, it doesn't, honey. You're both going 100 mph and you're exhausted by the time you get to be alone together. I was never married so I can't speak from experience, but I can tell you that I've seen lots of young couples on the same hamster wheel you're on right now. It will get better. The twins are getting easier to manage and me and Bonnie are getting better at it," her aunt joked.

"You two are phenomenal and I don't know what we would do without you. You being gone for a whole month just about undid me. Don't go away for so long again!" she demanded in a joking tone.

"How are things going with the new girls?" Aunt Etah asked. "Were the interns a good idea or a bad idea?" She'd been following things closely, even from her cruise. Helping Kelsi secure the little guest house had made her invested in the outcome of the overall project.

"It's going pretty well for the most part. I feel like they're learning and we're getting a lot of work out of them. I can't say at this point whether I'd want to hire any of them on full time, but that's why they have nine months to prove their value to me," she explained.

"How's Kelsi holding up?" Etah asked with a chuckle.

"I don't know why you encouraged her to live with the girls," Tally kept her eyes on the road but shook her head vigorously. "That was a terrible idea. She complains constantly."

"But she hasn't moved out, has she?"

"No, she hasn't even suggested it."

"Exactly. She's fine. Kelsi likes to help people and make their lives easier. Chances are she is just taking on more than she should with the interns. Once they've been here a little longer, she'll relax," Etah said.

"From your lips to God's ears. I've heard entirely too much about the bathroom habits of interns lately."

***

Mitch got home late that night, but Tally was still up, working on her laptop at the dining room table, when he came in.

"How was your day?" she asked him, as if they were a perfectly normal married couple seeing each other after work.

Mitch bent over and planted a kiss on her lips, and then he sat down in a chair next to her.

"Did Etah make it home in one piece?" he asked.

"She did. And she had a wonderful time. And she met a man." She watched for his reaction and was not disappointed. Although it took a second to dawn on him what she was saying.

"Really? Etah met a man?" Mitch grinned. "Wow. That's great." He said it like he meant it.

"His name is Beau Morris and he's from Atlanta. And he's into art and she's into him. I think it's adorable," Tally said. "I can't wait to meet him."

"Be careful you don't scare him away by threatening to leave the twins with her when he's around," Mitch sounded like he wasn't joking.

"I doubt Etah would want to date anybody who didn't want to hang out with Molly and Moody," she said. "They're her favorite little humans."

"We'll see."

"So, what exciting things did you do today?" Tally asked, getting up from the table to fix glasses of wine for both of them.

"I met the rest of the team we're working with on the new task force," he said. "It's some of the same federal agencies, but entirely different divisions and people. The guys running this task force are with HSI – Homeland Security Investigations. It's part of the Cultural Property, Art, and Antiquities program created to combat the smuggling of art and antiquities."

"You don't sound excited about it," she observed, setting a glass of wine down in front of him and taking her seat again.

"I'm not *not excited* about it, it just sounds kind of boring. At least the part they want me and Joe to do."

"And that is?"

"Mostly observation at the port and at some specific galleries that are suspected to be involved," Mitch said. "Really, Tally, it's not that different from what we've been doing for the past year, we're just watching for something different. It'll be a crate of artwork getting shipped instead of a cargo box of girls arriving."

"And that doesn't sound as exciting to you?" she asked, silently cheering to hear he wouldn't be going undercover or doing anything else she'd have to really worry about.

"We'll see how it turns out – it's not forever – they're trying to catch a piece of stolen artwork that is allegedly being shipped out of the United States before the end of this month. There's a black-market buyer waiting for it in Brazil or somewhere like that," he explained.

"I guess I didn't realize that art smuggling was a big problem," Tally admitted, a thoughtful look on her face. "I mean we've all seen it in the movies, but you don't really hear about it in real life."

"Most of the stolen artwork is sold privately to uber-wealthy collectors who can barely show it to anyone anyway. It's ridiculous," he told her, shaking his head. "A lot of it gets used to fund criminal enterprise or exchanged for political favors."

"Seriously?"

"Yeah, I guess one of these paintings can fetch enough money to fund multiple terrorist attacks, so that's a consideration, too. Art is just another way to hide money and move money around for nefarious purposes," he explained. "I still have to finish reading the briefing book tomorrow to get a handle on all of this. It's not something they really talked about at the academy. But it will be something on my resume that's not on the other guy's resume, I guess."

"That's for sure. And you get to stay here on Jekyll Island for the foreseeable future, right?" she asked.

"Correct. I'll be able to return to the other task force when this one is done with me, as long as the other task force still exists. You never know with how things operate with the feds," he explained.

"Well, I hope it turns out to be less boring than you think. Joe's working it with you?"

"Yep, he's my partner again," Mitch confirmed.

"So, no matter how lame the assignment is, at least you know it won't be boring," Tally pointed out.

"That's the truth," he chuckled. "My job is never boring."

"Kinda like weddings?" Tally teased.

"Yeah, but hopefully with less drama and tears."

Chapter 13

The residents of Jekyll Island were serious Georgia Bulldogs football fans. University of Georgia flags flew in front of a number of houses, and some diehard fans got much more creative, displaying their enthusiasm by putting inflatable Bulldogs and giant footballs with the Georgia logo on the side in their front yards.

"I think there are more Georgia decorations in people's yards than Halloween decorations," Liz complained one morning as she made coffee in the office.

"Probably," Kayla agreed. "But look at the average age on the island."

"She's right. There's not a whole lot of trick-or-treating going on here. The families with kids usually bring them around to the few houses giving out candy in their golf carts, but I think they do their real trick or treating in a normal neighborhood over in Brunswick," Tally explained.

"Plus, we have the Shrimp & Grits Festival on the island, right around the same time, and that's more than most of the residents can handle," Kayla added.

"She's right," Tally agreed. "Jekyll during Shrimp & Grits is like DC on the 4th of July. Some people love going to it, but a lot of others just plan to be out of town every year. Jekyll Island is a zoo with an extra 40,000 people on it."

"Is the festival cool?" Katy asked. "I've heard about it, but I've never been."

"It's awesome," Tori told them. "We came down from Charleston one year for it and had a wonderful time. But that was back before the pandemic. My mom said she'd heard it's not the same anymore."

"It's still a great festival, but your mom is right. It's not the same as it used to be," Tally admitted. "There are a lot of things that have changed on Jekyll since I first came to live here."

The women sat down around the table in the office and started the staff meeting they'd all been avoiding.

"Let's do Brubaker/Sherman last," Kelsi suggested. "I think it's going to take the most time, and some of this new stuff I need to tell you about will likely derail us. Just trust me," she told them with a smirk.

"Uh oh," Kayla said. "I don't like the sound of that."

Tally passed around an agenda, and her team picked their way through the events that were scheduled through the rest of the year. There was nothing on their calendar for the better part of December because Tally had a firm rule about that. But when they got through all of the weddings they needed to do for the rest of the year – except Brubaker/Sherman – Tally told the girls about something new they needed to put on their calendars.

"Okay so I had dinner at Bonnie's house with Etah and Roberta last night," she began. "It was just us girls – Tom had to work, and Mitch didn't get home until after we were finished."

"Of course," Kayla said sympathetically. She knew how hard Tally and her husband struggled to live on the same schedule.

"But being just girls, I heard lots more local gossip than I usually get when the guys are around."

"I bet," Kelsi nodded.

"And I also heard about this ridiculous volunteer plan that Etah and Bonnie have cooked up."

"Huh?" Kayla asked, sounding puzzled. Kelsi said nothing but didn't look any more clued in than anybody else.

"Yeah, it started back before Etah left on her cruise," Tally explained. She took a sip of her coffee and a breath before she continued. "Bonnie has been volunteering at the Mosaic Museum for the past few years, and she wanted Etah to do it with her after she retired. She gets all sorts of cool invitations through her volunteering, and she wanted Etah to be her wing-woman."

"But Etah already had another plan in mind. She'd done her research and found out that Goodyear Cottage and the Friends of Historic Jekyll Island throw some of the best events, so she told Bonnie she was going to join those groups, and they could tag along with each other to everybody's events without both of them having to volunteer at all the different organizations. She joined the Jekyll Artists and signed up to volunteer there."

The girls around the table nodded as if the plan made sense to them.

"And then Aunt Etah met a man with an interest in art on her cruise and suddenly she's a lot more interested in the arts on Jekyll," Tally told them with a straight face, waiting for their reactions.

"She what?" Kelsi asked.

"No way!" Kayla blurted.

"Yes way," Tally laughed. "His name is Beauregard, and he lives in Atlanta. He's a retired band director."

"Beauregard? How old is he?" Liz joked.

"Younger than Aunt Etah," Tally surprised them all. "She calls him Beau. It's really cute the way her face lights up when she talks about him.

She said he's going to come visit her on Jekyll in the near future, so we'll have to plan a barbecue or something to give everybody a chance to check him out. Not gonna lie, I'm very curious."

"How come your million-year-old aunt can get a date but I can't?" Liz whined.

"Because you never want to leave Jekyll Island!" Tori replied quickly. "The only men here for us would be sugar daddies, and I don't think my parents would approve of that." She was serious and Tally and her senior planner were struggling not to laugh.

"I dunno, how much money would my Jekyll sugar daddy have?" Katy asked.

"Alright, let's stop right there. I did not bring three Anna Nicole Smiths to the island for the semester," Tally joked, referencing a young model who had become famous for marrying a wealthy elderly man named J. Howard Marshall.

At their age, Anna Nicole Smith was stripping to pay for her child that she'd had out of wedlock when she met her sugar daddy in the club where she worked. They were married for a few years, and he left her most of his money when he died. The world watched Anna Nicole Smith's very downward spiral on reality TV during her public battle over Marshall's estate with his sons. Her story ended tragically when she died of an overdose just months after her son, Daniel, died of the same thing.

Tally looked around the table at five blank faces and realized she'd used a reference that none of her Millennial or Gen Z employees understood.

"Look it up," she ordered all of them. "Anna Nicole Smith is a pop culture reference you should know. Plus, her reality show was hilarious and well worth binging. Actually, it was awful, but it was impossible to stop watching it. Sort of like a train wreck."

"Can we please talk about the Brubaker/Sherman wedding now?" Kelsi asked. She glanced at the time on her phone as she made the request.

"Absolutely. What's going on with that? I saw some wild emails flying around yesterday," Tally said with a hint of a smile.

"Yeah, how's that going?" Kayla asked. "Did you figure out what was going on with the bridesmaid dresses?"

"Unfortunately, I did. I spoke to her mother, Vera, last night and honestly, I don't really know what to do with this one. Figured we could put our heads together."

Tally put down her pen and sat back in her chair, focusing her full attention on Kelsi. "What's up?"

"You all saw the email I got from that bridesmaid who is a cousin, Julie Musitano?" Kelsi asked. Everybody around the table nodded.

"Well, I got a few more emails like it the next day – all worded similarly enough that I don't think I'm being a conspiracy theorist when I say this: I believe Kortney's bridesmaids have banded together to send a message to the bride," Kelsi continued. "From what I have read – and I haven't called any of these women because I'm not ready to get yelled at – but from what I read in the emails, it appears that Kortney ordered size 8 bridesmaid dresses for all of her attendants, regardless of what size they actually are."

Kayla gasped audibly. "No way."

"Way," Kelsi nodded. "We had three more dropouts today. What's interesting is that everybody who has resigned from the wedding party is a relative. I wondered right away if this was an intentional move by the bride to get rid of some dead wood."

"Really?" Kayla asked, sounding doubtful. "Are all of her friends a size 8? Did anybody know she was going to do this?"

"Apparently not, from the tone of the emails. Two of the girls wrote that they'd rather waste the money they spent on non-refundable plane tickets than stand up for a bride who had treated them so disrespectfully."

"Ouch," Liz said.

"Big ouch," Kelsi agreed. "I tried to talk to Kortney about it yesterday afternoon, but she sent me a really bitchy text about how busy and important she is, and asked that I handle any problems myself that weren't 'a house on fire' and use my own best judgment."

"Yikes," Kayla said. "That could get awkward."

"Right? I called Vera last night to find out what was going on. That also may not have been the best decision I made this week," Kelsi said and sighed loudly.

"Why?" Tally asked.

"Because I think people in Alaska could hear Vera shrieking about it all the way from Chicago."

"So that's what that sound upstairs was," Katy said with a snort. "I thought maybe you had broken the house rules about bringing boys home."

"Smartass," Kelsi said, giving her a look. "It turns out that Kortney cut a deal with her mom when they were wedding dress shopping and she probably pulled this little stunt to get out of her end of it. It turns out that Kortney has seven bridesmaids because her mother agreed to buy her a wedding gown that was three times what they'd budgeted if Kortney would invite her girl cousins to be in the wedding.

"But Kortney didn't want any of her cousins in the wedding because she doesn't socialize with them and doesn't feel like she fits in when they do a girls' night together, at least that was the reason that she gave her mother at the time. But really, she doesn't want any bigger girls in her wedding pictures. I think we all know what she was up to now when she told us about paying for their dresses."

"What?" Tori looked completely confused while the other girls around the table were nodding.

"She did it to screw with her cousins," Katy turned to Tori and explained what the rest of the wedding planning team had already figured out. "She knew the size 8 dresses wouldn't fit them, so she sent them to incentivize her cousins to resign from the wedding party. Rude as hell, but effective," she shrugged. "She couldn't leave them out and get the wedding gown she wanted, so she had to make them get mad and quit."

"What did Vera say when she finished yelling about it?" Tally asked.

"Vera never really stopped ranting on our call," Kelsi admitted. "She's fired up. Her sister called her after we finished talking and went off about how mean the dress-size thing was to her daughter. She sent me an outraged text demanding that I talk some sense into her daughter."

"And did you try?" Kayla asked, sounding sympathetic.

"I'm still waiting for Kortney to find time for me in her busy schedule," Kelsi replied, deadpan.

"You're kidding," Tally said.

"I wish I were. But there's also some good news to report," she teased.

"What's that?"

"The other three girls received their bridesmaid dresses and said they fit," Kelsi reported.

"Thank God for small favors," Kayla said.

"Thank God for small bridesmaids is more like it," Kelsi shot back. "Her sorority sisters must all be tiny from what Vera said."

"Have we seen a picture of the dresses?" Tally asked, curious.

"Oh yes, we have," Kelsi replied, pulling a piece of paper from her file and dropping it on the table where everybody could take a look.

"Wow," Kayla said at first glance.

"I love it," Tori told them. "That's the perfect cerulean blue for Tri Delts."

Kayla and Kelsi both looked at the intern from Charleston as though she'd grown a second head.

"What?" Tori asked in an innocent voice.

"You can't be serious. I've seen more fabric in bathing suits," Liz told her, picking up the picture of the bridesmaid dresses to get a closer look. She shook her head.

"What she did was messed up," Liz continued, sounding a bit like she was lecturing Tori. "She intentionally humiliated women who had agreed to stand up for her on her wedding day. This dress wouldn't look good on anybody over a size 8 – it would probably be indecent on anybody with boobs."

"Well, it's the perfect color, anyway," Tori wasn't going to turn her back on her favorite bride yet. The sisterhood connection was obviously strong, and it made Tally glad she'd gone to Georgetown University. It didn't have a real Greek system to screw up all of her priorities.

"So, Kortney is down to three bridesmaids. What will that mean for Mike's side of the aisle?" Tally asked.

"Vera said she didn't know what Kortney was thinking on that, so I straight-up asked her if any of the guys in the wedding party were fat," Kelsi said.

"You did not!" Tori looked horrified.

"I hope she did," Tally interjected and looked at Kelsi hopefully.

"I did. And I think that's when it clicked for Vera that it wasn't just about Kortney not fitting in with her female cousins. She didn't want any fatties in her wedding. Period," Kelsi told them.

"Would you rate this better or worse than the brides who tell their girlfriends to lose a certain amount of weight before the wedding?" Katy asked. "Because that happens all the time. My sister was in a wedding like that once and she couldn't eat for a month beforehand or the dress wouldn't have zipped."

"I would have dropped out of that wedding," Kayla declared. "I don't like anybody that much."

"Me too," Kelsi said. "Definitely. I like food more than most of my friends."

"We know," Tally said and winked.

"All humor aside, how would you suggest that I handle this?" Kelsi asked Tally in a serious voice. "Kortney and I get along fine but that's because I don't challenge her on anything. I let her mother do that and then she takes the fire for it. I do not want to have to get involved in this dress fiasco."

"Don't," Tally agreed with her. Kelsi looked seriously stressed out over this and that annoyed her. She watched the young wedding planner wrap and unwrap her hair around her finger and, finally, put the end of a piece in her mouth to chew on. Kelsi only did that when she was really worried, Tally knew.

"This dress mess is not our problem unless we make it our problem. And we're not going to do that," Tally told the younger girl. "We were hired to plan and execute the wedding, and we're going to do all of that perfectly. We have no obligation to manage wedding party matters before they all get here. We don't know her friends. While I understand why they reached out to you versus the bride, it was the wrong thing to do, and it put you in a bad position with Kortney."

"I know all of that. How can I fix it?" Kelsi asked.

"You can't," Tally replied.

"No way," Kayla agreed. "These girls knew Kortney had a mean streak because they grew up with her. They probably suspected she was up to something when she told them she'd ordered the dresses without sending anybody to get measured for them. That's not how it works. So, any one of them could have gotten upset then, but apparently didn't. They waited to see what trivial baloney Kortney would throw at them before they made their exits."

"Don't do anything with the bridesmaids' emails. Don't even follow up about a conference call with Kortney to discuss them," Tally advised. "Just forward the emails to Kortney and her mother with a note that says something about it being inappropriate for you to handle the wedding party problems. Copy me. You've already talked to Vera, so it won't come as a surprise to her."

"What if Kortney calls me to yell? I'd really like to avoid that."

"If you're really concerned, put her number in your cell phone so you can avoid her calls. Don't call her back unless her message is about something else. And even then, try to reply via text or email if you can get away with it," Tally said. "We have our final wrap-up planning call with Kortney and her mom next week, anyway. It's going to come up, and I'll handle it then. In the meantime, you keep doing what you're supposed to do, and make sure you've triple checked the lists for this particular bride," she said in a warning tone. "We cannot afford to have her catch a mistake. She'd like nothing more than to take out her life's frustrations on us in a nasty Wedding Wire review. And we've worked too hard for that to happen."

Everybody nodded in agreement. Wedding Wire was to wedding planners what their "permanent record" was to schoolchildren. It could make or break a young business.

They reviewed their calendars for the next week and sorted out a few conflicts.

"Kortney's group will start arriving on Wednesday, but her activities start on Thursday at The Wharf," Tally said to nobody in particular. "I've got plans on Thursday night."

"I don't think we'll need you for anything on Thursday," Kelsi said. "Unless you need to come bail me out because I tried to kill our client."

"Don't do that," Tally advised. "It's terrible for our reviews."

"I've got you," Yaya yelled from inside her office, about 10 feet away from their meeting table. She came out and sat down with them to comment on everything she'd heard them saying. "I'll bail you out, *mija*. I've got your back on this. In fact, the way my week has been going so far, I'd like to volunteer to solve this little problem for you, if you want. I haven't been to Horton Pond in a while."

Everybody laughed. Yaya was famous for threatening vigilante "Viequenses Justice" on anyone who made her angry. Horton Pond was a big watering hole in the marsh where a large family of alligators lived. There was a viewing platform adjacent that was super popular with tourists. Most residents only mentioned Horton Pond when they were joking about offing somebody.

"Thank you so much for your kind offer, Yaya," Kelsi said with a laugh. "But you'll be too busy fighting with flowers on Sea Island that weekend to help feed the bride to the alligators on Jekyll. I'm sure the wedding itself will be fine. I'm just dreading the unavoidable drama that's going to be the result of this dress thing."

"Vera said that her sisters were threatening to boycott the wedding because their own daughters were so upset," she reported.

"I don't blame them," Kayla said. "Being a bridesmaid is a pain in the ass. And it's expensive. I'm only willing to extend myself that far for a few special people. Kortney would never be one of them."

"Definitely not," Kelsi agreed.

"Stay focused on the wedding plans and let the chips fall where they may in Chicago. It's entirely possible that all of her cousins will be here by the time Vera works things out. She's the one who insisted that Kortney ask them to be in her wedding, and she will have egg all over her face if she lets her daughter get away with this. Anybody want to place a bet on whether the mother of the bride has already ordered replacement dresses for the offended ladies?" Tally asked.

"Can you do that with less than a month's notice?" Liz asked, looking genuinely baffled. "Wouldn't they have to find something off the rack that fit?

"You can have anything you want on your wedding day – including four bridesmaid dresses made on the rush – if you're willing to spend enough money," Tally replied.

"Well, that's the good news in all of this," Tori declared, prompting the other women to look at her quizzically. "At the very worst, she'll have fat bridesmaids in cerulean blue. And her colors are going to look awesome. The tiki torches that she chose for her ceremony aisle will be wrapped in cerulean tulle and have gold ribbons streaming from them. And all of the table linens at the reception will be cerulean blue. The table décor at Eighty Ocean will be silver, gold, and cerulean blue, too. We're swirling wide gold ribbons around the bases of clusters of tall sterling silver candlesticks and using handmade cerulean tapers in all of them." The intern looked at her list to continue but Kelsi cut her off.

"Tori, I appreciate your enthusiasm, but if you say 'cerulean' one more time, we're taking you to Horton Pond with Kortney," Kelsi threatened. "Just call it blue, please. Before you make all of us nuts."

"Okay," Tori agreed, but her face said she didn't understand. Tally had noticed that she looked like that a lot of the time.

"That's it for today," Tally declared. "I've got places to be and toddlers to see. I can't believe the twins are turning two in January. We need to start planning that party."

"Upstairs at Tribuzio's again?" Kayla asked.

"Probably. We have to figure out the theme first. They're so little that it doesn't really matter but I want to have a proper party and get good pictures," Tally told them.

"You're not going to top last year's pictures," Yaya told her. "When Molly picked up her entire cake and put it on Moody's head," she started laughing and couldn't finish her thought.

"Let's hope we don't top that," Tally agreed. "We had to hose them off outside on the deck before we could bring them in the house for naptime."

"Oh my!" Katy laughed. "Sounds like it was quite a party."

"It's always a party at our house," Tally laughed. "It's either a party or an asylum, and as I am a professional wedding planner, I prefer to believe that I'm hosting events."

Chapter 14

The interns were bickering before Kelsi had her coffee, and that was against the morning rules at intern house.

"Why are you yelling this early?" she asked as she stumbled down the steep staircase into the interns' living space. She was relieved to see the bathroom door open and dashed into it before somebody could beat her there. Sharing a small bathroom with three other girls was the worst part about this living arrangement. But the free rent thing definitely outweighed the little inconveniences.

"Tell Kelsi what you did," Katy told Liz in a harsh voice.

"I put up an inflatable Ohio State Snoopy in the front yard," Liz said. "I don't think it's a felony, even in Georgia," she added sounding miffed.

"Wait what?" Kelsi was so confused. "Let me pee really quick and then you can explain."

After she'd used the bathroom, Kelsi followed the girls outside in her pajamas. Everybody else was dressed, which was weird because they weren't supposed to leave for another hour yet. Usually, somebody downstairs was still snoring at this time of the morning.

"Why is everybody up so early?" she asked nobody in particular as they made their way around to the front yard.

"Because Liz is rude as hell," Katy replied quickly.

"She woke us up with her stupid project this morning," Tori explained. "She pretty much tossed us out of bed."

"I said I was sorry," Liz snapped at her.

"You still woke us up," Tori snapped back.

"For real, Kelsi, she rocked the damned bunk bed to try and pull a box out from underneath," Katy reported. "I could have broken my neck falling from the top bunk because of that stupidity." She sounded mad and she wasn't cutting her intern partner any slack this morning.

"I was trying to wiggle-jiggle the box out from under the bed without waking you guys up. I'm sorry," Liz said again. This time she sounded like she actually felt badly for waking them up.

"If you'd waited til we were up, we would have helped you," Tori said. "I think the Snoopy is cool."

"Snoopy?" Kelsi asked, more confused than she'd been when she heard the girls arguing.

"See?" Liz pointed across the driveway to a red inflatable Snoopy doghouse with a big Ohio State logo on the side of it. Snoopy himself sat atop his house like a comic strip. The only thing missing was Woodstock.

Just then, Susan McLemore came out of her house across the street to collect her copy of *The Brunswick News* from the driveway. "It looks great," she called to them, making Kelsi chuckle. All the girls waved back at her and shouted morning greetings.

"Well, if it doesn't bother Susan, and she has to look at it every time she walks out her door, then it's okay with me. But if the Jekyll Realty people get annoyed, we'll have to take it down," Kelsi determined, thinking out loud.

"I don't care about the stupid Snoopy," Katy said. "I'm just really mad that I lost an entire hour of sleep after I bothered to shower last night so I could sleep later this morning." Her tone had changed, and she wasn't sounding as accusatory as she had a few minutes earlier. Kelsi figured it probably had to do with the fact they were all standing there staring at a giant Snoopy together.

"I'm really sorry about the way I did all this," Liz told her roommates, sounding sincere this time. "I didn't think it through all the way. I've been meaning to put him up for a couple of weeks, and we keep getting home from work after dark every night. I set my alarm for super early today so that I could put him up and be ready for work on time. I didn't think about needing to turn on lights and how much noise I was going to make."

"Okay, is everything forgiven now, ladies?" Kelsi asked, trying not to sound as annoyed as she felt. "I'm going to go get ready for work and I'd expect all of you to be ready to go before I am, since you blew me out of bed." She sounded annoyed but that was okay, she thought. Sleep was sacrosanct for Kelsi and having the interns disturb her had started her day out badly.

She saw that the interns had read her annoyed tone correctly and tried to fix things before everybody ended up having a bad day together.

"While you're waiting on me, you might think about what kind of costumes you're planning to wear to the Halloween Costume Party at Tribuzio's Grille. They give out prizes for the best ones," Kelsi told them. "There's a group costume prize, too. If you ladies feel like doing some bonding."

She saw Liz roll her eyes and headed upstairs before the other girls could silently express their opinions, too.

Chapter 15

Etah Davis straightened her skirt and then slowly made her way up the front steps of Goodyear Cottage, home to the Jekyll Island Arts Association. It had been years since she'd been a regular volunteer anywhere. She'd occasionally done shifts at soup kitchens and shelters when other reporters were going to be there. But for the vast majority of her years as a wire service news reporter, Etah had covered news stories in places where a woman wasn't welcome to engage with the community in that way.

She got up to the top of the steps and reached for the doorknob. It was locked. She was confused and wondered what she was forgetting. She was glad she'd remembered to bring the three-ring binder she'd been given at the front desk training session. She pulled it out, read the first page and groaned. Then she trudged back down the stairs and around to the side of the building where the keys were kept in a lockbox.

"Apparently, I'm working alone today," Etah said to herself as she fiddled with the lockbox. Once she'd liberated the keys, she let herself in through the kitchen door and then locked it behind her.

"I'm not sure what they're thinking letting a new volunteer run things alone," she said aloud as she wandered through the historic vacation home of the Goodyear family, trying to find all the light switches they'd been shown at orientation. She remembered seeing that kind of light switch in homes when she was a child, but she'd never lived anywhere that had an electrical system that old before. *Neat, and sort of frightening*, she thought.

The art gallery and its accompanying gift shop looked beautiful with the morning sunshine pouring through the wavy glass of the original windows. She heard noises coming from the basement of the building and realized that the members of the pottery guild were probably downstairs working. She remembered that the weavers might be upstairs, too. She'd have to look at the building's daily schedule. Goodyear Cottage had a lot of regular member traffic that wasn't there to shop.

Etah opened up the binder again to see what else she needed to do. The volunteer guide said she should turn on the music in the gallery and check around for anything that looked dirty or needed to be straightened. She did – she even checked the powder room - but everything looked like it had just been cleaned and polished. It was far tidier than her own home, for sure.

At 12 o'clock on the dot, Etah unlocked the front door of the historic house on Millionaire's Row in the Jekyll Island historic district and put the "Open" flag in its holder beside the front door. She folded her arms across her chest and stood contently for a few minutes, enjoying the fall breeze and the lack of tourists on the sidewalk. A slow day with few shoppers was exactly what she wanted to see on her first day behind the cash register.

***

Two hours into Etah's first volunteer shift, Jackie Becker came flying into the gift shop with her arms full of things that couldn't be easily identified.

She said hello to Etah as she rushed through and then came back out to chat a few minutes later, after she'd dropped everything at her desk in the kitchen beside the computer that was the brain of the shop.

"Has it been busy?" Jackie asked.

"Not really. A few looky-loos shortly after we opened but that's about it," Etah reported.

"Pretty normal for an off-season Wednesday," Jackie replied. "I'm glad you're volunteering at the desk here. We need more new faces getting involved at Goodyear."

Etah had met Jackie and her husband, Bruce, shortly after they arrived on the island to renovate one of the homes across the street from Susan McLemore on Old Plantation. They'd been flipping houses for years in Florida and decide to make Jekyll Island their retirement spot.

Jackie knew everything about everything at Goodyear Cottage. She'd been on the board of the Jekyll Island Arts Association for years, and she was credited with singlehandedly turning the Merry Artists Holiday Market into a massive revenue generator and popular regional arts event. On top of that, she managed the shop inventory and was constantly answering calls from volunteers with questions about how to do their jobs. Fortunately, she almost always had the answers.

"Here ya go," Jackie dropped a pretty envelope on the desk in front of Etah. "I'm getting my Pie Night invitations out early this year because if I wait until we're neck-deep in Merry Artists prep, I'll change my mind about throwing the party." She laughed as she said it, but Etah knew the tall blonde woman wasn't really joking. She'd worked so hard on Merry Artists the previous year that she'd made herself sick. Etah knew her friend didn't plan to do that again.

"Pie night!" Etah crowed. "I love Pie Night, and I've missed so many because I was traveling for work. I'll be there!"

"Pie Night is always the same night every year – you should put it on your calendar," Jackie reminded her. "The Thursday before Thanksgiving so that we can eat all the different kinds of pie that we want. We're always too stuffed to do that after turkey on Thanksgiving Day, and everybody working Merry Artists will be too tired to care. That's how the tradition got started."

"Well, I think it's a wonderful tradition, and I'm very happy that I'll be here this year. I'll have to coordinate with Bonnie so that we don't bring the same kind of pie again," she laughed.

A few years earlier, both Bonnie and Etah had baked their famous apple pie recipes that were basically identical. Each woman claimed the recipe was hers, but they didn't really know where it had originated. It had caused a laugh amongst their friends. Etah was determined not to be accused of pie plagiarism again this year.

"Is there any chance you're available to pick up an extra shift or two in the next few weeks?" Jackie asked.

Etah had seen the pleas for desk help in the emails from Jekyll Artists.

"I could add a Tuesday or Thursday for a few weeks, but I help out with Tally and Mitch's twins a lot, so I can't be too unavailable. I'm having way too much fun playing with my grandbabies," she smiled

"That would be great," Jackie was quick to the accept the offer before Etah had a chance to think twice. She whipped out her phone and, in a few clicks, Etah had signed up for the Tuesday desk shifts for October and November.

Oh, she's good, Etah thought. She hadn't meant to commit herself to so much volunteering out of the box but somehow, Jackie made you want to help her out. So, she would.

Jackie left a short while later and Etah kept busy with the slow trickle of tourists who wandered into the shop. She sold some pottery and several copies of local author Pamela Bauer Mueller's most famous book, *Splended Isolation*.

Etah had done her studying and was able to lead one of the couples on a tour of the historic Goodyear Cottage, explaining how it was one of the only homes built on Millionaire's Row at the Jekyll Club that actually had a kitchen. Most of the families had taken all of their meals in the Main Dining Room in the club house, and so their homes only had small butler's pantries. It was one of the quirks of the famous moguls of the Gilded Age who had spent their winters on the tiny island off the coast of Georgia, and Etah found it fascinating.

At 4 p.m., Etah brought in the flag and locked the front doors. Her new gentleman friend, Beau Morris, had intimated that he might find the time to drive down to Jekyll to surprise her over the weekend and she needed to get home to straighten up. It wouldn't do for her new friend to catch her with lingerie drying in her powder room.

She packed up the tote bag she'd carried her magazines and snacks in and then carefully made her way through the historic home, making sure to turn off all of the lights as she went. She wasn't about to be the person responsible for causing the historic Goodyear Cottage to burn to the ground because of a wiring problem in the night. The artists would probably vote her off the island.

Chapter 16

Beau did come to visit on Friday evening, and he didn't leave until Sunday morning, Etah was ashamed to admit. She was glad that Tally was busy with weddings, or she knew she would have had to introduce her gentleman caller to her niece. They were too close to hide something that she hoped would become a more serious relationship.

Meeting Beau had been random. She and her travelling companion, Scarlett Branson, who she'd known since her White House reporting days, had opted to be seated with other passengers at their dinner table in the ship's big dining room. They'd get bored with just each other after a few days, they joked.

Beau had been traveling by himself, and had been seated at their table, along with a family from Ohio. He and Etah recognized each other's Georgia accents immediately and struck up a quick friendship. She and Scarlett had really enjoyed listening to him play the piano, guitar, and any other instrument he could talk the ship's entertainers into handing over to him. By the time they disembarked in Florida a month later, Etah was wishing Atlanta wasn't a five-hour drive from Jekyll Island.

Her new friend had explained on the ship that although his training had been focused on music his entire life, he also had a keen interest in the visual arts. They'd visited several museums together when the ship stopped in places that had historic significance and worthwhile spots. They'd talked about the local music and art festivals they'd attended in their youth – neither had been at Woodstock and both of them regretted it. Etah had been delighted to learn that her new friend was also very familiar with the art scene in the Golden Isles in the 1950s and 1960s.

"My aunt and uncle had a house on St. Simons Island when I was growing up, and I spent more time there than at my own home in the summer," he explained. "My cousins were just one year older, and one year younger than me, and we ran like wild things all over the island. Back then it wasn't nearly as developed as it is now."

Etah heard him sigh and understood exactly how he felt.

"I remember. I've always loved St. Simons – not as much as Jekyll, mind you – but it's such a pretty place with such rich history. If it weren't for all the people and the traffic, I'd like to live there," she joked. There was a subtle snark in her tone that gave away her true feelings on the matter.

"But it's worth it to go over because the Literary Guild of St. Simons brings in such wonderful authors," Etah continued. "And when I was a child, we'd never have missed Sunshine Fest. It was the highlight of the summer," she recalled, smiling softly. "I've missed a lot of the community events over the past 30 years. And it seems like some of my favorite things to do on the island have gone away with time."

"A lot of things in our lives seem like that now," Beau agreed.

They felt the same way about a lot of things, Etah learned during their long talks on the ship and while wandering through ruins on Greek islands. It wasn't just about coming from the same generation, although that helped. They both remembered life with rotary phones, before the

Internet, and were of the generation of parents who had to be reminded by Cher and other celebrities to make sure their children were home by 10 p.m. Neither of them had their own children, which Etah thought was a little unusual.

Raising Tally hadn't been normal parenting, at least as far as Etah was concerned. She'd been fortunate the little girl was self-sufficient and had enough confidence to survive being pulled from her home and school and moved more than 800 miles south at the drop of a hat after losing her mommy and daddy. If Tally hadn't been mature enough to be sent off to St. Margarets when her parents were killed in that terrible plane crash, Etah would have given up her career traveling to raise her.

Etah looked at Beau in the orangey-glow of the sunset. He had thick white hair and a nicely-trimmed mustache. It would have been good if he were a little taller, but she figured she was shrinking anyway so at some point they'd even up. Anyway, height didn't matter when you were in bed. She'd told Tally as much in the car on the way home from the airport and had laughed until her belly hurt at her great-niece's reaction.

"Too soon?" she'd asked, grinning.

"Way too soon," Tally said, giving her aunt the side-eye.

"Sunshine Fest? Wasn't that a Bill and Mittie Hendrix festival?" Beau asked, bringing Etah's thoughts back to the present. They were sitting on her balcony watching the sun set over the Jekyll River. The condos by the marina were the only residences on the island with a sunset view this spectacular. She missed her oceanfront house that now held Tally's family, but the sunsets on this side of the island more than made up for it. Plus, she could enjoy her former view on the days she was babysitting Molly and Moody.

"Sorry, I was just remembering..." she didn't explain what she was re-membering, and Beau didn't ask. They were both of an age where almost everything reminded them of something, and it would take all day if they shared all of those thoughts. "Yes, Sunshine Fest was a Bill and Mittie thing. Really more of a Mittie thing since she was the one who did all the organizing and ran the business side of things. But people came from all over the United States to see Bill Hendrix and take classes from him. Anything Mittie planned for Bill was sold out as soon as it opened. She was a real dynamo."

"Did you know them?" he asked, sounding impressed. Etah nodded proudly but knew it wasn't really an impressive claim because absolutely everybody who had ever spent time on St. Simons Island had met Bill, Mittie, or one of their children at some point during their visit. The Hendrix family was everywhere. And they also had a beautiful home on Amelia Island, just over the Florida border. Tally's parents had died in a plane crash just off Fernandina Beach there, not far from where the Hendrix's house had been.

"Yes, I knew both of them, but I knew Mittie better because we were on several of the same committees back in the day," Etah said. "She and I both walked our shoe leather off helping campaign for President Jimmy Carter one summer."

"Really, you were a liberal back then?" Beau chuckled.

"I'm not a conservative now," Etah shot back, not wanting to be labeled.

"You're closer to a Republican than a Democrat, my lady," he replied with a chuckle. "You want legalized pot and gay marriage, but you don't like handing your hard-earned money to the government to use on people who don't feel like working for it. I'd say you're a pretty solid Blue Democrat – or moderate Republican – you can choose whichever you find least offensive, of course. But you and I are alike, Etah. And they don't make them like us anymore."

"That's the truth," she agreed. Beau lifted his wine glass to clink a toast, and she met him in midair. They settled into a comfortable silence while they watched the shocking orange ribbons of sky fade to a coral, and then pink, before they eventually disappeared into the water beyond the Sidney Lanier Bridge.

Chapter 17

"I swear to God, this wedding makes me want to elope," Kayla told Jake when they finally sat down to eat dinner the night before the Brubaker/Sherman wedding group was to arrive on the island.

"We had the usual pre-game meeting," she continued, cutting into her steak like she meant to hurt it. "And that didn't go as badly as it could have, but there were things that should have been done that weren't. And when you add to it the wedding party crisis... there's a lot for those girls to juggle this weekend."

"Tally's still planning to let the interns run the wedding?" her fiancé asked, a puzzled look on his face.

"Yeppers."

"Why?" It was obvious her veterinarian husband-to-be was not as business savvy as he was good looking, she thought.

"Because we are hoping all of these girls succeed in our program and become wedding planners for a career. We hope some of them will actually want to be hired and have demonstrated the ability to learn so that when their internships are up, they're staying on as planners. If we don't start letting them run things, they won't learn," Kayla explained, in between shoving bites of food in her mouth. She realized it had to look terrible and made an effort to slow down. "I'm sorry – I didn't have time to eat anything today. I kept meaning to run next door to Love Shack but I never got a break."

Love Shack was the little carry-out restaurant inside the Jekyll Market. It was known for its famous fresh fried wild Georgia shrimp, but Kayla really had a thing for their Brunswick stew. Plus, the stew was easier to grab when she was in a hurry – you had to wait while they fried up the shrimp.

"Maybe you should start packing a lunch?" Jake suggested sensibly.

"I should. It's just that I've tried doing that in the past and it always turned into a rather nasty science experiment if I don't remember to deal with the Tupperware."

"Ew," Jake said.

"Exactly. I actually spend less money when I buy when I'm hungry during the day, rather than trying to pack stuff I'll be in the mood for when I'm hungry. I'm not that great at meal planning, as you know," she reminded him. "Besides, it gives me an excuse to take a breath and get out of the office for a few minutes. At least I go out and get lunch most days. Today wasn't a normal day."

"Tell me about it," Jake encouraged her.

"This is Kortney, the bride I told you about who ordered the dresses too small for her bridesmaids on purpose," she began.

Jake made a face. "I remember."

"Well, we're down to just three bridesmaids – her sorority sisters that she wanted in her wedding. And she's happy as a little clam," she said. "Kelsi said she told the groom – who was participating in a planning call for the first time ever last night – that he had to demote a few of his groomsmen to ushers and he didn't even flinch. He was like 'okey dokey.'"

"To be fair, you've got to remember that his buddies who got out of having to stand up at the ceremony were probably thrilled. Guys hate that stuff," he opined, not for the first time. "I mean, I've done it for a good friend and I'm sure I'll do it again at some point, but it's a pain in the ass and it ends up being super-expensive now that everybody wants to go somewhere fancy for the bachelor party," he complained.

"I blame brides for that, by the way. It was the women who started this 'take me somewhere cool for my last wild night' bs, and now it's spread across the aisle to us guys, too," Jake continued, almost on a rant. "I mean isn't renting the tux enough? Now we're expected to pick up our share of the groom's plane ticket and trip to Vegas or Cancun or wherever."

"You don't want to have a destination bachelor party when we get married?" Kayla giggled, knowing full well that wasn't Jake's style.

"Absolutely not," Jake said firmly. "Actually, I was talking my buddy, Andrew, about it, and we both agreed that when we get married, we'd be perfectly happy with a beach day and a barbecue. But don't let that stop you from doing something epic," he added quickly, knowing even as he said it that Kayla wasn't that kind of woman.

They sat there in a companionable silence, finishing up the steaks that Jake had grilled and had waiting when Kayla finally got home from the office, two hours later than she'd guessed when she left for work that morning.

"You know, if we want to get married anytime in the next two years, we're going to have to set a wedding date," Kayla said carefully, not wanting Jake to think she was suddenly turning into one of *those* brides. "We're booked out two years right now, and it would be more, but Tally drew a hard line there. She said that she has to stay flexible because the twins are going to be a handful when they hit school age. She hopes to be staffed up enough that she can run things and not have to go to events by then, but she's afraid to book that far ahead without really knowing what's going to happen in her life."

"Do you think they're going to have more kids?" he asked.

"I'm not sure. She doesn't talk about having more kids, yet. And I've never heard him say anything. I doubt they're even in bed at the same time often enough to make another baby."

"Well, that's just sad," Jake said.

Kayla nodded in agreement. "I know. And that's why it's so hard for me to keep pushing for the St. Simons office expansion. I know Tally is at her absolute max and she's not wrong about us needing to staff up before expanding, but I also know that St. Simons is ripe for a new local wedding team after Kelsi's old boss sold to one of the big destination management companies. They've been slammed so much on Wedding Wire that it's surprising they're still in business here. Only a seriously sloppy bride would consider hiring them."

"I thought the whole point of destination management companies was that they weren't here and just sent people on site when they needed to. At least that's how Kelsi explained it to me when she was let go," Jake said, looking confused.

"You understand it correctly. It's just that you can't really run destination weddings that way. It's fine for business conferences and big events, where the planner goes in for a day to confirm the client's selections for the hotel. But when it's something as personal as wedding, those bigger, off-site companies usually come up short," Kayla told him.

"For example, somebody who came in from Atlanta or New York to execute a wedding wouldn't know where to find a tailor or seamstress on the fly for a wardrobe emergency on a weekend. Same with being able to get the florist to go back into their shop to remake a bouquet for a dissatisfied bride. We do that sort of stupid stuff all the time because we own the flower company, too. But when you're dealing with a flower vendor out of Savannah who has a bunch of other wedding orders to fulfill the same day, they're not going back in to change up a bouquet that was made exactly as the bride ordered. We do," she said.

Jake still didn't look like he got the difference.

"We can triage any crisis, Jake. Remember how we met? Best Man ate the wedding rings? I got your number from Mitch and called you based on the reference that you've treated state patrol dogs. Somebody from out of town would have ended up at one of those weird emergency vets we always read about on social media."

"I see," he said, but he obviously didn't.

"Okay, so being a DMC – destination management company – means that you serve massive regional areas rather than specializing where you are located. It would be akin to doing a virtual vet appointment for your pet," she paused more a minute to let him think. "If you have a horse with colic, do you want the vet that lives nearby to check on him or do you want a vet in Atlanta to dial it in, so to speak? A virtual vet wouldn't know the patient even if you could do an animal exam that way. Same thing with wedding destinations.

"Tally's company has most likely done so well because she's the only wedding planner who is actually based on Jekyll Island. The hotels have in-house planners, but most of them are thrilled when they find out the bride has an outside planner. It means they don't have to do any work except coordinating with the banquets team after the other planner tells her what the couple wants," Kayla continued.

"A planner who is at the destination can tell them when it's too hot out to carry poppies, or if they're trying to plan an outside happy hour at the buggiest time of year."

"I think I understand," Jake nodded. Kayla figured he was playing along so she would stop trying to educate him on her industry, and she didn't blame him. More nights than not, she came home venting about what some crazy client had done.

Last week, she'd spent four hours constructing a wedding ceremony that should have taken her 15 minutes, and she'd come home in a foul mood.

"Suzy missed her last three deadlines for getting their ceremony plan to us," Kayla had complained that night once she'd sat down on the couch for a little tea and sympathy from her fiancé. She put her feet in his lap, and he started rubbing them without her having to ask. *Mmmmm, this is love,* she thought.

"But she finally sent it to you?" Jake asked.

"Oh, she sent it to me," Kayla groaned. "And sent it and sent it and sent it. I swear to God, I think Siri was writing the wedding ceremony via text." She smiled at that and then started chuckling.

"Seriously, Jake. I saw the email pop up with the header OUR CER-EMONY and I thought she'd done her homework. Then I saw that it was one of like 50 emails. And I am not even exaggerating when I say it could have been more. I lost track.

"I had to copy, paste, every line from every message and put together a wedding ceremony."

"You're kidding! Wow, has that ever happened before?" he asked.

"No. If it happened regularly, I'd have quit and become a funeral director by now," Kayla joked. "There's no way that wedding ceremony was what she actually meant to send. I went in and revised the heck out of it and put some stuff in that she'd missed – like the whole 'you may kiss the bride' part. But I guess it doesn't matter. If I had to guess, she has no idea what she sent us," she started laughing.

"Why did I sit there and fight with it for so long so she wouldn't notice changes? Oh my God." She was laughing and shaking her head. Jake smiled at her, but he wasn't in on the joke.

"It's okay," Kayla patted his hand. "I appreciate that you let me rant and that you sit here listening to all of this. I hope, for your sake, that when we get married, I won't act like a ninny."

"Speaking of which," Jake began.

"I know, I know. It's just a tough decision – do we wait until next summer to get married in Iowa at the church I grew up in or invite everybody here? Kelsi's here, but your parents are in Arizona and they travel constantly. Which means they won't mind coming wherever we get married, but first we have to find a weekend they aren't already booked," Kayla said.

"Yeah, that's pretty much accurate. Sorry," it wasn't the first time Jake had apologized for his parents' blasé response to the big news from their progeny. His mother, although sweet, was terribly self-absorbed. Jake and Kayla's engagement announcement had been met with lukewarm enthusiasm and a demand to be given a wedding date as soon as possible so they could make sure they were available. Kayla had been a bit shaken by it.

"My parents like you a lot, so don't even worry about that. They just checked out on parenting when I went away to college, and they've never really checked back in," Jake explained. "Mom still acts like she's the president of a sorority, and Dad is either on the phone with his investment guy or golfing. Those are his two main activities. Lucky for them, Kelsi and I are both normal grownups. They get away with their lifestyle because we don't need them except for major life events."

"It's a little strange but I sort of envy them."

"Oh, me too," Jake said quickly. "I just wonder what will happen when one of us has kids. Like, will they suddenly become grandparent material, or will I be the dad from the sad Hallmark movie explaining why grandma forgot a birthday? Ya know."

"I don't think they'll be that bad. Remember when Kelsi was taken captive last year? They flew out here as fast as they could," she defended her future in-laws.

"Actually, what I remember more clearly is that as soon as they made sure that the situation wasn't fatal, they ditched us and went up to Savannah for a few days of shopping."

Kayla remembered that, too. It had seemed a little strange at the time, but when Kelsi and Jake didn't say anything about it, she figured it was just how the Brooks family rolled.

"Do you want a big wedding, Jake?" Kayla asked her fiancé for the first time. Everyone had just assumed that the wedding planner would have a big hometown wedding in Iowa. Just not on Walleye Weekend. Kayla had taught all of them that it always rained in Okoboji on Walleye Weekend.

Kayla realized she had slid deep into her own thoughts for a moment and hadn't heard Jake's response, if he'd answered her question.

"I mean, did you always figure you'd marry a woman who wanted a big wedding and so that's what you wanted? Or do you think that's what I want and you're giving in to me on everything even though it's not really what you want to do?" It wasn't the first time she'd accused him of letting her win too often. But this time she meant it when she said she didn't want to bigfoot him. They were going to marry each other for life, in good times and in bad, so theoretically, they should be able to get through planning a wedding together.

"I honestly never thought much about it," he finally said. "I mean, Kelsi's my older sister so I've played wedding more times than I can remember. And sometimes I had to be the bride," his huge grin told her it was a very happy memory.

"I think I always imagined a big-ish wedding in Okoboji, but I never imagined I'd be living in Georgia when I got married," she chuckled. "Now that I've planned almost 100 weddings, I've got to be honest. While I love the idea of marrying you, I hate the idea of planning my wedding, dealing with my family and your family, juggling all the opinions at my office, and everything else." She stood up and started pacing while she spoke.

"Just thinking about planning our wedding stresses me out more than 100 crazy clients. Knowing what I know now, I don't even want to plan my own. I wish I had a wedding planner," she ranted, her voice going up a few notes at the end. "I know it sounds ridiculous," she was quick to say.

"Nope. Doesn't sound ridiculous. I've been a little worried about things being over-the-top just because Kelsi won't let you do it any other way," Jake said, supportively. "It's a weird situation you're in. Most people only experience the chaos of a wedding once or twice. You've been laughing and crying through them for five years already. I'm surprised you haven't tried to go out on disability from the PTSD."

"Right?" she laughed. "But that's what is so weird. I love planning events – I love being the one who can triage any problem, and I adore having them tell me it was exactly what they wanted afterwards. I just don't know what I want, and I don't want to have to triage my own wedding." Her voice was getting louder again, she knew. She'd bet she looked like teenager having a tantrum the way she was pacing back and forth in the dining room.

She stopped and looked at Jake. He was sitting at the table watching her with concerned blue eyes, his hair mussed from running his hands through it repeatedly as he'd listened to her.

"Do you still want to marry me?" she asked.

"Of course, I do, you big goofball," he said and got up from the table. In two steps, he'd wrapped his strong arms around her, and she fell into the hug. "Why wouldn't I want to marry the most amazing woman in the world?"

"Because she's too crazy to plan her wedding to you," she said. "This is just stupid. We should just pick a date and go for it."

"Or we could elope," Jake suggested, pulling away from Kayla and looking her in the eyes.

She paused and took a moment and then caught herself slowly nodding in agreement. Then she started nodding more aggressively, causing her dark blonde ponytail to bounce.

"You know what, we could," she finally said. "We really could. My parents wouldn't care, to be honest. They'll still have my sister's wedding to pay for eventually. As long as we let them have a party for us back home afterwards, they'll be fine."

"Will you be fine if we elope?" he asked, still sounding concerned.

"Absolutely." Kayla's decision was made.

Chapter 18

Kelsi and the interns were already buzzing around the Jekyll Weddings office when Kayla got there on Thursday morning. And she was in early. The Brubaker/Sherman wedding party was due to arrive on Jekyll Island at noon, and some of their guests had arrived the night before to start their extended vacations. Everyone on the team had been going full speed since Monday.

Kayla had dropped off some of the welcome bags on her way home last night to save the interns almost two hours of work – she'd never understand why some wedding guests insisted on staying on St. Simons Island for a wedding on Jekyll. Or even worse, Sea Island. That posh, private getaway could only be reached by going all the way to the other end of St. Simons – it was solidly 45 minutes from Jekyll Island if there wasn't any traffic. And there was always traffic on the causeway to and from St. Simons on a nice weekend. It was beautiful over there, but it geographically undesirable from a wedding weekend standpoint. That was why Kayla felt so strongly that Jekyll Weddings needed to expand to brides wanting weddings on St. Simons and Sea Island. If they had an operation over there, it would be a huge moneymaker.

She and the interns had been loading up their vehicles in the parking lot at the same time the night before, and when she'd overheard them grumping about going all the way to Sea Island to deliver welcome bags, she decided to show some mercy. Yes, it was going to add about an hour to her trip home – Jake's house was just a few minutes away once she'd crossed the Jekyll causeway and she was going to have to go all the way over to St. Simons first – but it was worth the extra effort to help them out. The girls looked overwhelmed by the 190 fully-stuffed welcome bags they had to deliver to hotels and private vacation rentals all over Jekyll before they would be finished for the evening. She could easily drop off the bags for the guests staying at The Cloisters and save them a huge hassle.

Everyone at Jekyll Weddings appeared to be busily working on their own to-do lists and, if you didn't know what the vibe was usually like, the business appeared to be a well-oiled machine. Each of the women greeted Kayla and kept going on what she was focused on, without a blip in the process.

Wow, this is exactly what we were hoping to accomplish with the interns, Kayla thought. But she didn't say it aloud because she wasn't about to jinx them.

Kelsi had taken the lead on the "Great Intern Experiment," as Tally's Aunt Etah started calling it, and Kayla had benefitted from the tutelage the college girls were receiving 24/7 from her bestie. She and Kelsi had been winging it since Katy, Liz, and Tori arrived, but so far that approach was working. Kelsi's decision to live with the interns in the little cottage she'd found for them on Jekyll had turned out to be a blessing for Kayla and Tally. It meant that the interns had somebody as their role model during their Jekyll internships. It was hard for them to complain about doing something hard that their boss was doing with them. And as long as they were ready to go in time, Kelsi was happy to chauffer them around the island.

She set down her bags and reached over to give Kelsi a hug where she was sitting. Kelsi was frowning at her laptop while clutching a mug of coffee. She smiled and hugged Kayla back but didn't initiate a conversation because she was in the middle of trying to figure something out, obviously.

Kayla and Jake hadn't seen nearly as much of Kelsi as they usually would since the interns arrived. Kayla had assumed that Kelsi would hide at Jake's house more, just to get some space from the college girls she worked with all day. But making the upstairs of the cottage her own private space had worked out well, and Kelsi was rarely at her brother's house unless they had something planned. That meant Kayla and Jake had been able to figure out the whole living together thing in a more normal way, without his opinionated big sister telling them both what to do – not that she didn't love his opinionated sister. It could have been really hard being engaged to her work wing-woman and bestie's brother if they didn't have separate spaces after hours.

Yaya was zipping around, in and out of her office, reading off her flower forms and prepping one long table with all of the supplies she'd need for the St. Simons weddings on Saturday and Sunday. It was fun to watch her. She rotated between Spanish and English as she muttered, but Kayla and Kelsi knew that if she was muttering in Spanish, she was using obscenities.

Flowers would start arriving from Yaya's favorite supplier, Potomac Floral Wholesale, by late morning and then they'd all have to step carefully around the space. Buckets filled with water were already staged around the perimeter of the room, out of the way but still a dangerous trip-hazard to a wedding planner carrying a stack of something that blocked her view of the floor in front of her.

Another prep table was set up for Tally to make the Brubaker/Sherman wedding bouquets and centerpieces, complete with the crazy ribbons that Kortney had insisted should be tied on everything. The tables didn't need any other identification to keep things sorted – one glance and everybody who had been working on Kortney's wedding knew exactly whose décor was whose. She had sent hundreds of yards in a variety of sizes for all three colors of ribbon and Yaya had sorted the ribbons out on the table by size and color.

Sadly, Kortney's high-budget wedding would have been an elegant affair that resulted in tons of marketing videos for her wedding planners if she hadn't felt the need to turn it into a sorority event. That was everybody's opinion except Tori's. And she was still acting like Kortney had a direct connection to Christ himself.

"Looks like she sent plenty of ribbon," Kayla noted with a smile that made Kelsi and Yaya chuckle. Liz and Katy rolled their eyes. They've both been having nightmares in silver, gold, and blue for a week.

"I like the ribbons," Tori said, as if she felt a constant need to defend the client who was her sorority sister. "The cerulean is beautiful."

"It's blue," Katy corrected her, sick of the Delta Delta Delta nonsense that Tori had been spouting since they'd started planning Kortney and Mike's wedding. "Just plain blue."

"You probably think it was okay for her to send the too-small dresses to her cousins, too, don't you?" Liz asked with snark in her voice. "After all, they were *cerulean.*"

"I do agree that may have been a little bit over the top," Tori conceded.

"A little bit? She intentionally did something mean to women who had agreed to stand up for her," Liz sounded outraged.

The girls were sitting across from each other at one of the worktables and Kelsi and Kayla made eye contact over their heads. Kayla raised her eyebrows in question at Kelsi, and Kelsi responded with a ginormous eye roll. Kayla nodded to confirm the message had been received.

"Okay seriously, ladies – tacky ribbons aside," Kelsi held up a hand to silence Tori, who had opened her mouth to object. "Kayla and I really don't want to listen to this garbage today. Be a little more professional, please."

"I get that we all have opinions about the brides we work closely with, and we tend to express them whenever we want around the office. But this is a big wedding for us – a huge moneymaker since Kortney and her mom have had such ridiculous requests – and we can't risk anybody getting the impression that we don't love and adore the bride," Kayla explained patiently with a serious expression on her face.

She knew she was lecturing the girls, but her point was important. If a wedding guest or family member overheard anybody on the wedding team saying something derogatory about the couple, the bride and groom would find out about it. You couldn't undo that sort of mistake, and that's why so many companies refused to do internships. Kids had to be taught. And yes, Kayla considered these young women all to be "kids," still.

"We all have our favorite brides," Kelsi backed her bestie up. "But the bride who is on Jekyll Island for her actual wedding is the *only* bride that matters during her wedding weekend. And she should feel like she is 'the favorite' of everybody on our staff. Get it?"

"We get it," Katy said, and Liz nodded.

"That's what I was doing," Tori claimed, sounding more than a little put out. "Is it wrong that I'm excited she's finally coming to get married?"

"Not at all," Kelsi assured her. "But you have to keep in mind that you like Kortney solely because she was in the same sorority as you at another school, and she hasn't been easy for the rest of us to work with over the past few months. You're not exactly helping us get in the right chill frame of mind to deal with her."

"I can be the one who deals with her," Tori suggested. "And I like her because she's an impressive businesswoman with excellent taste. And she's been a lot of fun to work with."

"You shouldn't be left alone with her," Liz interjected. "You'll probably try to figure out a way to tie those hideous ribbons onto her wedding gown."

"They aren't hideous. I might even use the same colors at my wedding," Tori sounded petulant. Liz and Katy groaned and made faces.

Kelsi didn't blame their bubbly Tri Delt intern for being so excited about Kortney's wedding and she felt the need to deliver an attitude adjustment to the rest of them, too.

"You're right," Kelsi agreed, nodding at Tori. "They just look funny sitting there. And we're being bitchy because we're tired and a little stressed out. I'm sure it will all come together beautifully when we set it up." She was lying, big time, because the Brubaker/Sherman wedding was definitely going to look like a silly sorority dance and everybody except Tori knew it.

Kortney had chosen to carry her color theme throughout all of her events, from the welcome party to the farewell brunch the day after the wedding. Tablecloths would either be cerulean or white – depending on the venue – and the napkins would be the opposite. And the big silver and gold wired ribbons would be swirled around everything they could be, and tied onto everything else.

The Brubaker/Sherman welcome party was being held tonight at The Wharf on the historic side of the Jekyll Club. The entire restaurant was blocked off for their private event from 8 to 11 pm, and Kortney and Mike's guests would be served a giant raw bar and offered a selection of drinks from a top-shelf open bar. Each guest would be handed a glass of the event's signature drink, Hairy Buffalo, upon arrival. Just thinking about that made Kayla laugh. She'd been sitting in the room when Kelsi was doing that planning call with Kortney and the interns.

She heard Kortney telling them that Mike wanted to serve his fraternity's signature punch, made with Everclear 190-proof, at one of their wedding events. Kortney claimed to have already put the kibosh on the idea, but Kelsi stopped her.

"You know, when you have a groom who doesn't have a lot of opinions or hasn't had much input in the planning, it's my experience that we should pay attention when he actually asks for something he wants," Kelsi began almost diplomatically. "So maybe we could figure out a way to have his fraternity punch at *something*, if not the actual wedding reception."

"Good God, Kelsi," Kortney replied, sounding shocked her wedding planner had disagreed with her. "They usually made this poison in the bathtub or a trash can."

"It doesn't have to be their recipe, Kortney. We can have the bar make up a tasty rum punch that has a splash of Everclear in it and call it 'Hairy Buffalo' just to satisfy his nostalgia. And we can serve it in fancy glasses, too. Why don't we do that for the welcome party?" Kelsi suggested before the bride could object. "You figured that some of the older relatives and business friends of your parents wouldn't come to The Wharf anyway, so why not make the kickoff party something that Mike would really enjoy?"

Kayla had been impressed by the way Kelsi was handling the difficult bride, and she'd tuned out their meeting and gone back to working on whatever was in front of her. But she'd noticed the Hairy Buffalo signs on the supply list this week for the welcome party and had to laugh. Score one for Mike and Kelsi.

"Who's delivering the bride and groom's welcome basket?" Yaya asked, holding the enormous gift basket in her arms. It had already been shrink-wrapped so it would hold together – otherwise, the wine bottles and posh snacks would slide all over the place when it was delivered.

"I've got it," Tori volunteered. "I want to see if I can put it in the room myself and make sure everything is perfect up there. And I wrote a special welcome note to Kortney on our sister stationary."

Kayla was briefly impressed. Liz made a face behind Tori's back.

"And I figured I could tie some cerulean ribbons on the front door of their suite to greet them," Tori added with a grin, giving Katy the side-eye.

"Fine, do it," Kelsi said, sick of listening to the girls. She was trying to create the client schedules for Kortney and Mike, and she needed to concentrate.

Jekyll Weddings had a very specific way of doing things that Tally had learned from Isabelle, back in her days at Vieques Weddings. It worked in the Caribbean, and it worked on Jekyll, so Tally still made everybody do it the same way.

Every wedding had a master schedule that included every single detail of everything for the wedding weekend. That was the schedule that everyone on the wedding team would have on their clipboards. Then whichever planner was responsible for running that wedding had to break it down into the vendor and client schedules, too.

Vendor schedules only had the very basic information that the vendors needed. Setup time and teardown time for each event – with the details the DJ needed for music cues included for the wedding reception. All of the clients' and guests' details were stripped out of the document. She'd made the vendor schedules a week ago and sent them to everyone individually. And she'd confirmed them already.

The client schedule was the opposite – it only had the wedding activities themselves, and anything else the bride or groom had to do, like be ready for pictures to start at a certain time. There was nothing about the wedding setup on the bride's schedule because that would give her the ability to watch what was happening and worry if things appeared to be behind.

The bride and groom were each given a copy of their wedding weekend schedule when they arrived on the island, along with a copy for every member of the wedding party and the parents of the bride and groom. The wedding weekend would run on that schedule with no deviations, regardless of how late somebody important showed up to an event. The only people who could actually delay something by not being ready were the bride and groom. And if they caused the wedding events to start late, everything would still end at the same time, even if they'd barely had a chance to get the party dancing.

Kelsi had reviewed the detailed schedule with Kortney on the phone during their last call and gotten everything blessed that needed to be. Nobody should be surprised by what time they were expected to be somewhere, if Kortney had done her part and told everybody where to be. Kelsi wondered what the odds were that Kortney had actually done that, and figured it wasn't terribly likely. She made a mental note to try to talk to both the maid of honor and the best man individually at the welcome party, to make sure they'd gotten and understood the schedules.

Chapter 19

Kayla had a hard time not telling her best friend about the impending elopement while they were getting ready for Kortney and Mike's wedding. It had been a few days since she and Jake had made the decision to elope, and last night, they'd booked their trip through the travel agent Jake's buddy used rather than the one who helped Tally coordinate large wedding groups. Kayla had planned to call her contact at that agency, but Jake convinced her not to, pointing out that travel agents didn't have any more of a confidentiality agreement than wedding planners. There was a big chance that somebody at the travel agency on St. Simons would accidentally let the cat out of the bag if they were asked to handle the arrangements.

"You know, we can do this ourselves," Kayla pointed out. "We don't really need a travel agent."

"Oh, but we do," Jake corrected her on the spot. "Travel agents will make sure everybody knows we're on our wedding and honeymoon, and we'll get special treatment everywhere we go because the travel agent will flag us as VIP. Plus, you have no free time to do anything right now and I'd rather have your available minutes to spend with me than searching online for the cheapest airfare to Las Vegas."

"I thought we'd agreed on Puerto Rico," Kayla was confused.

"We also talked about Glacier National Park, but the time of year was wrong."

"Oooo I loved that idea. Do you think we could go up there in our wedding clothes next year when the weather is good and have professional photos taken?" Kayla asked. "I bet we'll photograph better when we're not feeling all stressed out anyway."

"Honey, if you'll agree to marry me anywhere, I'm happy to take wedding pictures with you in a hundred places. I promise," he told her sincerely.

They'd sent an email to his friend's travel agent that night and had their reservations booked within 24 hours. Easy peasy. Hard to believe they were actually going away to get married.

She hadn't decided on what to do about a wedding gown, yet. Kayla had always imagined a traditional wedding gown, but not something big and poofy. She wished she could talk about her plans with any of her girlfriends, or her sister, Anna. But she knew that once she told somebody, everybody would find out.

She and Jake were eloping after her last wedding in December and then going directly to Okoboji to celebrate Christmas with her family. Their friends believed they were taking an extended vacation – way overdue because they both had horrific schedules. Jake had been the one to approach Kelsi about taking care of the animals at his vet practice. He and another nearby vet usually covered for each other, but this was a longer trip than he'd normally take, and he needed somebody at the property to make sure everything was fine. He rented out stable space in his barn to several local equestrians who did all their own care and feeding, but sometimes, the owners would call him in a panic, needing Jake to cover them if they couldn't get there in time. Kelsi would have to be Jake for the last two weeks of December.

His sister said she didn't mind. Their parents were going to be in Europe for the holiday markets, something new her mother had discovered in their retirement. And Kelsi said that staying at Jake's house would feel like a vacation after four months in the guest cottage with the interns. She'd lounge around and binge all the reality TV she'd gotten behind on during fall weddings. She was pretty sure she'd built up a whole season of one of the "Below Deck" shows, and she wanted to re-watch "The Gilded Age" before the next season dropped. All the talk about it surrounding Kortney's wedding had her intrigued.

So, with that, Kayla and Jake's wedding had been planned at the El Conquistador Resort in Fajardo, Puerto Rico. Once Kelsi had agreed to house-sit, the only thing left for Kayla to do was find a dress. Jake couldn't get his wedding clothes until she figured out how dressed up she was going to be. So, figuring out her wedding attire had to be a priority.

Chapter 20

Korney and Mike's welcome party was a hit, Kayla reported to Tally via text after she went by The Wharf to see if she was needed on her way home from the office. She'd stayed late at Jekyll Weddings to help Tally and Yaya process the 15 boxes full of flowers that had arrived that afternoon. It wasn't difficult work, just precise and time consuming. Some flowers came with nets over the blooms that had to be removed so the blossoms could relax, others had to be stripped of their thorns, one stem at a time. Lilies had the messy stamens inside them that had to be removed carefully, by hand, so they didn't stain the wedding party's clothing.

Every stem had to be cut on an angle and then placed in water that had been treated with preservative to keep the flowers alive longer. It was all a chemistry experiment. If the hydrangeas started to wilt, there was a spray bottle of emergency magic for that, but it only worked half the time.

The empty flower boxes would be stripped of the strapping and padding materials, and then the lids were set inside the box bases to reinforce them before the finished centerpieces were set inside for transport, with padding shoved tightly in between the vases to keep things from sliding around.

Kayla stayed until all of the centerpieces for the Brubaker/Sherman wedding and the St. Simons weddings were finished. Yaya and Tally would do the bouquets the next day – some of the flowers were too delicate to be assembled earlier than a day ahead of the wedding.

"It looked like everybody was having fun, including Kortney and her mom," Kayla texted. "Heading home now unless you need anything else."

"Go home. Drive safely and I'll see you mañana," Tally wrote back.

***

The wedding guests were rockin' outside on the deck of The Wharf as the clock slowly approached 11 o'clock, the time the event was scheduled to end.

Kelsi approached Kortney, who was chatting with some friends over by the bar, and waited for a chance to get her attention.

"Did you want something?" the bride asked her a moment later. Everybody in her circle turned to stare at Kelsi and she prayed she didn't have a booger in her nose or something between her teeth.

"I just wanted to check in with you and see if you needed anything from me before the party wraps up," Kelsi said, sounding much nicer than she was feeling. "We're done here in about 15 minutes."

"That's fine," Kortney said, and turned back to her friends. *Alrighty then*, Kelsi thought. But she kept her mouth shut and went to let Liz, Katy, and Tori know that they could start packing up discreetly.

Once the clock struck 11, all bets were off. Half of the restaurant staff had to leave on time to get home and relieve babysitters. She touched base with Vera last, and the mother of the bride thanked her for a beautiful event.

"The Hairy Buffalo signs were hysterical," the mother of the bride said, pointing to the bar. "I'm glad you let a little bit of Mike's personality into the weekend."

"Me, too," Kelsi agreed.

At the stroke of 11, without further ado, the interns began helping the service staff pull the tablecloths out from under the plastic to-go cups that everyone had been given at last call. Kelsi and Tori shoved all the décor into tubs while Liz and Katy ran loads to the parking lot like they were trying to set land-speed records.

The goal was to get the heck out of the party venue as fast as possible. If the wedding planners didn't move quickly, they'd get stuck at The Wharf answering drunk-people questions and helping to find transportation for the wasted wedding guest who got left behind by his drunk friends. Or worse, driving him back to his hotel. With Kelsi's luck, he'd be one of the guests staying over on Sea Island. She'd warned the girls that if she had to take any guests home, they were going along for the ride with her. That news seemed to incentivize them to get everything loaded before the clients could even notice they were leaving.

"We did it," Katy said, as they shut the back of the van after Kelsi brought out the last box with the signage from the bar. It was 11:07. Katy fist-bumped her boss as she got into the flower delivery van and then reached back to do the same with Liz and Tori. All of the interns looked wired up from the success of a good event.

"Nice job, all of you. But don't start celebrating yet. We haven't gotten to the difficult stuff," Kelsi warned them. She wasn't being dramatic – they had a formal rehearsal dinner tomorrow night in the historic Jekyll Island Club Hotel, and the invitations had asked the guests to dress for a dinner in the Main Dining Room in 1890.

"Interesting twist," Tally had commented when she saw the detailed invitations Kortney sent out. "I like it though. Telling them to dress in a certain era is fun. It's just a pain in the ass for the rehearsal dinner since you girls will obviously have to costume it up, too."

"Seriously?" Kelsi asked. Then she made a note. It was just one more thing she needed to put on her supply and to-do lists for Brubaker/Sherman.

"Cool!" Tori interjected, always excited about anything to do with her sorority sister's wedding. "Can we choose our own outfits?"

"Yep, I'm serious. And yes, you can, as long as you use good judgement. I have final approval on all of it," Tally said. "The service staff at the club have something appropriate for Gilded Age dinners, and you ladies would stick out like sore thumbs in your 2025 fashions."

"What do you want us to wear?" Kelsi asked, not sound as enthusiastic as her intern.

"We'll find something," Tally assured her. "I'll buy each of you a dress that would work because I have a feeling you're going to need them again in the not-so-distant future."

"Why?" Kelsi looked horrified. Costumed weddings were few and far between and Kelsi had hoped the trend would stay that way.

"Remember that wedding planner from DC I was talking to about historic weddings?" Tally asked.

"Sure." Kelsi nodded.

"I liked her a lot. I think we might try to help her out with some of her weddings. And if we do, I can almost guarantee you that we'll need some historic wedding planner ensembles in our wardrobe," Tally explained.

"Maybe we could get matching demimondaine outfits," Kelsi suggested innocently, wondering if Tally would know what she was talking about. "It would make us easily identifiable to the wedding guests."

"No, Tally. We are not going to dress up like the high-class prostitutes of the Gilded Age, but thank you so much for the suggestion," Kayla replied from the other end of the table where she was working on her own project.

"It was just an idea," Kelsi said, pretending to have hurt feelings but unable to stop herself from grinning. "Party pooper."

****

Kelsi drove straight home from The Wharf after the welcome party. She parked the flower van in the middle of the driveway, relieved that the owners were having the interior painted this month and so nobody was renting the house.

She was pooped. And there were three more days of events to go for these clients. She was halfway to the little cottage in the back yard they called home when she heard yelling out front. She turned around and ran back to see what was happening.

"What's wrong?" she asked Katy, the first of the girls she encountered in the driveway.

"Snoopy is gone."

"Who?"

"Liz's Ohio State Snoopy. It's missing," Katy pointed to the spot where the front lawn met the street. Liz had her flashlight out and was searching around on the ground where her football inflatable had been when they left for work that morning.

"That's weird," Kelsi said. "Nothing ever gets stolen on this street. The Beckers next door said they accidentally left their garage door open for an entire week once when they were up in the mountains, and the only thing that went in it was a raccoon."

"Maybe a raccoon took Snoopy," Katy proposed.

"Probably," Kelsi agreed and walked over to where Liz was to tell her to lower her voice.

"Everybody around here went to bed hours ago, Liz. Let's not wake them up," she said. She saw that Liz had tears streaming down her face.

"We need to call the police!" Liz actually got louder when she said it, not quieter, Kelsi noticed.

"You can make a police report in the morning," Kelsi said, trying to make her intern feel better. "Somebody probably took him as a joke. Everybody around here is a Dawgs fan. He'll probably show up in a picture on the residents' page tomorrow drinking a beer and wearing a Georgia football jersey."

"Well, I don't think it's very funny," Liz said.

"Don't Buckeyes have a sense of humor?" Kelsi asked. "My brother's a Buckeye and he would think a prank like that was hilarious. He once helped a buddy mow a giant O into the perfect grass in the front yard of a friend who rooted for Michigan."

"Grass grows back," Liz argued. "Snoopy is gone."

"I'm pretty sure that Snoopy will be back," Kelsi said and stifled a yawn. "And I think it's a good idea to report him missing tomorrow. But we can take care of it super-fast if we call Tally in the morning and she passes it to Mitch. If we call the police tonight, we'll have to wait til whomever is on midnights for the Georgia State Patrol feels like moseying over here. And I, for one, just want to go to sleep."

"Me too," Tori was quick to add. "I need my beauty sleep before I deal with so many sisters again tomorrow. I hadn't thought about how much pressure I'd feel from the sisterhood during this wedding."

Katy looked at Tori like she'd announced she felt pressured to join the aliens in outer space and shook her head. Instead of telling Tori what she thought of her "sisterhood stress," she turned to Kelsi and said, "I'm ready for bed, too." And then started walking to the cottage.

Kelsi silently thanked her as she walked in her path. She wasn't up for refereeing another discussion about the advantages and privileges of being a Tri Delt sister yet again.

$$Chapter\ 21$$

The Brubaker/Sherman wedding weekend continued on without too much drama. Kelsi checked in with Kortney on Friday morning to make sure she'd enjoyed the welcome party. Then she confirmed that the hotel's shuttle buses would run constant circles between the beachside Jekyll Ocean Club and the riverside historic Jekyll Island Club, from an hour before the rehearsal dinner until an hour after. The bride wanted her guests to feel like royalty, she said. And royalty didn't wait for a bus.

Kelsi had texted Tally as soon as she woke up to tell her about the missing Snoopy inflatable. Tally had been at first confused, and then amused, but promised to talk to Mitch or his dad, Tom, who was actually assigned to the Jekyll Island trooper barracks, and make sure somebody caught up with Liz to take a report at some point over the weekend. And she offered to put Snoopy on a the side of a milk carton and post it on the residents' Facebook page, in case anybody had seen the kidnappers in action.

"That's not the worst idea," Kelsi told her. "Liz is pretty upset about it. She bought him in the campus bookstore. He's a little bit different than the ones you can buy online."

"Got it. I'll talk to Mitch when he gets out of the shower."

"Okay, thanks. See you at the office," Kelsi signed off.

***

Kortney and Mike's rehearsal dinner was absolutely gorgeous. If not for all the cell phones in the guests' hands, you might have believed that it was actually 1890 on Jekyll Island. It certainly looked like something from the set of the popular television show about the era. The vast majority of the dinner table lighting came from exquisite five-armed silver candelabras in the center of each table, which burned tall gold tapers. And the table linens were all the exact right shade of blue. The ceiling lights were dimmed to mimic the gas lighting that may have been used back in the days when dinner tables at the Jekyll Club were occupied by the Goodyears, Astors, Pulitzers, Rockefellers, Morgans, Vanderbilts, and Fields families, who were club members and spent their winters on the tiny Georgia barrier island.

The only negative of the evening were the costumes the wedding planning staff had to wear. And Kelsi knew it was her own fault. She'd done this to them all by herself. She stepped out of the view of the guests to scratch under the dress where the cheap tulle was irritating her thighs.

Kayla had been right, of course, when she suggested they consider dressing as the staff from that era, rather than party guests, so they'd be able to move around more easily. But Kelsi hadn't listened. She'd gotten wrapped up in the interns' enthusiasm when they found an online shop with dresses that were meant to be Gilded Age Halloween costumes. They were gorgeous and Kelsi could imagine dressing up in them. So, she'd poo-pooed Kayla's objections and picked out a dress for her friend instead.

Now, an hour into wearing the tight-fitting bodice with ribbons and a corset that created a bustle in the back, Kelsi knew she regretted her decision, big-time. The interns were too amped up to notice they were miserable, but she'd seen Kayla frowning and tugging at the corset under her arms and she recognized the problem. The inexpensive lacey fabric on the costume corset was irritating Kelsi's skin, too. And the cheap polyester made the yards of dress fabric sticky and hot. By the time this rehearsal dinner was over, Kelsi would be lucky if Kayla was even speaking to her. Only Tori, who had found a perfect cerulean dress with silver and gold on it, wasn't complaining out loud by the time dessert was served.

"Now I understand why the staff wore those Amish-looking dresses with pinafores," Kelsi admitted as they were trying to carry the supplies back out to their vehicles after the event. "This is a royal pain in the ass to work in."

"I told you so," Kayla said in a tone that told Kelsi she was more amused than angry with her.

"I know you did."

"Now you've gotta figure out how to tell Tally that we're going to need new dresses for the events we have to work for that Daisy lady," Kayla said, smirking.

"I may just pay for them out of my own pocket. It would be less humiliating than explaining to Tally that I'm an idiot and the dresses I picked gave us a rash."

Kayla laughed. "You do whatever makes you happy, Kelsi. I've always got your back. Otherwise, I wouldn't be standing here dying in this monstrosity. I would have already killed you and changed into something normal."

"Understood. We won't do this again. Thanks for letting me live," Kelsi told her sincerely.

"I couldn't kill you or I'd have to deal with Kortney's wedding tomorrow and that's your circus and your monkeys." Kayla chuckled.

Chapter 22

Etah and Beau had lunch with Bonnie Durham and Susan McLemore on the porch at Zachry's Riverhouse on Saturday afternoon. She'd hoped she'd be able to convince her great-niece to join them at the riverfront restaurant that was walking distance from her new condominium at the Jekyll marina, but Tally had a massive wedding on the island and a bunch of flower commitments over on the other islands. Etah had wanted to introduce Beau to Tally before all of her friends met him, but she'd finally given up earlier today when her niece cancelled on her yet again.

"I'm sorry, Etah," Tally said when her aunt picked up the phone. "I'm not going to be able to get away for lunch today. There's too much going on around here, and I need to call my father-in-law about a missing Snoopy on top of it."

"A what?"

"A missing Ohio State Snoopy inflatable," Tally slowed down and spoke in a patient tone, realizing that Etah was clueless. "Liz put it up in their front yard for football season and it disappeared while the girls were working the rehearsal dinner last night."

"Are they sure? That seems very strange. I've never heard of yard decorations being stolen," Etah said. "I'll have to ask Susan if she saw anything." Susan lived directly across the street from the intern house.

"Well, they're sure it's gone. I agree it's strange, but I don't think it's malicious. I'm thinking maybe he'll pop up on Instagram wearing a Georgia Bulldogs shirt or something. It's got to be a joke. But the interns are worked up, and I need them to be totally focused on this wedding today, so I promised I'd handle it."

"Maybe it's the same lady in a convertible who used to steal the new plantings out of the Jekyll Island Authority gardens," Etah joked.

"High crimes and misdemeanors on Jekyll Island, for sure," Tally said. Then she shifted gears. "Please give Beau my apologies – I really do want to meet him as soon as we can work it out."

"I'm going to call Bonnie and Susan to see if they're available to join us. It's time to reveal my gentleman friend to the island."

"I'm so jealous," Tally said. "But have fun."

"You know where we'll be if you have two minutes to stop by," she told her niece.

***

Etah was scrolling on Facebook a couple of hours later, while she waited for Beau to arrive, when she happened upon Tally's latest post on the residents' Facebook page. She couldn't help laughing. Tally had shared a picture of an Ohio State Snoopy on the side of a milk carton, and posted the following message:

"MISSING SNOOPY ALERT! Ohio State Snoopy was kidnapped from our interns' front yard on Old Plantation sometime yesterday evening. There has been no ransom demand. The inflatable toy is sentimental to our intern, and she would really like to have it back. She said Buckeyes have a sense of humor, and if Snoopy is returned, unharmed, by midnight tonight, all is forgiven and no questions will be asked. By the way, the neighbors have cameras and GSP is working on the footage."

Etah read it twice and couldn't resist sending a screenshot to Tally with a bunch of ridiculous emojis indicating how hard she was laughing at the post. "That was brilliant. I bet he'll be home before they get back from the wedding tonight," she texted.

"Let's hope so," Tally replied with an emoji of her head exploding.

Chapter 23

"Such lovely fall weather," Bonnie commented in between bites of salad. She and Susan had been waiting when Etah walked across the street with Beau at half past 12. Etah could tell they were appraising her friend as she introduced him to them.

Susan was very friendly to Beau and immediately began playing the who-do-you-know game, looking for mutual friends they might have in Atlanta, where she spent quite a lot of time visiting her children.

"I haven't spent a lot of time in Atlanta over the past 10 years," he admitted. "I retired when the school shut down in 1999, and my wife, Mary Catherine, died four months later from an aggressive pancreatic cancer. We were both only children, our parents were all dead, and Mary Catherine and I had never been blessed with children," Beau told the women.

"After she was gone, I started traveling to all of the places that she and I had planned to go after I retired," he continued. "My wife loved the one cruise we took together about 20 years ago, and so I try to find ships going to the destinations that were on our bucket list. It's a little bit like she's traveling with me" he said with a soft smile.

The women were impressed with his vulnerability. Etah reached for his hand and gave it a squeeze.

"That's how we ended up meeting on the Med cruise I took with my girlfriend," she explained to the girls. "Beau convinced me to get off the ship more and explore some very cool galleries with him in Italy, Greece, and Spain. I never would have known most of them were there, let alone how to get tickets."

"I have a membership in an organization for art aficionados who like to travel, and I get the most wonderful tips about galleries in unlikely places there," he explained.

"It was more than just travel tips that you shared with me, Mr. Morris," Etah argued with him. "I *never* would have known how to get tickets to the Canellopoulos Museum in Acropolis, and that became a highlight of my trip."

Beau had taken her a luncheon and gallery opening at private museum housed in a neoclassical three-story mansion built in 1894 as a residence for the Michaleas family. She'd marveled over the incredible paintings on the ceilings of the rooms on the top floor.

"I'm not familiar with that museum," Susan said. "Tell me about it. Maybe Gil and I will go. He's finally retired and we are going to start traveling more."

"The Michaleas mansion was expropriated by the Greek state in the 1960s and 1970s. It was finally restored and expanded to permanently house the Canellopoulos collection," he explained to the ladies and then stopped and pulled up a picture on his phone. He passed his phone to Susan. She looked at it and nodded, then passed the phone to Bonnie.

"That new part of the museum was added in 2007," he continued his lecture. "Architect P. Kalligas designed the new wing at the behest of Alexandra Canellopoulos and the Paul and Alexandra Canellopoulos Foundation."

He sounded a bit like he was reading from a travel guide as he reported the details to Etah's friends, but she figured it was because she'd made him explain the special museum he'd taken her to for several other people already.

Beau was so handsome that he could get away with a lot more than most men. He was tan and had a thick white shock of hair and a healthy mustache to match. But it was trimmed most fastidiously – not like the young men today. And he always dressed like he was going to the club, suits or jackets and slacks – she'd noticed he preferred double-breasted – and sometimes a fedora that went with his outfit if it was a particularly hot and sunny day.

"Anyway, Beau managed to get us tickets to a fabulous gallery opening there that took place one of the days we were in port," Etah told her friends. "It was a special gallery show of jewelry from all periods, made from gold, silver, bronze, and glass. It was all gorgeous. You should have seen the security!"

Their lunch went quickly – everybody ordered shrimp po' boys except Bonnie, who'd ordered a salad with fresh grilled scallops. Wanting to linger so they could chat some more, Etah suggested that they order a couple of slices of the restaurant's famous pie – perhaps key lime and the peanut butter – and share it between them. The suggestion was greeted with enthusiasm.

"How are you enjoying volunteering at Goodyear Cottage?" Susan asked Etah.

"It's a fantastic organization," Etah replied with a big smile. "In fact, I need to talk to Jackie and the other powers-that-be at Jekyll Artists because

I have an idea for something that would definitely increase traffic to the opening of Merry Artists this year."

"Oh really? What's that?" Bonnie asked.

"I was telling Beau about how I'd been friendly with Bill and Mittie Hendrix," she began.

Bonnie cut her off. "Bill and Mittie were friendly to everybody on St. Simons and Jekyll. I lost count of the number of times they invited all of us back to their place after a gallery show or community event. There was always a party at the Hendrix house."

Her friend sounded a little bit huffy, and Etah was amused. Was Bonnie preening for Beau? They'd both been single forever and the sudden appearance of her new friend might have upset her best friend's apple cart.

"That's true," Etah conceded. "I've told Beau that we all knew Bill and Mittie, and several of us had taken painting classes from him. But my point was that I've kept in touch with Bill and Mittie's daughters. The youngest one, Emily, was the realtor who helped me buy my condo at the Moorings."

"Do I know her?" Susan asked.

"Of course you do. You probably taught her and her kids," Bonnie said. Susan had recently retired from teaching at Glynn Academy, one of the local high schools, and she knew everybody, or their cousin, because she'd taught so many of them. "She goes by Emily Hendrix Slaughter. She's a realtor with Avalon on St. Simons Island now."

"Do you remember when she worked for the summer driving the red Jekyll Island Authority tour trollies for tourists? She wasn't very old – she'd probably just gotten her driver's license when she had that job," Etah couldn't help laughing at the memory.

"I remember when she was just a little bitty thing, and she used to come along when her father flew his plane to Jekyll to teach painting lessons on the beach," Bonnie said. "I took several classes on the sand with Bill

Hendrix, and if I remember correctly, Emily may have kept an eye on my boys during a couple of those classes. I believe his older daughter was already grown up and gone by then, so it had to have been the younger one."

"Probably," Etah agreed. "I was telling Beau that I think it's a shame that there's nothing up on the walls at the Jekyll Island Arts Association to honor Bill Hendrix's legacy on Jekyll. Everybody always talks about what he did on St. Simons but as time goes by, some have forgotten that he meant just as much to the arts on our island as he did next door."

"There's not much permanently up on the walls at Goodyear, is there?" Susan asked. "We used to go over there all the time, but now we only go for gallery openings now and then. Is there something to see there that I haven't seen already 100 times?"

"No, there's not, because it's such an active arts community that there's really no space for permanent installations on the first floor. The walls and stands in the gallery hold the latest show, and the rooms that make up the gift shop are packed with merchandise made by local artists," Etah explained. She'd learned a lot since she started volunteering for the arts group. "They bring down the Fiore statues from upstairs for Art Fest in the spring, but that's about it."

"That's a shame. But it makes perfect sense," Bonnie agreed. "They have the same problem in the Mosaic Museum. More exhibits than space, and more things being added to the collection each year." She been a docent at the Mosaic Museum for longer than Etah could remember. Etah had been Bonnie's date to a dinner or show more than once when the shop manager gifted her with last-minute tickets to something the authority was hosting.

"So, I had an idea," she continued and Bonnie and Susan both frowned. "I thought maybe I'd ask Emily if she'd loan me a few of her late father's paintings for a pop-up exhibit at Goodyear Cottage during Merry Artists Holiday Market."

"That's a neat idea," Susan said. "I'd love to see some of Bill Hendrix's paintings again. They used to be all over the place on St. Simons, but after he died, the family put most of it away. The only Hendrix pieces you see anymore are hanging on walls of Golden Isles art collectors."

"Exactly. That's why I thought that if we had a one-weekend-only viewing of a one of his more famous paintings - or a few of them, I'll take whatever Emily is willing to loan us – everyone in the Golden Isles art community would want to see them," Etah explained. "I don't think of it as a fundraiser exactly, although it would be wise to have a Jekyll Artists' donation box in the room where the art is shown. More of a way to get a lot more people to put the opening of Merry Artists on their calendars."

"Doesn't everybody already know about Merry Artists?" Bonnie asked, looking at Etah strangely. "It's been the same dates for years and years."

"Yes, but there's more competition out there now. That Crafts in the Village thing across from the St. Simons Welcome Center is a good example. It's a lot harder to motivate people across the Sidney Lanier Bridge when they have something similar happening right in front of them," Etah said. "I think having a Hendrix pop-up at opening weekend would drive a lot of traffic to us if we put it up on the billboard." At that, all of the women at the table made faces. Susan rolled her eyes.

"I know, I know. I hate it, too. Why they felt the need to switch the historic, neon year-round resort sign for that billboard escapes me," Etah sighed.

"They couldn't get the neon replacement bulbs anymore," Bonnie volunteered. "It was getting too expensive to light the thing up. You hate anything that changes, Etah."

"That's not true. I just think that sign was a piece of art that should have been kept and restored," she argued.

"I told Etah that I think she should promote the Hendrix artwork to all the local art schools. Heck, she should notify all the universities in Georgia – Bill Hendrix taught art classes at all of them at some point, I'd imagine – and let them know about the three-day show. It might attract a whole new audience for Merry Artists," Beau told the ladies in an animated voice.

"That's an excellent idea," Susan agreed. "It's the sort of thing art teachers and professors give extra credit for, going to see a legendary artist's work on display."

"I need to talk to Jackie about it. But before that, I need to ask Emily if she'd be open to loaning us a painting or two, because if she's not, I'm just wasting our time," Etah said to shut down the conversation. "It's sort of a crazy idea this close to the opening of Merry Artists anyway. I have a feeling the powers-that-be at Goodyear Cottage may not be as enthusiastic as you ladies were."

"Talk to Emily and then take it from there," Beau advised her. "Don't start borrowing trouble. It'll find you on its own."

"Is that the truth?" Etah laughed. Then she excused herself to use the restroom so that she could drop her credit card off at the bar and avoid an awkward situation with the check at the table.

She had invited everybody to lunch, and she didn't feel comfortable making Beau pick up the tab, which of course, he would because he was a southern gentleman who was at lunch with three ladies. As much as Etah considered herself a southerner, she was also a seasoned international news reporter, and she hadn't lived the last 30 years in a world where men were expected to always pick up the tab. She wasn't about to start living that way now. To the best of her knowledge, Beau had plenty of money. But so did she.

Chapter 24

Kortney's aunts had kept their pledge to boycott her wedding, but that was probably for the best. It would have been more drama to have the mothers of the bridesmaids who dropped out of the wedding party sitting in a row in the family section, at least in Kelsi's opinion. Vera didn't need to feel them all glaring at the back of her head. Regardless of her daughter's bridezilla-esque behavior in the run up to the wedding day, she was the mother of the bride. She was here to celebrate Kortney, and she shouldn't have to worry about defending her daughter from criticism at her own wedding.

At the end of the day, Kortney had gotten exactly what she wanted, three perfect size-eight sorority sisters standing up for her in cerulean. It looked and felt a bit staged. But that didn't matter for their purposes, and she made that point to Liz, Katy, and Tori during setup.

"We were hired to plan and execute her wedding, not get involved in her relationships with her friends and cousins. That's overstepping unless something blows up right in front of you at a wedding event," Kelsi explained, looking pointedly at Tori.

"I just think it's sad," Katy said. "I wonder what she'll think about when she remembers it in 20 years. Her perfect wedding pictures or the fact that her family wasn't there?"

"Pretty sure this bride is going to be all about the pictures," Liz said and made a face.

She wasn't wrong.

***

Tori was in her element getting ready for Kortney's wedding, despite being told she couldn't wear one of her cerulean dresses to work the event.

"But it's one of her colors," the intern protested. "I thought it would be perfect. I had my mom mail it to me to wear," she added, as if that would change Kelsi's opinion on the appropriateness of it.

"I get what you were trying to do," Kelsi softened her tone because Tori hadn't done anything wrong and she didn't want to give her the impression she had. It wasn't a hard, fast rule, she was just making a judgement call. She needed the college senior to understand their place at these events. "But in this case, when the shade of the color is so very specific, I don't think you should wear something that matches the bridesmaids.

"You don't want to give the impression that you're in the wedding party, versus on the staff for the event. Even if you're in the same sorority," Kelsi added, before Tori could remind her that she was a Delta Delta Delta for the umpteenth time.

Liz and Katy hadn't worn blue, silver, or gold, Kelsi noticed. Liz was wearing pink and Katy was wearing coral. Nobody would mistake them for members of Kortney's sorority, and that was exactly how it was intended.

***

After three months of chaos leading up to the Brubaker/Sherman wedding, it was a remarkably uneventful weekend. None of the guests did anything too atrocious, and all of the vendors brought their game. Jekyll Weddings executed four days in a row of flawless events that were utterly forgettable, except for the rash from that stupid bustier that was still bothering her.

Kelsi had been proud of the way Tori handled herself with the wedding guests. Kortney had introduced her to the bridesmaids as a "sister" at the start of the weekend, and when all the Tri Delts at the wedding reception got together for a group photo, they'd included Tori in one of the shots. They'd also invited her to join them on the dance floor to sing a sorority song.

Tori's reaction to the invitation had been priceless. Her face lit up like she'd just won a Grammy for best song of the year, and she did that *"who me?"* thing with her hands on her chest.

The interns had run the wedding events all weekend, under Kelsi's supervision. Kayla had been a second set of eyes and hands at the big events, but Kelsi told her she could skip the farewell brunch on Sunday and sleep in, if she wanted to.

"Honestly, if I didn't need to be here to wrap some money stuff up with Vera tomorrow morning, I'd be lobbying Tally to let them run the brunch without a babysitter," Kelsi told Kayla, as they stood in the shadows together at the reception watching the action on the opposite side of the room.

Liz had just announced the cake cutting and Katy was guiding the bride and groom through how to hold the knife for pictures. Tori was busily setting up the candy buffet in the lobby so that every guest would pass by it on their way out. She'd remembered that it needed to be ready to go right after the cake cutting and took the initiative on her own before Kelsi reminded her. She arranged a pretty favor table with a variety of containers filled with fancy candies in the wedding's signature colors. The bride had custom-ordered blue M&Ms with their initials on them to satisfy her need for something close to cerulean. Each jar of candy had a silver scoop in it and the guest would fill up glassine bags that had been printed with the couple's initials and wedding date. Kelsi had to admit that the entire setup looked really fun and festive, despite the strange candy colors.

"If you're sure you don't need me for the brunch, I'd love to have a whole day off on a weekend," Kayla readily agreed, bringing Kelsi back to their conversation.

"Go for it. I fully intend to be done here by one, and back in my bed by two. You'd spend that much time getting here and back. Don't bother."

"Thanks, Kels." Kayla had a huge list of things to do in her own life and getting the day back meant she would get some of that done. If Jake would even let her get out of his bed after he found out she didn't have to go into work. She smiled to herself, and her best friend caught her.

"Tell my brother he owes me." Kelsi winked at her.

"He knows he does."

Chapter 25

Etah and Beau had a romantic weekend together on Jekyll. They'd eaten a very early dinner at Driftwood Bistro on Saturday evening and then she'd taken him on the sunset dolphin cruise. The tour boat went from the historic wharf down to the Jekyll Sound and back, while the captain explained about how the location of the island played into the need for an Intercoastal Waterway during World War II.

"At the time when German U-boats began sinking American merchant vessels right off the coast of Georgia, historians say that one-sixth of the world's wealth was gathered on Jekyll Island. It became a genuine concern that the millionaires would be targeted by the Germans, and that it would lead to the fall of the U.S. economy," the captain explained as they floated along the coastline.

He said the members of the Jekyll Club had been advised to evacuate the island after several merchant vessels were sunk by U-boats that were much closer to the Georgia coast than anybody anticipated.

Then he explained that the famous Sharktooth Beach they were passing was man-made. "When they dug the waterway, what they dredged from the bottom had to go somewhere. The sharks' teeth that get found so frequently by visitors to Jekyll aren't new, they're what was dug up from the bottom around here 75 years ago. Meaning they're probably hundreds of years old, if not thousands."

"That's interesting," Beau murmured to Etah.

Afterwards, they'd gone home and had a nightcap on her balcony. Beau was headed back to Atlanta in the morning, and he hadn't made plans for a return visit to Jekyll yet. Etah didn't want to worry that he was losing interest in her already, but it was a genuine concern. She was old and ornery and despite her best efforts, she no longer considered her boobs and butt to be assets. She wasn't immature enough to wonder what he saw in her, but she also hoped the intellectual connection they had was going to be stimulating enough to keep his interest.

The next morning, Beau joined her for coffee and pastries and then took his leave to beat traffic home. She walked him to the door and kissed him goodbye, and then she went into her office and grabbed a pad of paper before she returned to the kitchen table and picked up her phone.

She looked at her watch. *Darnit*, she thought. Emily would still be in church this Sunday morning. The Hendrix family had attended church on St. Simons forever. Etah sent the busy realtor a text and ask her to call first chance she got after the service.

She busied herself making a list of places where she'd advertise the gallery, online and with flyers on bulletin boards. If Jackie could be convinced to allow them to have a little reception at the end of the first day of Merry Artists, she was sure she could fill Goodyear Cottage with Bill Hendrix fans who would likely spend a fortune in the gift shop when they came to see the artwork.

Merry Artists was an all-consuming event for the volunteers at Goodyear, and she'd known from the beginning that in order to get permission for a reception, she would have to present Jackie with something that required absolutely no work by the Elf Squad who were running the holiday market. Those volunteers would have been running flat-out the entire week ahead of the opening, and some of them would have probably worked most of Thanksgiving Day, too. She was going to have to ask her niece to do her a big favor for this one. She needed the staff of Jekyll Weddings to carry the ball for the event if she got it approved.

She had just finished her second cup of coffee when her phone rang. Etah smiled when she saw Emily Hendrix Slaughter's name light up the display.

"Hi Emily. I caught you at church, didn't I?" Etah greeted her.

"You did, but I was happy to get your message. I feel like I haven't seen you in way too long," Emily replied.

"Well, I'd like to come talk to you about an idea I have, if you've got a few minutes to have coffee with an old lady in the near future."

"I'd love to see you. I'm babysitting my grandchildren this afternoon while Jenna meets with a client." Emily's daughter, Jenna Garwood, owned Scout Proper Designs on St. Simons Island, an up-and-coming interior design firm. Etah knew she also sold real estate with her mother. "Would you want to come over here? I could do any time after 3 today because two of them will be down for a nap then."

"I'd love to. And I'll stop to get coffee for us on the way," Etah said. "Text me your Starbucks order when we hang up."

"Yes, ma'am," her old friends' daughter replied respectfully.

Chapter 26

The next few weeks flew by at Jekyll Weddings – fall always moved faster than any other season, in Tally's opinion. The Shrimp & Grits festival weekend had been a total zoo, but Kayla's idea to only book elopement packages that weekend had worked out beautifully.

For the past few years, Tally and her team had struggled to find venues and vendors for wedding events during the biggest festival weekend of the year on Jekyll Island.

Last year, listening to her stress out about it, Mitch had proposed that she just cross Shrimp & Grits weekend off her wedding calendar and go to the festival instead. He said he could take some time off too and they'd take the twins to enjoy the chaos. He and Tally could listen to the music on the big stage while Molly and Moody danced in the grass.

"I wish we could afford to do that," Tally admitted. "But we can't. That's why I booked weddings during the festival the last couple of years. I couldn't afford not to and still pay everybody. But Kayla hit me with an idea that might just work. It might even give me time to go to the festival with you and the kids for one of the nights."

The subject had come up ages ago – right around Shrimp & Grits last year – when Jekyll Weddings got two consultation requests for the next Shrimp & Grits on the Monday morning after the festival.

"I hate Shrimp & Grits weekend," Tally muttered as she looked at their big calendar on the wall.

"What if we didn't do any big weddings that weekend, but instead we marketed deals for elopement packages? Like 'come to Jekyll for Shrimp & Grits and say *I do* while you're here,' or something like that," Kayla proposed.

"We'd have to do several elopements in order to make up the difference."

"I know. But those are easy-peasy compared to a big wedding when there are no venues or hotel rooms to be had because everything's booked two years out for the Shrimp & Grits Festival. I think we should assume there are people who are coming to the festival who might want to get married. So, let's market to them rather than brides who haven't started planning trips here yet," Kayla explained.

Kelsi agreed it was a good plan and Yaya blessed it, too. She'd have a lot of bouquets to make, but not all the time-consuming centerpieces of a big wedding weekend. It was win-win as far as she was concerned.

At their next staff meeting, Tally signed off on the plan and started posting a series of promotions for getting married during the next festival weekend. They offered discounts to couples who were booked before the end of the year, and their calendar was full before last Christmas. It was a great way to make money and not struggle to make wedding events happen in the midst of a bigger event.

As a result of Tally's early push to book those dates, Jekyll Weddings had 12 separate elopements over the festival weekend. Four per day on Friday, Saturday, and Sunday. They'd assigned each of the interns one wedding on each of the days to be entirely responsible for – and Kayla took the fourth. Kelsi floated between the interns' elopements to make sure everything went perfectly. Tally was on-call from the festival if they needed her, but they hadn't. Everything ran perfectly once the clients got through the ridiculous line at the gate to get onto the island.

Chapter 27

It had not been easy for Etah to convince Jackie that showing the Bill Hendrix artwork was a good idea on the opening weekend of Merry Artists. Etah had to make a lot of compromises and promises to get her on board. For example, it would be a one-evening-only showing of the Hendrix artwork at Goodyear, instead of the three-day show she'd originally planned.

Etah proposed a nominal ticket fee of $5 online in advance, or $10 at the door, with the proceeds going to the art class program at Goodyear as a contribution in the Hendrix family's name. Everyone knew Bill Hendrix had never been about making money with his art. His legacy was in teaching art. He was famous for only having charged his art students on Jekyll $20 for six lessons on the beach, back in the days when he had to fly over to teach them, before there was a bridge.

"It'll just be about 90 minutes long," Etah promised Jackie. "I found the cutest silver plastic cups to use for serving my famous Jekyll Juleps. And I'll call and order a bunch of fancy cookies that say Merry Artists and Goodyear Cottage on them to offer people in line. They'll all be wrapped individually because I imagine a lot of people will just pocket them to eat later."

"What are Jekyll Juleps? You can't serve alcohol," Jackie reminded her for the tenth time after she'd granted the permission for the pop-up gallery show.

"We wouldn't dare," Etah promised, crossing her fingers behind her back and thinking that what Jackie didn't know wouldn't hurt her. Officially, they'd be serving a virgin version of her famous spiked muscadine cider with all the ingredients except the Fireball whiskey she usually put in it. The spiced cider tasted much better with a shot of something in it, of course. But she didn't say that to Jackie. What was in her and Bonnie's flasks at the event was their business. She wasn't going to check anybody else's purse, and they could stay out of hers.

Etah distracted Jackie by telling her about how she had met with Emily to look at her father's artwork that she was loaning them for the pop-up gallery on Black Friday. They chose one of Emily's favorite oil paintings from her father's more modern period to be the main event. It lived on her great room wall. It had never been publicly displayed, to the best of Emily's memory. Not that it mattered. Even if folks had seen it before, they hadn't seen it in more than 40 years unless they'd been to a party at the realtor's house. None of them had been able to find any record of its existence on the Internet.

She'd also shared a series of pen and ink sketches that had ultimately become her father's popular notecards that were sold at the Island Art Center. The ones that were drawn on Jekyll Island would be displayed, along with the big painting.

"I'll get you permission to do this, Etah, but you can't break any rules or do anything that's going to get me into trouble, too," Jackie warned her.

"I would never!" Etah held a hand to her heart as if she were offended and then winked at her friend. Jackie just shook her head.

Chapter 28

After she got Jackie's quasi-permission for her Hendrix gallery, Etah texted Tally to find out where she was, so she could go talk to her in person about helping pull the whole thing off. Tally replied that she was at home. So, Etah got into her golf cart and buzzed directly over to the house on Tallu Fish Lane that had been hers for so many years. She let herself in quietly so as not to disturb the napping twins and found her great-niece in the kitchen.

"Hey Aunt Etah," Tally gave her a warm hug. "Will you be staying for dinner? We're having leftovers. But they're good leftovers because they're from Bonnie's house." Mitch's grandmother's cooking was legendary and there was always a Tupperware of something yummy in their fridge that had originated across the street.

"I'd love to, but I can't. I have too much to do. But I need your help with something, and I wanted to ask you this favor face-to-face," Etah said with a serious tone, sitting down on one of the barstools at the kitchen counter.

"What's up?" Tally asked. She stopped what she was doing and gave her aunt her full attention.

"You're going to kill me," Etah warned her.

"That's highly unlikely. Why would I kill you? I need you to babysit," she joked.

"Because I just committed you to helping me pull off an event at Goodyear Cottage on Black Friday," Etah said quickly.

"*This* Black Friday?"

"Yes."

"Ew. That's soon," Tally said, immediately dreading whatever her aunt was about to ask her.

"I'm sorry."

"What kind of event?" Tally asked. She would do anything for this woman who raised her, but she really hated the last minuteness of all this.

"It's a pop-up art gallery at Goodyear Cottage. It's only 90 minutes and then it's over. We just do the online promotion and handle the traffic through the gallery to make sure it goes smoothly. I'll run the cash register for anybody who shops Merry Artists while they're there," Etah said, and then went on to tell Tally exactly what she had in mind.

Etah explained that Goodyear Cottage would close at 4 p.m. as usual on Black Friday, and that they would set up the pop-up gallery after closing. The Hendrix art exhibit would open at 5 p.m. with Tally's staff checking tickets at the door. Etah said she'd give them change to have on hand for anybody who needed to buy tickets the night of the event.

"We won't be turning anybody away who wants to see the gallery," she told her niece. "Even if they don't have money for a ticket. The tickets were just a good way to fundraise for arts classes. That's something Bill Hendrix truly supported." She sounded wistful when she talked about it.

"Did you take art lessons from Bill Hendrix?" Tally asked.

"Oh Lord, no. My art is in the written word. You know I can't even draw a stick figure," Etah laughed. "But I spent plenty of time waiting for my friends to finish up their classes, or their homework, back in the day. I remember when Bonnie and two other neighbor ladies stood in her backyard painting that big live oak tree for half the summer," she chuckled at the memory.

"So why the sudden interest in showing the Hendrix artwork?" Tally asked, looking at Etah with a serious expression.

"I'm not entirely sure," Etah was honest. "Spending time with Beau and visiting those museums reminded me of what the art scene used to be like in the Golden Isles, back before there were so many people. And I missed it.

"I think I feel like showing his artwork – especially these pieces that have been hidden away for so long – will kick off a much-needed art renaissance in his memory on Jekyll Island. It was just an idea, but then I told Beau about it and I was committed. He'll be here, by the way, to help us the night of the pop-up gallery. Really, I'm mostly counting on him to help me set it up in an attractive way."

"Does he have gallery experience?" Tally figured she had a lot to learn about Etah's gentleman friend.

"Just a little. But when I went back to Emily's house to measure all the artwork for easels, he went with me. And he had all sorts of ideas about how we could display the different pieces. Emily showed him some other paintings she has in her home, and he got all excited about future galleries. He knows a lot more about the Hendrix artwork than I do, it turns out."

"Was Hendrix that big in Atlanta?" Tally asked.

Etah shrugged in response. "Maybe. I have no idea," she admitted. "But Beau spent his summers on St. Simons and that's how he knows so much about Golden Isles art. Now let's get back to event planning."

She explained that she wanted Tally to act as a hostess when guests arrived at the front doors of Goodyear Cottage and then funnel them the right direction through the house. The art exhibit would be displayed on easels in the dining room, and the traffic to see it would be routed through the gallery, into the dining room, and back out to the front through the butler's pantry attached to the kitchen. Etah hoped that people would impulse shop the Merry Artists items displayed all around them while they waited in line, if there was a line.

She planned to man the cash register the entire 90 minutes, since she was the only member of their team who was a trained Goodyear Cottage shop volunteer. She hadn't wanted to ask anybody else to come help because they were all signed up for long shifts through the holidays. And Etah had promised Jackie that her plan didn't require anything from anybody who was already overloaded.

She proposed that Tally's interns would man the Jekyll Julep and apple cider donut station, which would be set up at the bottom of the stairs so visitors could get a drink and snack while they waited in line to see the artwork, or on their way out afterwards. Etah also planned to order extra fancy cookies for the event and leave a bunch of extras behind in the kitchen for the volunteers working Merry Artists the next morning.

Tally agreed that her team would take care of all the setup and cleanup and said they'd bring the tables and linens needed to make it all happen. Etah explained that everything at Goodyear Cottage was already in use for Merry Artists and nothing should be moved. Fortunately, her niece was the best party planner in the area, and had everything under control, even on short notice. All Etah would have to do was show up, smile, and hopefully, run a lot of transactions on the cash register.

"We'll be there to set up at 4 o'clock on the dot. I'll ask Mitch to help if he's not working because those easels and pictures probably weigh a lot," Tally offered.

"That would be great. I truly appreciate you doing all of this at the last minute for me, Tally."

"I know you do," Tally said, and closed the gap to give her aunt a big hug. Just then, Molly let out an ear-piercing shriek from the down the hall to notify everyone that she was awake. "Mommeeeeeeeeeeeeeeeee!"

"You want to repay the favor?" Tally asked Etah with a smirk. "You go get them changed into clean diapers while I finish putting dinner together."

"Anytime," Etah chirped and jumped up from her chair on a mission.

Chapter 29

"I have to admit it was a good plan, if Etah had a little more self-control," Tally was telling Yaya the next morning when Kayla got to the office. A minute later, Kelsi and the interns swarmed into the back room of Jekyll Weddings. It was chaotic for a few minutes. Tally stopped trying to tell her story while everybody got their coffee and notepads, but she picked it up again once everybody was settled.

"Good morning, beautiful ladies!" she greeted her staff, sounding perkier than she felt. "I was just telling Yaya that Etah has signed us up to help her with an event on Black Friday."

"This Black Friday?" Kayla asked, gulping.

"That's what I said, I promise," Tally replied. "I think she's been bored with retirement so far, although how she gets bored with Molly and Moody all over her a couple days of the week is a mystery. But that was the problem – she needs more to keep her busy."

"How does your aunt being bored equate to all of us working a holiday we were supposed to have off?" Liz asked, sounding a little bit miffed.

"Nobody *has to* work this event, Liz," Tally said, pointedly looking at the intern who had asked the question. "But anybody who is here that wants to *volunteer* to help out will get my undying appreciation."

She paused to let everybody absorb what she'd said and make the appropriate faces.

"I know. I agree, it's a pain in the tush," she told them. "And I guess nobody at the art association was too excited about it either because they'll be busy opening up Merry Artists.

"But you know Etah," she continued, directing her words at Kelsi and Kayla. "Tell her she can't do something, and she'll find a way to make it even bigger and better than her original idea."

"Oh boy," Kayla said, grasping where her boss was going with the story. "I adore Etah, so I don't mind. But I bet you're ready to kill her, considering that's in a couple of weeks."

"She's not really asking us for that much help," Tally conceded. "She just needs us to handle the social media promotion and make the signage for whatever she's putting together. We'll be there to take tickets, pass cookies and punch, and generally play hostesses. And we'll act like we're having a blast if anybody is taking pictures," Tally added.

"It's a little pop-up art gallery of some paintings by an artist friend of hers who has been dead a long time. But his family started the whole arts scene over on St. Simons and everybody still knows his name. Etah is friends with his daughter and she's loaning the artwork. Nobody has ever seen some of it, so she's hoping there will be a lot of interest from the Golden Isles art community. It's only going to be a 90-minute event at Goodyear Cottage."

She went ahead and tasked Kelsi with promoting it and Kayla with coordinating for the night of the gallery event.

"Her new gentleman friend is apparently into art and will be there to help set up the gallery on Black Friday," she announced. "It's going to be up to us to move all the tables and easels and do all the work. Goodyear has to look like we were never there when we leave that night."

"That doesn't sound too bad," Kelsi said. "I wasn't going anywhere for Thanksgiving weekend anyway."

"Neither was I," Kayla said. "Jake and I are cooking our first Thanksgiving dinner together, but that's about it for my plans. I'm sure he won't mind escorting Kelsi and I to Goodyear Cottage for a gallery."

"You might consider having Jake come over early that day or even the night before," Tally suggested. "You could both stay in one of Bonnie's guestrooms, or with Etah, if you wanted. The gate to Jekyll will be a nightmare on Friday with Merry Artists and the first night of Holly Jolly Jekyll. You'd do well to avoid that."

The Holly Jolly Jekyll light display was one of the biggest money makers hosted by the Jekyll Island Authority every year. The ads claimed the island put up something like 10 million lights, but friends who worked for the JIA said it was more than that. Somebody had lost track while counting, somewhere around the 10 million number, and that's what they'd stuck with. The light display, the golf cart light parade, brunch in the main dining room of the club with Santa, lunch with the Grinch, and hunting for Treasure Balls in January and February were some of Tally's favorite memories growing up on Jekyll, and she was determined to do all of them with her children. Every year.

Tally had refused to plan weddings over the Christmas holidays since she first opened her company because she never wanted to miss any of the island's fun activities because of work. She planned a few Christmas parties every year for friends of her aunt, but she didn't market that stuff too hard because she didn't want to spend her holiday season at somebody else's party.

"Are any of you planning to go home for Thanksgiving?" she asked the interns.

"I am," Tori chirped. "I'm actually leaving the Monday before – I got Kelsi's permission when I was hired – because we have a sorority event that week that I absolutely must not miss."

"Totally understandable," Kayla said, making a note. "What about you?" she asked Liz and Katy.

"Count me in," Katy said. "It's not worth flying back to New York for the weekend with all the flight delays that will probably happen."

"I'll be here and I'm happy to help on Black Friday," Liz said, changing her tune from before. "But I already have plans to watch Ohio State's game against Michigan that Saturday. I've found a Buckeye Bar in Brunswick that will be showing the game. I figured it was better to watch it off Jekyll if I was planning to scream obscenities at the TV. And I am," she told them.

"Good idea," Tally agreed. "Okay, so I'll let Etah know that she can count on us to help with this art thing and that all of us, except Tori, will be there for the big event and can help her run things. Etah told me to invite all of you to Thanksgiving at Bonnie's house. You certainly shouldn't feel obligated, but I can tell you from experience that her holiday meals are amazeballs. And she always sends you home with leftovers."

"Count me in," Kayla chirped.

"I thought you and Jake were going to cook Thanksgiving dinner to-gether?" Kelsi pointed out.

"We were. When I thought I had Thursday and Friday off. Now I don't, and we've got an invitation to a fantastic meal we don't have to cook. I see this as win-win," Kayla explained.

It sounded as if everybody would be coming to Mitch's grandmother's house for the holiday and Tally made a note to warn Bonnie that she'd extended the invitations.

"Okay, now let's get focused and talk about our paying clients," Tally said, and opened the file in front of her.

Chapter 30

Mitch was home with the kids early that afternoon when he got a text from his new boss, Whit Butler, the special agent in charge of the Homeland Security Investigations Atlanta field office. He and Joe had met Agent Butler at the first task force meeting in Atlanta, and they'd seen him on Zoom a few times since, but he'd never actually spoken directly to either of them. That was why the little hairs on the back of his neck stood up when he saw Agent Butler's name pop up on his phone.

"Need you to go to NYC tonight. Things are happening," the message read.

Well, that's as vague as you can get, Mitch thought. The stolen artwork they were investigating was taken from Atlanta, the task force was in Brunswick, and now they were going to Manhattan. He assumed somebody would fill him in when he got there.

Before Mitch could organize a text response to Agent Butler, he got another message.

"You're both booked on the 7 pm JetBlue flight out of JAX. Don't miss it. Your contact will be waiting for you at arrivals. I'll email you more info to read on the flight, so you know what you're headed into."

"Count me in," his partner, Joe Moody, replied in what Mitch then realized was a group chat with his boss.

"Me too," Mitch typed quickly and hit send. Then he looked at his watch and groaned. It was supposed to be his day to spend with Molly and Moody. He'd just gotten the both of the twins down for naps in their own cribs a little while ago, and he'd planned to tackle a few of the items on the honey-do list that Tally had been keeping on the fridge door. But that wasn't going to happen now.

Tally was busy in meetings with potential clients all afternoon – it sounded like she was drowning in brides. She'd said as much when she swept out the door that morning and Mitch had taken it as a hint that she didn't need to get silly texts from him all day while he was hanging out with the twins. He didn't want to bother her with this sudden change to his schedule. Ultimately, she wouldn't be able to come home unless nobody else could help them out. And even then, she'd probably tell him to drop Molly and Moody off at the office where Yaya and whoever else was around could pinch hit. It was his responsibility to solve the problem.

So, he called his mom.

Roberta picked up her phone on the second ring and was thrilled beyond measure when her youngest son asked for her help.

"I'm on my way," she said.

"I can drop them off," Mitch offered.

"Don't even worry about it. I'll come to you. That way Tally doesn't have to worry about coming to collect them later. I'll need to see if she's got any other holes in her twin-sitting calendar while you're gone. I'll be happy to take them."

"You're the best," he told her, meaning it. His mom was always willing to watch her grandchildren, even on short notice, like today.

"Don't you forget it. Go get packed and I'll swing through the kitchen and pack up some of the chocolate chip cookies I baked for your dad last night for you and Joe to munch on the plane," she said. "This is exciting, Mitch. Going to New York City for work. Bet you didn't expect to be doing this when you signed up for the state patrol."

"I do a lot of things I wasn't expecting to do as a trooper," Mitch said and laughed.

***

Mitch stopped to pick up Joe in Camden County on his way to the Jacksonville airport.

"Don't sit on the cookies," Mitch told his partner as Joe swung into the passenger seat of the truck after tossing his overnight bag into the back.

"Cookies? What kind?" Joe picked up the container that had been sitting on his seat and opened it. "Mmmm chocolate chip. Tally make these?"

"Nope. My mom made them. She came over to watch the kids when we got called out," he explained. "Check and see if we got that email from Butler yet. I want to know what's so important in New York."

Joe tapped away on his phone. "Jackpot. We have a few emails from the boss. This first one is a news article."

"What's it say?" Mitch asked.

"Lemme read it." Joe was quiet for a few minutes. "Okay, so there was a big art heist in Manhattan a couple of days ago. Man, the thieves were ballsy. They smashed the glass doors to the gallery on Madison Avenue with a hammer. It was all caught on security camera."

"What did they steal?"

"A $100,000 painting that was sitting on an easel in the gallery. A Chagall," Joe told him.

"Never heard of it," Mitch said.

"Marc Chagall was considered one of the three major masters of the 20th century," Joe told him. "Picasso and John Miro were the others, in case you were wondering."

"I take it you're reading that and didn't just happen to know who he was?"

"Absolutely," Joe chuckled. "Get this – it doesn't sound like these were experienced art thieves. Cameras caught them making their getaway in a beat-up Honda Accord and they had a hard time stuffing the artwork in the back. There's a video."

"I'll watch it later. What else?"

"As messed up as the getaway was, they didn't catch them," Joe reported. "The briefing paper from the boss says that there's a concern that the Chagall is slated to be shipped out with the other items we're already watching for. We're on our way up there because that Chagall is more important than anything else we're watching."

"It sounds like it's going to be interesting, although I'm not clear on how we're supposed to help track it down. Guess it just depends on what's already happening in their investigation," Mitch said. "We're the new guys in this so I'm going to do a lot of watching and listening."

"Sounds like a plan," Joe agreed. "Can I have a cookie?"

"Yeah, but only if you give me one, too."

Chapter 31

Jackie Becker loved to host Pie Night on the Thursday before Thanksgiving every year. It was a fun tradition that she and her husband, Bruce, started after they moved to Jekyll Island and had finished renovating their new home. Every invited guest was asked to bring their favorite pie to share, and Jackie and Bruce put out an elaborate top-shelf, self-serve bar in their kitchen that would become a favorite place to hang out during the evening.

For Jackie, Pie Night felt like the beginning and end of her holiday season. She'd been running the Merry Artists Holiday Market for the art association for so many years that it had replaced Christmas as the priority of her December. By the time Christmas Eve and Christmas Day finally arrived, Jackie was usually too wiped out to care. And Bruce dearly missed the fun they used to have together during the holidays when his wife wasn't volunteering full time.

By Christmas, four weeks into Merry Artists, Jackie would have jumped in her car at least 10 times to run over to Goodyear Cottage and fill in at the cash register for somebody who hadn't shown up for their volunteer shift. It was exhausting on top of the constant intake of new merchandise for the market and staging the new things in the sale areas.

She'd promised her husband that this would be her last year at the helm of Merry Artists, but she knew that was only a half-truth. They hadn't found anybody willing to run it for next year yet, which meant she didn't have a new person to mentor and teach the ropes for next year. Whoever ultimately took it on would need her guidance pretty much all the way through the process. When she'd told her husband as much, he'd agreed to stop giving her a hard time about it if she allowed him to book a cruise to somewhere exotic that left the second week of December. He said he didn't want them to come back home until after New Year's.

"If they haven't figured it out by then, they'll have to do it without me," Jackie promised. But she made sure they were scheduled to travel on a cruise line the touted its excellent at-sea wi-fi and wireless service.

She hoped that next year, Pie Night wouldn't be accompanied by the sense of overwhelming dread she couldn't help feeling when she looked her calendar and the growing pile of Merry Artists submissions waiting to be checked into inventory in the kitchen at Goodyear Cottage.

"Are we ready?" Bruce asked, coming into the kitchen. "You look beautiful as always," he told her and planted a kiss on her lips. They'd been married for more than 45 years and could read each other's minds most of the time.

"We're ready," she smiled and handed him the drink she'd just mixed for him. The doorbell rang before he'd taken his first sip. He took a slug and set the glass down on the counter.

"I'll get that while you mix a drink for yourself, before you're too busy dealing with our guests," he said, heading for the front door. She saluted him to his back, but she was smiling. And she smiled even bigger a moment later when she heard their good friends, Jim and Theresa LaPean, greeting Bruce in their foyer.

***

The party was in full swing, inside the house and on the back patio, almost two hours later when something made Jackie stop mid-conversation with her friend Stella to do a doubletake in her own kitchen. Her instincts told her something was off, but it took her a few seconds to realize what it was.

There were pies and cakes set up on the dining room table, and also on the countertop of the kitchen island. She scanned both areas and saw there were no empty pie dishes or dirty cake plates, there were plenty of clean cocktail napkins and forks, and everything appeared to have been sampled. That was when she realized what had set off alarm bells in her head. She stepped back into the dining room and checked that table, too, to confirm she wasn't imagining things.

She wasn't. Somebody had cut a circle and taken the center out of every single pie at the party.

"What's wrong?" Stella asked, having realized Jackie wasn't listening anymore to her story about her daughter-in-law's behavior at a recent family gathering.

"Look at the pies," Jackie pointed. "Who would do that?"

It took Stella the same few seconds to process what she was seeing, and then she started laughing. She looked around but didn't find the person she was looking for. "Is David Fisher here?" she asked.

"He stopped in briefly," Jackie said. "He brought a pizza. Said it was his favorite kind of a pie, which we all already know because he posts so many pictures of it on Facebook."

David and his wife, Julie, owned an architectural photography firm that was one of the most well-respected in the country. They were only on Jekyll for part of the time. In addition to filming new buildings and construction all over Georgia and its surrounding states, David also considered himself a bit of a pizza and barbecue connoisseur, and he regularly posted about the hole-in-the-wall spots he found during his work travels.

"Why?" Jackie asked, sounding suspicious. "Why are you asking about David?"

"This looks like something he might have done," Stella said. "I feel like I've heard stories." She didn't elaborate and she didn't need to. Because that was when Bruce came into the kitchen to mix another drink for somebody.

"Who cut circles in every single damned pie?" Jackie asked him in a low voice.

"David Fisher. He says it's the best part of the pie and nobody else had taken it yet, so he helped himself," Bruce said nonchalantly, like it was perfectly normal for a party guest to do something that bizarre. "He really liked that cheesecake." He gestured toward a sideboard where Jackie had placed the two cheesecakes that guests had brought.

"Of course he did," Jackie shook her head but kept smiling. Stella laughed like it was the funniest thing she'd heard in ages. The cheesecakes hadn't fared as well as the pies, when it came to David's creative cutting techniques. What remained on the cake stands looked like a sea turtle had nested in it, she thought. But it was done and she couldn't undo it, so she made herself a drink and went into the living room for a distraction.

Somebody was telling a story to a group of guests, and everybody was laughing hysterically.

"What did I miss?" Jackie asked as she joined them, leaning against the doorframe.

"Have you heard about the great treasure ball mystery?" her neighbor, Sarah O'Neil, asked.

"The what?" Jackie thought she'd misheard.

"All of the 'island treasures' for the 2024 Jekyll Island Treasure Hunt have gone missing," Sarah explained. "My son, Eric, heard about it at work today. He works for one of the contractors that's helping put up the Holly Jolly Jekyll lighting all over the island."

"All of them? How many were there? Where were they?" Jackie asked, still confused.

"Well, that's the problem, isn't it?" Murray Jordan picked up the story where he'd left off when Jackie walked in. "Seems that the all the glass globes from Mark Ellinger's shop out west, Glass Quest, were delivered to Jekyll Island last week. It's the last year Mark's doing the treasure balls on commission for the authority, so this was a special order and bigger than usual, I heard."

"Lucy Johnston at the Jekyll Island Authority signed the manifest and took delivery of them last week. Like she does with everything that comes in for the JIA shops and sales inventory," Murray continued.

"Right," Jackie nodded.

"Lucy says that she told Dougie Stonewall to put 'em on a storage shelf out of the way because they won't even stock them into the shops until after Christmas, and he did. She saw him loading them."

"So, what's the problem?" Jackie asked.

"I heard that somebody on the JIA board made a special request for one of the balls," Sarah volunteered. "And it landed on Lucy's desk. So, she went out to get a ball for the VIP, but she couldn't find them."

"And Dougie is out of town on a Carnival Cruise to Alaska and won't be back until just before Thanksgiving," Murray started laughing.

"But this board member wants the treasure ball this week. It's for something special he's doing – God only knows what – and the executive director's secretary promised she'd take care of it. And now half of the admin staff of the Jekyll Island Authority are out digging through warehouses," his wife, Carol, had to pick up the story for Murray because he was laughing too hard to continue.

"Oh, it's a hot mess at the JIA offices," Carol said in a serious voice. "They know the balls are there, somewhere, but where they are is anybody's guess. Seems that Dougie was in a rush before leaving on his trip and may have failed to enter some information into the computer."

"And he told everybody he wasn't going to be reachable on the cruise because the fees for Internet use at sea were so high that he and his wife had decided to take a digital vacation. He won't get his messages until their ship returns to the port in Seattle after the 12-day journey," she reported.

"Well, that's a nightmare," Jackie said, only chuckling because it wasn't her problem. She had been on the hunting end of things a few times when artists came to retrieve artwork and couldn't find it. It was the worst position to be in.

"Well, nobody on grounds or in landscaping can help look for it because they're all trying to finish putting up the Holly Jolly lights, and so Lucy had to get a bunch of admin people to help her. She made a list of everywhere they store things, and they're searching one building at a time," Murray had regained enough control of himself to continue the story. "Turns out they use a lot of old buildings for storage. Gonna take a while to check them all he chuckled. "Another fantastic use of our tax dollars, right?"

"It seems like that might be a big waste of time, since Dougie will be back eventually, and the balls are not actually needed until January," Stella's husband, Roger, opined.

"Lucy said as much, but she doesn't have a choice with the boss's secretary breathing down her neck," Murray said. "If it was me, I'd go buy another danged treasure ball in the shop at the Jekyll Info Center. But she seems to think that somebody could find out that it's not one of the new ones, and she'll get in big trouble."

"Well, I hate that for her," Carolyn James joined in. She'd been sitting on the couch, quietly listening to everybody else. "I hate that somebody is spinning in circles trying to do something that doesn't benefit the residents of Jekyll Island in any way."

Etah spoke up from the wing chair where she was sitting. "It's strange. Lots of things getting lost or stolen on Jekyll these days. Somebody stole a big Snoopy off the front lawn next door."

"Is that what happened to it?" Jackie had noticed the football decoration was gone and just assumed its owner had taken it down. "That's so strange."

"The McLemores' Ring camera across the street caught video of a car stopping in front of the house on the night Snoopy was taken, but you couldn't read the plate number or see it very well," Etah told the party guests, who were all listening intently. This gossip was even better than the treasure ball mystery because everybody knew the glass globes would be found eventually.

"The camera only caught enough to see it was a four-door sedan. But Mitch took the footage into work with him today and was going to ask one of their computer people to try and enhance it," Etah told them.

"Are you sure it wasn't a football prank?" Jimmy Dyer asked, his expression skeptical.

"It's got to be a joke," his wife, Laura, agreed.

"That's what the girls thought at first, but it has been a couple of weeks, and he hasn't turned up or been posted on social media wearing a Michigan or Georgia jersey, so maybe it really was just stolen," Etah said with a troubled look on her face.

"I hope not," Jackie said. "That would mean we have to remember to shut our garage door when we leave town." She was joking and Bruce caught her eye and winked. "Now that Rocky Raccoon isn't the only concern in the neighborhood."

The rest of the party chatter was mostly soft-core gossip. They shared news about which chefs had been replaced at local restaurants between the summer and winter high seasons. And there were rumors that all was not paradise over at the island's award-winning tennis center. Everybody already knew that the pickleball people were mounting an aggressive campaign to get some of their courts installed on the island. All 16 courts at the Jekyll Island Tennis Center were red clay and not appropriate for the plastic wiffle balls that were used for the newer, popular game.

On top of that, tennis players worldwide had been pushing back against the migration of pickleball courts into tennis clubs, and most tennis players on Jekyll felt the same way. Pickleball was much louder than tennis, due to the hard paddles and plastic balls. And the players stood closer to each other on the shorter court, and so they chatted, loudly, much more than they would usually talk during a real tennis match. Tennis players complained when tape was added to mark out pickleball courts on established tennis courts. None of them wanted to share a court with people playing pickleball – it was too distracting and annoying.

However, JIA liked to make money, and they saw a profit center in adding pickleball courts that would be available for rent by tourists and locals alike on Jekyll. Right now, all the pickleball players on Jekyll were spending money to play on St. Simons Island next door and the authority hated to see money drive over the causeway. Everybody figured JIA would add pickleball courts to the island eventually. But if you based progress on how long it took to build the new bath house at the campground or even the new public safety building, the tennis players had no competition to worry about for a long time.

***

Jackie was exhausted when their last guests finally took their leave from Pie Night. It had been another successful party if you didn't count the fact that nobody wanted to take home any pieces of pie or cake. It was hard to sell leftovers that were missing what many considered to be the best part. It almost looked like somebody had taken two or three bites off the tip of each piece. She shook her head and smiled. It had probably made perfect sense to David to eat the centers. He was an artist and his brain worked differently. Or so they said.

Bruce had already triaged the bar mess, and the dishwasher was chugging away. Jackie had used disposable plates, napkins, and silverware, and she'd stayed on top of the discarded ones all night. She was absolutely exhausted, but she forced herself to keep going with the promise of the massages she'd scheduled tomorrow afternoon for them both with their friends Laura and Jimmy, who owned Beach Life Massage.

Once she wrapped up the remaining mangled pieces of pie and cake, she slid it all into the fridge and turned off the kitchen lights. Whatever she hadn't gotten to yet would be waiting for her in the morning. Bruce was probably already in bed upstairs waiting on Jackie.

Chapter 32

Kayla had started to doubt the wisdom of eloping without telling anybody about their plans, but when she told Jake she was worrying, he told her she was being silly. She'd gone dress shopping by herself on St. Simons when she was over there for a vendor meeting a week earlier, but she hadn't seen anything that she wanted to try on.

Then yesterday, she poked her head into Brittney's Closet to say hi to her friend, Rozell, and spotted the perfect dress. Brittney's Closet was a popular dress shop across the street from Jekyll Market, owned by Brittney and Rob Tribuzio, the same couple who owned two restaurants on the island. All of the girls on the Jekyll Weddings staff had a few outfits they'd purchased during the big sales at monthly Sip'n'Shop events at Brittney's Closet.

"You playing hooky?" Rozell asked when Kayla came in. Then she walked around the counter to deliver a big hug. "How's the wedding business?"

"You know exactly how it is this time of year," Kayla gave the older woman a knowing look. Rozell had planned weddings on Jekyll Island for years before semi-retiring and taking on Brittney's Closet.

"I definitely do. And I'm really glad that I'm busy stocking hairy Santa sweaters and fun evening bags now instead of trying to talk a certifiably crazy bride out of doing something stupid," Rozell said, and Kayla knew she meant it. Wedding planner burnout was a very real thing. Tally's mentor, Isabelle, was an excellent example of that. She'd never gone back to event planning after the storm wiped out Vieques Weddings.

"What's a hairy Santa sweater?" Kayla asked.

"Oh, you'll see. We sold out of the first ones the day they arrived. I'm expecting another shipment tomorrow. Want me to set one aside for you?"

Kayla smiled and shrugged. "I think I need to see what a hairy Santa sweater looks like before I commit."

"You'll be sad when they sell out again," Rozell warned. "Now what can I help you with today? Or did you just come in to see me because you heard I'd gotten a couple of dozen oatmeal cookies from Jekyll Market this morning?"

"You did? I didn't know you could buy cookies from them by the dozens," Kayla was perpetually amazed by everything that could be had at the Jekyll Market.

"I have a connection," Rozell winked.

"Of course you do," Kayla said, and helped herself to two cookies from the container her friend held out to her. "I need a white dress and that sundress over there caught my eye."

"What do you need a white dress for in November?" Rozell asked suspiciously.

"Some stupid client with a white wedding theme. It's not until spring. But the one dress I've worn to work white weddings for the past couple of years has a big stain on it, so I've been looking for something new. And that caught my eye," she walked over to look at the sundress up close.

The dress came in white, pink, and light blue, but Kayla was only interested in the white version. It was sleeveless and when she looked closer, she saw the fabric was actually a sheer floral overlay with a white lining. She loved it.

Kayla pulled a medium off the rack and handed it to Rozell. "Okay if I try it on at home tonight and exchange it tomorrow if the size is wrong? I need to run back across the street for a conference call now." She pulled out her credit card and put it on the counter.

Rozell moved quickly and a few moments later, Kayla was dashing back to Jekyll Weddings with her own wedding gown carefully packed in pink tissue paper in a Brittney's Closet shopping bag.

Chapter 33

"Hey honey," Tally greeted her husband when her phone buzzed late on Friday night. "We could have used you around here today."

"Oh really? What happened?" Mitch asked. He had been in New York for almost a week and hearing his wife's voice made him homesick.

"We had to break into a bedroom at a rental house on Beachview after the father of the bride accidentally locked all the wedding clothes inside it," Tally explained. "First time I've had that happen. I'll have to ask Isabelle if it ever happened at one of her weddings. I swear, I think I've seen it all and then something even more ridiculous happens."

"Did you call a locksmith?" Mitch asked. The solution to the problem seemed relatively simple.

"Didn't have time. He locked them out of the master bedroom about 30 minutes before the wedding ceremony. The bride was hysterical. And her brother had been pre-gaming a little too hard and he hurt himself trying to save the day and bust the door down," she told Mitch. "It was a total cluster when I got there. But we had to get into that room because the string quartet and the photographer and videographer were all running on time and my clients would have had to pony up a whole lot of extra money if they'd had to delay things by an hour or more because the bride couldn't get to her wedding gown."

"Sounds like a mess." Mitch smiled as he said it. Tally's behind-the-scenes stories about her weddings always came from a worst-case perspective. He thought she was hilarious.

"Everybody was so worked up that a really silly, small problem became a crisis of epic proportions. When I arrived, the bride's father was yelling at Kayla because she hadn't been able to get them into the room yet."

"That's ridiculous. She's not a locksmith," Mitch said.

"She might become one after tonight," Tally laughed. "But your dad was the one who finally saved the day. I called him on his cell phone in a panic, and he came right over."

"Did he knock the door down?" Mitch asked, wishing he'd been home for the excitement and feeling a little left out.

"Nope. He did even better. He checked and found one of the bedroom windows unlocked. He boosted me up and I climbed in and unlocked the door from the inside."

"Go Dad," Mitch crowed.

"Seriously. I don't know why I hadn't thought to check the windows myself. Kayla didn't think about it either, but she was trying to hold it together while the father of the bride screamed at her."

"I'm glad my dad could help," Mitch said.

"Me too. Although they're still going to have to buy a new bedroom door for that house. Her brother really mucked it up, even if he didn't get it open," Tally reported. "What about you? When are you coming home? We miss you."

"We're booked on a noon flight tomorrow, so I'll be home in time for dinner. Are you working tomorrow night?"

"We have weddings all weekend, but Kelsi and Kayla have them under control and I don't have to be there unless something goes sideways," she told him. "So, I'll plan to feed you when you get home. Maybe we can even have a date night afterwards, if the kids ever go to sleep. The twins will be so excited to see you. Molly looks for you every time she wakes up."

"Aw. That makes me feel bad that I've been having so much fun up here," he said.

"Have you really had fun?" They hadn't had many long conversations since he'd been gone. Tally and Mitch were both super busy and most of their chats had involved updates about Molly and Moody.

"Not really. It's been interesting, but I'm not sure how the two investigations actually link together. I'll tell you more about it tomorrow night," he promised.

"Have a safe trip home. Text me before you take off, and when you land," she reminded him.

"I will," Mitch said. "Don't stay up too late working just because I'm not there to drag you off to bed."

"I'll try not to," she said and chuckled as she hung up the phone. He knew her too well.

Chapter 34

The weddings on the Saturday and Sunday nights before Thanksgiving went off easily compared to the wardrobe nightmare on Friday afternoon. But that didn't mean they'd been free of drama and surprises.

Kayla was still laughing and in a fantastic mood when they finished teardown from the Sewell/Framingham wedding reception on Sunday evening. When Tori said she could catch the last train up to Charleston if she left right away, Kayla offered to drop the intern off on her way home. Tori had been talking about this trip back to College of Charleston for a not-to-be-missed sorority event every day for the past couple of weeks.

"What did you think of that wedding?" Kayla asked the bubbly intern as they cruised down the Jekyll Causeway. They'd worked together on most of the planning with Mary Elizabeth Sewell and Noah Framingham, but the bride and groom had brought a surprise with them that even their planners didn't know about. Kayla and Tori had watched it all unfold but they hadn't had time to talk about it yet.

"That was crazypants!" Tori laughed at the question. "I totally didn't see that coming."

"Right?" Kayla laughed, too. "That was definitely a first for me. I don't think it's ever happened at one of Tally's weddings either. We'll have to get her to ask Isabelle," she said, referring to Tally's former boss in Vieques. Isabelle lived in Vermont now but visited regularly. She usually stayed with Etah now that Molly and Moody's cribs occupied the guest room. There was usually nothing that could happen at a wedding that Isabelle hadn't seen before. "Maybe we'll finally stump her."

"Here we are, doing this super-religious wedding for these high-dollar Southern Baptists. Super-long wedding ceremony conducted by important Baptist pastors imported from six counties away. Three days of events with no alcohol, technically speaking," Tori listed off the rather conservative details of the Sewell/Framingham nuptials. She added the caveat onto the no booze thing because it had been obvious from the get-go that not all the members of the wedding party were on board with the dry weekend.

"I was so afraid that the best man was going to say something outrageous during the toasts," Tori said. "He was so clearly inebriated before the wedding ceremony even started. Now I know why Mary Elizabeth insisted that they put those fancy-dancy water bottles in the welcome bags. It was camouflage for the cocktails!"

"That was pretty brilliant. I had no clue until we saw them all carrying them around at the welcome party. Nobody needed to bring a water bottle to a restaurant," Kayla said.

"I guess Mary Elizabeth wasn't drinking," Tori said with a laugh. "At least I hope she wasn't."

It had been a rather normal weekend, up until the second half of the wedding reception. In fact, things were going so smoothly when the shit hit the fan that it took a minute for the wedding planners to realize what was happening right in front of them.

"We wanted to thank everybody for coming," the groom said, and then tapped the microphone to get everybody's attention. He was standing with the bride near the DJ booth and had obviously appropriated the microphone. The room quieted.

"Was this planned?" Tori asked Kayla.

"Nope. Shhh," Kayla held a finger to her lips. It didn't matter if this moment was unplanned, the clients could do whatever they wanted at their own wedding reception.

"You all think you're here just to celebrate our wedding tonight, but we have something even more exciting to share with you," Noah looked at Mary Elizabeth and smiled. "Do you want to tell them?" He offered her the microphone.

"You tell them," she said, pushing it back at him. They were cute up there, and the smile on the bride's face was infectious. Kayla found herself smiling with them.

"Okay, I will. Guess what everybody? Mary Elizabeth is pregnant," the groom paused for effect, "and we have a baby due on Valentine's Day," he announced, his voice full of enthusiasm.

Noah and Mary Elizabeth looked toward their families expectantly and got no reaction whatsoever. After a pause, their friends started cheering and clapping, and the wedding planners joined in, hooting the loudest for the couple. But their parents remained seated and silent at their dinner table, and a few minutes later, Tori nudged Kayla to point out the bride's parents slipping out the back of the venue.

"Way to kill a party, eh?" Tori remarked.

Kayla had rolled her eyes and gone to do triage with the obviously emotional bride who had just realized that her parents were walking out of her wedding. Tally always said that surprises were a bad thing at weddings and tonight had certainly proved that true. The funny thing was, Kayla had always thought about it in terms of somebody trying to surprise the bride or groom, not the happy couple dropping a whopper on their families at the reception. She hadn't had an "if, then" plan for when the bride and groom intentionally ruined the festivities at their own wedding reception.

Tori bought her train ticket in the app and when they arrived at the Brunswick train depot, she was ready to go. Kayla leaned across the seat and hugged her intern.

"You did a great job with Mary Elizabeth and Noah, no matter how the evening ended. Give yourself an A+ for this wedding weekend," Kayla told Tori.

Tori grinned. "Thanks. I knew it went perfectly – up til tonight," she groaned. "But I really thought I was on my game. I double-checked my lists and my schedule, and everything went the way it was supposed to."

"That's why we're so uptight about the lists and schedules for your first few months," Kayla reminded her.

"I get it now."

"Have a great time at school, but don't have so much fun that you can't come back next week. We need you for the Scott/Browning wedding. It's big and complicated and we're all going to be there," Kayla told Tori.

"I know. I can't wait. It's my first flash mob at a wedding," Tori sounded like she was being initiated into a secret society. Kayla couldn't help laughing at her.

"Let's see if you still think it's a neat idea after you've helped coordinate it," she said. "Now get out of here before you miss your train."

Tori slammed the door shut and waved goodbye to her boss, before practically skipping her way into the station.

Chapter 35

Mitch's brother, Glynn County Police Sergeant Pete Durham, and his wife, Robin, joined Tally and Mitch for dinner on Monday night. They'd dropped their own boys off with Bonnie across the street and were looking forward to an adults-only evening with Mitch and Tally, but not until after Robin got in her quota of snuggles with Molly and Moody.

Mitch and Pete put the twins to bed while Tally and Robin got dinner ready together. Tally had baked a lasagna that she had stashed in the freezer, and she pulled the bubbling pan out of the oven and set it on the counter. Meanwhile, Robin assembled a Ceasar salad from the grocery store kit Tally had picked up at the Jekyll Market that afternoon.

Pete wandered back into the kitchen and Robin tasked her husband with opening and pouring the bottle of wine they'd brought as a hostess gift.

"Do we want glasses of ice water too?" she asked Tally.

"I don't. But if you do, go ahead," Tally replied. "I'm sticking to wine tonight. Wouldn't want to mix."

Robin laughed knowingly. "Pete, you might want to go ahead and open up another bottle to breathe. Pretty sure we're going to need it."

The first half of dinner, the couples caught up on everything that was going on with the family.

"Mom said you stayed with Tommy and Frank in Atlanta. I haven't seen you since that trip - how was it?" Pete asked. Tommy was their oldest brother, and Frank was two years older than Pete.

"Same as always. The only thing in their fridge was beer and leftovers. And not much of that," Mitch complained. "They didn't even have milk for coffee in the house because they like the coffee from the corner shop."

Pete laughed. "Predictable. Did they at least put clean sheets on the guestroom bed for you?"

"They *gave me* clean sheets to put on the guestroom bed for myself, so I guess that's something," Mitch chuckled. "But next time I go stay with them, I'm bringing my own clean towel."

"Ew," Robin made a face.

"They said they gave me a clean towel, but it smelled kinda sour," Mitch said.

"Probably clean but left in the washer for two days before they put it into the dryer," Tally suggested. "You gotta sniff if you don't flip the loads the same day. And I can't picture Tommy or Frank sniffing."

They all got a good laugh out of that.

"Tell us about this new task force you're working on," Robin directed her question to her brother-in-law. "What were you doing up in New York?"

"Joe and I have been temporarily detailed to the Stolen Arts and Antiquities task force operating in this region," he explained.

"What's that?" Robin asked.

"Homeland Security started really cracking down on the trafficking of arts and antiquities about 10 years ago. There are long-term operations in place as part of the Cultural Antiquities Task Force in a lot of major cities where stolen art trafficking is a problem. But this area hasn't been on their target list in the past.

"But now Atlanta, Savannah, and Charleston's art scenes are coming into play as well," Mitch continued. "It's not just about actual thefts of art and antiquities, but more about what happens to those stolen items next. My boss suspects there's a lot of stolen artwork just sitting in temperature-controlled boxes at the Port of Brunswick. He says the thieves park stolen art all over the place while they're moving it around."

"Interesting," Pete said, and Mitch could see his brother's mind going full speed thinking about Glynn County having a stolen art problem he didn't know about.

"They think there's a link between the thieves who broke into the gallery in New York and stole the Chagall last week, and the art dealer who is arranging the sale of some other important artwork that was taken from a private gallery in Atlanta six months ago," Mitch told them.

"I think that sounds interesting," Tally told her husband.

"It is. NYPD's Major Case Squad has been working with the task force for a few years, but this latest theft of 'Eve' – that was the name of the Chagall painting," he explained. "This one was brazen, and the thieves caught on video appeared to be rather amateur. So, either the guys who have been doing this for years are slipping, or there's another art thief in play that our task force didn't know about."

Mitch told them that he and Joe would be in an office doing research initially.

"Good," Tally said. "Maybe that means you'll have a normal schedule for a few weeks."

"What's normal?" Robin asked, and everybody at the table laughed.

Law enforcement families created their own "normal" in order to cope with the demands the community put on their family members. Domestic violence and suicide attempts skyrocketed over the holidays, and as a result, police all over the country had to work while the rest of the world was celebrating. There wasn't a police family in America who hadn't celebrated Thanksgiving on the day before, or the day after, the actual holiday so that their law enforcement family member could be with them. And every cop wife has had to talk the children off the ledge on Christmas morning when they weren't allowed to open the stockings Santa left them "until Daddy gets off-duty tonight."

"I just mean that it would be nice to see him more than I have been," Tally said. "The twins are at an age where they notice he's not around. Molly keeps asking for him, and that gets Moody going. And unfortunately, Daddy doesn't have a job where we can go visit him."

"They'll be old enough for ridealongs sooner than you realize," Pete joked.

"That's the truth," his wife agreed. "You blink and suddenly they're in driver's ed. How does that even happen? I think Nate has a girlfriend," she said, referring to their oldest son.

"Oooo!" Tally interrupted her sister-in-law. "Speaking of romance, Etah has a boyfriend that she met on her Mediterranean cruise."

"No kidding? That's awesome," Pete said with a big smile. "I've never known her to date."

"Me either," Tally agreed. "It's pretty wild to think about."

"I think it's great," Robin added.

"Oh, I do, too. But I haven't met him yet because my schedule has been nuts. It's totally my own fault. Bonnie and Susan met him a few weeks ago and they both liked him," she reported.

"Guess you'd better make time, if it's getting serious," Robin told her.

Tally thought about it. "I don't know if it's serious exactly, but you're right about me needing to make time. He's going to be here for the pop-up gallery of Bill Hendrix artwork at Goodyear Cottage on Black Friday. I should make plans to do lunch with them that Saturday."

"Is he going to be here for Thanksgiving?" Pete asked. "Because if he is, we'll probably all get to meet him then."

"I don't know. I'll have to ask. The last few times I've chatted with Etah, we've been talking about Miss Molly and Mr. Moody and her upcoming art show more than her love life," Tally made a face. "I'm old and married – why does thinking about Etah having a love life give me an ick factor of 10?"

"Because she'll always be a parent to you and that's gross to think about," Mitch said in a soothing voice, and patted his wife's hand on the table. "I don't want to think about my parents either."

"Ew," Pete joined in the fun, making a gagging face. "Did you have to mention *our parents?* Was that really necessary?"

"Oh my God, you're all adults. Grow up!" Robin ordered them.

"Does anybody know if Frank is coming to Jekyll for Thanksgiving?" Tally asked.

"Bonnie would know if Tommy and Frank are going to be here," Robin volunteered.

"I'll ask her," Tally said. "I want to know if I should warn Kelsi to dress for success or just come comfy for a family Thanksgiving. I felt some energy between them on the beach last summer, but he never called her after they met. Maybe it was just bad timing."

"It was definitely bad timing," Robin confirmed. "She'd just been kidnapped by the guy she'd been dating. If she wasn't having trust issues, she should have been."

"Valid. But I don't wonder why Kelsi didn't chase Frank. I'm wondering why Frank didn't chase after Kelsi. He's not one to stand on ceremony because of another guy," Tally argued. "I just kind of expected that he would want to see her again."

"Maybe he does and he just hasn't had time," Pete suggested. "Let's see what happens if he's here. Don't push it or they'll both feel weird and nothing will happen."

"I wouldn't push it," Tally prepared to defend her record of setting people up. But Mitch put the kibosh on it before she could get started.

"Yes, you would, and you'd have the best intentions. But Kelsi works for you, and Frank is related to us, so let's tread very carefully with this one. It might be better for the rest of us if that connection didn't happen again. All of Frank's girlfriends end up going nuts."

"Hmm," Tally grunted.

"What?" Mitch asked.

"I hadn't thought about Frank's track record with crazy women," she explained. "Are you saying they weren't nuts before they dated your older brother?"

"That's exactly what he's saying," Pete confirmed.

Chapter 36

Thanksgiving dinner at Bonnie's house was an absolute zoo. Pete and Robin were there with their boys, and Tommy and Frank had come in from Atlanta. Roberta and Tom were managing the twins in the backyard while Tally helped the other women in the kitchen.

"Thank God for your parents," Tally told Mitch when they rolled across the street early that afternoon with a beach cart full of bottles of wine and other sundry items for the festivities.

Molly and Moody had waited for them at the edge of the driveway, as they'd been taught. But they were both craning their necks to see what was happening in the yard across the street. They held hands with each other, and Molly held Tally's hand, and they crossed Tallu Fish Lane together, with Mitch pulling the cart behind them. The minute the twins' feet hit the grass on the other side of the road, Molly let go of her mother's hand and the toddlers went racing off across the yard, squealing in delight and still holding hands, as they rushed into the arms of their grandmother.

Etah was already there when Tally arrived, stirring a pot of something on the stove. Tally peeked into it and sniffed.

"That smells amazing," she told her aunt.

"It's my Jekyll Julep recipe. It'll be ready in just a minute," she promised. "I just have to add the most important ingredient." Etah picked up a bottle of Fireball whiskey sitting on the counter next to the stove. "I'll set aside some for the kiddos first, but the true cocktail needs a little pep."

The Jekyll Juleps were ready by the time Kayla and Jake arrived at Bonnie's. Kelsi pulled up in her Pathfinder with Liz and Katy a few minutes later. When she jumped out of the car wearing a turkey onesie, everybody burst out laughing. The interns each had a giant turkey hat they put on their heads reluctantly, and Tally suspected Kelsi had bought the hats and was forcing the girls to wear them. *Good,* she thought. Public embarrassment builds character. Wedding planners had to do humiliating things on a regular basis to keep a party going, and wearing a turkey costume wasn't the worst thing Kelsi would ever do.

Then the lightbulb went on in Tally's head and she felt awful. She'd forgotten to warn Kelsi that Frank might be at Bonnie's for Thanksgiving. The realization came at about the same moment that Kelsi set eyes on Frank, who was standing on the porch of Bonnie's house, laughing at her with his nephews. Kelsi's face turned scarlet and for a second, Tally thought she looked like it was time to take her out of the oven. And then she felt badly for not warning her friend.

"Come have a Jekyll Julep," she greeted Kelsi with a hug and handed her a red Solo cup of Etah's special brew.

"What's in it?" Kelsi asked, eyeing the beverage suspiciously before taking a sip. "Hey, it's good!"

"I know. But it's pretty sneaky too, because you can hardly taste the Fireball. Be careful," Tally warned.

"Is this the stuff that we're serving tomorrow night at Goodyear?" Kelsi asked, downing the remainder in her cup.

"We're serving a virgin version of it."

"Remind me to put some little airplane bottles of Fireball in my purse," Kelsi joked.

"That's not a bad idea," Tally agreed.

Kayla and Tally ended up helping in the kitchen while the turkeys – that was Kelsi, Liz, and Katy – visited with Jake and Mitch's brothers in the backyard. It turned out the turkey onesie had been the perfect ice breaker. If Kelsi had been worried that it would be awkward to see Frank – it could have been weird because he'd asked for her number and promised to call when they met in August, but he never did – wearing a turkey costume had eliminated all barriers to conversation. Nobody could look at her without laughing.

"I'm glad everybody is here today," Tally told Kayla.

"I know. I almost miss Tori," she joked.

"She's not that bad," Tally shook her head. "She's got that perky enthusiasm that we need in a team member. Liz and Katy are much cooler and lower key, but Tori is the first one onto the dance floor when we need to get the party going. And sometimes that's more important than knowing when to keep your mouth shut."

"I can't argue with that," Kayla said. "Do you have a favorite intern at this point?"

"Not really. I like all of them. I want to keep all of them," she said pointedly. When Tally had agreed to the intern program, Kayla and Kelsi promised her they would evaluate the interns after the first few months and make sure they wanted to extend the internship throughout the remainder of the year. So far, none of the girls they'd hired had been a problem that they'd want to replace.

"If they all make it through the year, how many would you hire full time?" Kayla asked. "Would you hire all of them?"

"I can't afford all of them," Tally told her.

"You could if we opened St. Simons Weddings this spring," Kayla argued. "You could give me one of them and keep two of them to work for Kelsi on Jekyll. It would be perfect – we could get them all cross-trained on both islands – but have one planner assigned to work with me full-time over there."

Tally let out a big sigh. "I wondered when this was going to come up again." She smiled to let Kayla know she wasn't annoyed by her asking.

"It's just that if we are going to do it in the next 12 months, we need to start planning for it now. I'd rather have several St. Simons wedding clients booked under the Jekyll Weddings umbrella before we announce the company anyway. It'll look better," she said, looking at Tally hopefully.

"So that's the plan?" Tally raised one eyebrow.

"We get several requests for weddings on St. Simons every month, don't we?" Kayla asked.

"At least one a week," Tally conceded.

"If we could book half of those into big weddings on St. Simons, we'd have a full slate to show on our website within a month of launching. Heck, we don't even need a whole website – we can just make St. Simons Weddings part of the bigger Jekyll Weddings website. All the weddings in the Jekyll pictures have been executed by the same team of wedding planners," she pointed out.

"True. But we also have quite a few St. Simons pictures we can use on the site – we've done a lot of rehearsal dinners over there, too," Tally said. "Okay, here's what we're going to do. Let's go ahead and have you take over all client inquiries that want anything other than Jekyll. You take St. Simons, Brunswick, Sea Island and Cumberland Island."

"Have we ever done a wedding on Cumberland?" Kayla looked confused.

"Not yet. But if we're going to hire three more wedding planners, full time, then we're going to need to book at least as many weddings as we're already doing right now in order to keep the business in the black," Tally explained.

"Will the numbers be that close?" Kayla asked. She had no idea what Tally paid everybody else on the team. And although she knew what it cost to make a wedding happen, and how much the planning fee was based on the final budget, she didn't know how much profit Tally actually made on each wedding after she'd paid all the vendors and everybody on her staff.

"Yes and no," Tally explained. She refilled her own cup from the punch bowl Etah had put on the sideboard in Bonnie's dining room, but Kayla begged off when she tried to top hers off, too.

"We don't make much of a profit off our wedding planning services themselves. If you ever stopped to add up all the hours spent by each of us on a client, and did the math on it, it would just depress the hell out of you. We're not even charging them an hourly rate that equates to minimum wage. But we make money other places. Like flowers and rentals," she continued.

"That's why it's so important to push bigger flower budgets and other things we make money on – because when they buy those things through us, too, we make a lot more on each wedding. And when you add it together, it's very profitable."

"That's great," Kayla smiled for the first time in the conversation.

"Don't get too excited. There's not much money left when you deduct the cost of our overhead here at the office – that's utilities, insurance, stocking merchandise, and payroll for somebody to work the register in the gift shop. Plus, health insurance for everybody who we employ full time – that was the biggest add-on for me when we got it for you," she told Kayla honestly.

"I have excellent benefits through Mitch's department, and by law, I didn't have to provide insurance for my employees until we had a certain number working for us. But I didn't feel right about that, and neither did Mitch. We both believe having health insurance is too important for us to cheap out on. But when we add three more girls to the policy, it's going to cost a holy fortune. And we have to think about that at the outset."

"Did you say *when* we add three girls?" Kayla asked, afraid she was pushing her luck. "When, not if? Did I hear you correctly."

Tally smiled at her. "Yes, I said when. But we're not going to tell anybody about this yet. Not even Kelsi, okay?"

"Sure," Kayla agreed. She'd just add it to the list of things she couldn't discuss with her best friend, like her upcoming wedding to Kelsi's brother.

"I want to have our ducks in a row and be ready to extend offers to whichever of the girls we want to hire, all on the same day," Tally explained. "We have a really great team of women working for us as interns, and I don't want to create chaos by making them think some of them are going to be hired and others aren't. It's just not the kind of vibe I want to have around the office. If they weren't working hard, I'd say let's put that kind of pressure on them. But they're all busting their butts, and I don't think we can expect any more than what we're getting from them right now."

"I totally agree," Kayla told her boss.

"I'll start pulling the numbers together and see what's what on my end and we'll know for sure by year-end whether we can launch St. Simons Weddings this spring," Tally promised. "What I need you to do is think about who you want to take over there with you. Because if we're breaking up the team this spring, we need to have a plan for how we're going to make the whole process seamless."

"No wedding is ever seamless," Kayla pointed out.

"Maybe not the weddings, but the who process of splitting our planning team up and expanding to cover more islands has to be figured out before we try to do it or it will be a nightmare. This probably means we should start taking applications for new interns for next year."

Tally got called away to deal with Molly at that point, leaving Kayla to think about everything they'd just discussed. It was really happening. Her dream of running her own branch of Tally's company was going to come true, even sooner than she'd hoped.

Kelsi wandered into the dining room to refill her cup then, and she dragged Kayla back outside with her for a cornhole game with Jake and the Durham boys. Kayla tucked away her new good news in the back of her head, next to her own elopement plans, and focused on the present.

Chapter 37

As perfect as the fall weather had been on Thanksgiving, Black Friday dawned to torrential rain and wind, the result of a storm front that was making its way up the Atlantic. Tally had just groaned when she woke up to rain hammering the master bedroom's big glass window that faced the ocean.

"Did we know it was going to rain today?" she asked Mitch, not really knowing if he was awake, but suspecting the lighting and thunder had disturbed his sleep, too.

"I'm not sure. You're the one who usually checks," Mitch replied in a gravelly voice without raising his head from his pillow.

"We don't have a wedding this weekend, so I didn't care. And therefore, I did not check. And as a result, I will have to hang up all the beach towels that were sitting out on the deck. I was lazy after we got back from the beach the other day, and I just left them in a pile because they were dry," she pointed to a wet pile of colorful beach towels draped all over a lounge chair on the deck.

"It happens," Mitch said. Then he rolled over, turning his back to Tally.

"You know this storm is going to wake up the twins, if it hasn't already," she told her husband.

"They're not awake yet, and if you stop talking, we can both go back to sleep," he said into his pillow.

She was quiet for a few minutes, but there was no way she was going back to sleep. She got up and padded into the kitchen in search of her first jolt of caffeine. Any morning that began with coffee before Molly and Moody woke up was a good morning.

***

Etah stood in her living room looking out at the foul weather over the Jekyll River. This was not the kind of weather that one wanted to see on the first day of Merry Artists or Holly Jolly Jekyll. She hoped it would let up soon so that people wouldn't use flooded roads as an excuse to skip the annual festivities.

Beau was due to arrive any minute, if he hadn't been slowed up by the nasty weather. Etah had warned him that he'd want to be well ahead of the traffic coming onto the island to see the lights. She reminded him, not for the first time, that he should really just go online and purchase an annual gate pass for Jekyll Island, instead of paying the $10 gate fee every time he came to visit her. During Holly Jolly Jekyll, the gate fee jumped to $15, and it was just silly for her boyfriend to continue forking over the cash.

Her friend used cash for almost everything, she'd noticed. She chalked it up to him being old-fashioned, and the fact he'd been a band director at a high school most of his professional life. She'd been a world traveler and knew how to work the points in a hotel loyalty program before most people understood the metrics of frequent flyer miles. She did everything on credit cards and paid her bills online. Beau had mentioned writing checks to pay bills not long ago, and she'd had to bite her tongue to keep herself from offering to teach him how to pay bills in the 21st century. Their relationship wasn't to that point yet. He hadn't even invited her to his home in Atlanta yet, although he'd spent a significant amount of time in her condo on Jekyll. She tried not to read too much into it. He'd shared the home in Atlanta with his late wife, and he might feel strange about inviting a new woman into it. She could understand that.

Etah had picked up the fancy cookies from her favorite baker the day before Thanksgiving. Everything was packaged to stay fresh. The only thing left to do was transport it all over to Goodyear Cottage at 4 pm. Beau was going to help with that. She didn't have enough room in her car for the artwork and easels, in addition to the jugs of Jekyll Julep and boxes of cookies. Tribuzio's was going to deliver the warm apple cider donuts she'd ordered from them at 4:45, so they'd be fresh for the guests who came to see the gallery at 5 p.m. There was nothing to worry about, but Etah couldn't shake the uneasy feeling in her gut. She attributed it to the weather. Unloading everything from their cars into Goodyear Cottage in the pouring rain would be a nightmare. She grabbed a box of black trash bags from under her kitchen counter and set it on the front hall table. It would be better to bag the artwork than try carrying it in the open from the parking lot to the historic home. There were big tall trees arching over the pathways all over the historic district, and the chance that rain would drip on the artwork was too great to risk.

She called Tally. Her niece would make her feel better about their plans.

"Hey Etah," Tally answered the phone. "Did you know it was going to rain? I missed it somehow."

"I saw it on the weather last night, but I chose to wish it away instead of talking about it," Etah said. "That obviously didn't work. So now I want to make sure we have a plan to do this thing even if it's still storming out."

"Absolutely, Etah," Tally assured her. "Nothing to worry about. A little rain doesn't stop the Jekyll Weddings girls. We all have rain gear. I'm more worried about keeping the artwork dry."

"Me too," Etah confessed. "I have a box of big black trash bags ready to go over them."

"That's smart," Tally was impressed her aunt had been thinking ahead. Planning wasn't Etah's strong suit, usually. "Bring the box with you because we won't want to re-use the same bags to take the paintings back out afterwards. Too much chance of water on the bags getting on the artwork."

"Is Mitch going to be able to help us move everything?" Etah asked. She'd been really worried that Beau would have to move all the easels and paintings from the parking lot to the building himself.

"He's in, and he's asked Pete to help, too," Tally replied, easing some of her aunt's concerns. Tally knew that her team could pull off the entire event without help from anybody else, but she didn't remind Etah of that. Her aunt needed something to worry about. "We're all planning to meet you in the parking lot at 4 p.m. on the dot."

"Beau and I will be there with bells on, if he ever gets here," she griped to Tally. "He was supposed to be here almost an hour ago."

"The weather is gross. He's probably sitting in traffic. Call him if you're worried," she suggested.

"He doesn't like to answer his phone while he's driving. I'm going to wait a bit longer. I'm sure he'll stop and call me if he's going to be much later. He's usually a very punctual man."

"There's nothing he can do about weather and traffic," Tally said. "Don't borrow things to worry about until something bad actually happens. Isn't that what you tell me?"

"I hate it when you use my own words against me."

"I know. But it's too bad because you have so many great phrases I just can't help quoting," Tally teased.

Etah promised to text her after Beau finally arrived, and they said goodbye. Then Etah went into her bathroom and refreshed her lipstick. Her hair still looked great, so she didn't mess with that. She spritzed on some of the Jo Malone cologne that Beau had bought her on the ship.

"If he's going to make so much effort to be here, I'd better make it worth it when he arrives," she said out loud to herself, and then giggled. She wasn't used to this dating game, and she obviously needed more practice.

Chapter 38

Tally got a text from Etah an hour later, letting her know that her gentleman friend had indeed arrived on Jekyll Island, and that all was right with the world.

Tally showed the phone to Mitch and laughed. "She's like a teenager waiting for a boy to call."

"Cut her some slack, Tally. She gave up her love life for you for the last almost 30 years," he said, with a serious expression.

"She didn't have to," Tally was quick to defend herself. She hated thinking that her aunt had given up even more than she'd realized to raise her after her parents were killed.

"No, she didn't have to. But she did. She probably didn't have time for a romantic relationship with anybody. Think about it. She was here with you for every school break and then she flew out again, right away, to destinations unknown to cover peace treaties and wars and all sorts of other crazy international shit. How could she have had a relationship with anybody but you? She spent all of her free time with you."

Tally didn't say anything because she was thinking about what he said and knew her husband was right. Etah always made plans with Tally for her next school break from St. Margaret's before she was returned to boarding school for a new semester. Tally realized now that Etah was plotting her own business schedule at the same time. When she was a kid, it had been all about where Etah was going to take her and how many days they could get away. She always loved spending her breaks on Jekyll, too. But Etah had thought it was important to expose her to more arts and culture than that. So, they'd done spring break in Paris one year, and another time they'd taken a long train ride up through snow-covered Canada to see the Northern Lights. Every trip was some kind of adventure and Tally had loved every minute of it. It had never occurred to her that her aunt might have preferred to have a different traveling companion.

"Well, I'm glad she has a boyfriend now," Tally said, not wanting to dig deeper into how Etah's life might have been better if she hadn't been saddled with her great-niece. "And I'm looking forward to meeting him. You should run a background check on him," she joked.

"What's his last name?" Mitch asked.

"Morris. Beauregard Morris. I believe he was born in Atlanta, or somewhere nearby there," she added. Then she turned to Mitch. "Are you really going to run a background check on him?" She was grinning.

"I'm not going to call it in, if that's what you're asking," her husband replied. "But I might check for warrants when I have some down time this week." He chuckled and Tally knew he was joking. Or at least she thought he was kidding. He might not be. They'd all been a little skittish about new people since two of their team members last year had turned out not to be who they said they were.

Chapter 39

Etah and Beau ate lunch at her dining room table because it was still blowing too much outside to eat on the balcony, like she'd planned. She'd made shrimp salad and served it on freshly-baked croissants she kept in her freezer for exactly this purpose. Feeling particularly southern this morning, she'd also made a nice broccoli salad to serve with it instead of just putting chips on the plate like she'd originally planned. Etah knew how to cook, even if she hadn't had occasion to do much of it when she was traveling for work. And she was enjoying getting the opportunity to show off her culinary skills for Beau every chance she got.

"I hope it stops raining before we have to leave," she said for the tenth time since he'd arrived.

"Stop worrying. We'll bag it all up and it'll will be just fine," he reassured her. "I brought a tarp with me in case we needed to cover it, but I think the trash bags will work even better. Good thinking."

After lunch, Beau pulled his vehicle under the building so they could load up where it was dry. They carefully carried the big painting, and the four smaller prints, down to the parking garage. Then they bagged each one of them up before carefully placing them in the back of an SUV Etah had never seen before.

"Where'd you get this?" she asked Beau, gesturing towards the grey SUV.

"It's my neighbor's. I swapped him for the day because I figured you'd need more space than my sedan had," he explained. "Where are the easels? Do you want me to go get those, too?"

"They're actually already in my car and I can take them over. The boxes of cookies are sitting on top of them. I just have to drive carefully," she said. Beau shook his head at her. "If you can help me get those two jugs of Jekyll Julep down here and into my car, we'll be all set."

They used the cart she had for taking groceries up to her condo to bring the large plastic jugs of holiday cider down to her car. They fit one of the jugs in Etah's car and put the other on the front passenger seat of Beau's borrowed SUV.

"Now you have to drive carefully, too," she admonished him with a wink.

"I need to go back upstairs and lock up, and then I think we're ready to go," Etah said, slamming the door shut on the SUV.

"I need to use the restroom before we depart," Beau told her. "Why don't I go do that and then I can lock up for you. You can head over there now so we're not late. Just let them know I'm right behind you."

"Works for me," she bent over and kissed Beau soundly on the lips. He kissed her back after a second, but he looked surprised when the kiss ended.

"What was that for?" he asked.

"That was a thank you for being here to help me today," she told him, getting into her own car. "Now go take care of business," she giggled, "and hurry over to Goodyear Cottage. You know how to get into the back parking lot?"

"I do. Just go through the gate across from the Mosaic and take the first left around the little guard house," he said, smiling smugly as he proved he knew his way around.

"I'll see you there." Etah waved and put her car into gear, pulling slowly away so that she didn't upset the carefully stacked party supplies in the back of her car.

<h1 style="text-align:center">Chapter 40</h1>

Everybody was waiting for Etah when she pulled into the little parking lot behind Goodyear Cottage. The rain had blessedly stopped, but as anticipated, there was so much water coming off the trees above them that it still felt like a light rain was coming down.

Etah had just gotten out of her car when she heard a golf cart whiz up beside her and stop. It was Jackie Becker on her way home from surviving the first day of Merry Artists.

"Thanks again for letting us do this," Etah said.

"It's no problem. Just make sure you leave the place how you found it, and you lock everything up tight when you go. I saw you out here when I was leaving and I left the kitchen door unlocked for you. But you'll need to pull the keys out of the lockbox to lock it up when you're done," Jackie reminded her.

"Absolutely. I brought my binder with the closing checklist," she pulled the white notebook she'd been given at Jekyll Artists' cashier orientation and waved it at Jackie. "See?"

Jackie laughed at her. "I hope you have better traffic tonight than we had today. It was pretty slow for opening day."

"It was pretty gross weather. It took my friend Beau an extra two hours to get here from Atlanta because so many roads were washing out," Etah told her.

"Doesn't surprise me. They had the Sidney Lanier Bridge shut down for a while today, too," Jackie said, widening her eyes to express the dramatic move that had been.

"Wow, they don't do that until the wind is gusting at 40 miles an hour, do they?" Etah could only remember a handful of times the big bridge that ran from the Jekyll Causeway over to Brunswick had been closed.

"It's re-opened now, so hopefully you'll still have a good crowd tonight," Jackie said. "How many advance tickets did you sell?"

"Last time I checked, it was over 100. But I'd hoped it would be far higher than that," Etah admitted.

"That's $500 to put towards art classes that we didn't have before," Jackie said, trying to make her friend feel better about her efforts. "I'm sorry I can't hang around and help you out."

"Please don't even worry, Jackie," Etah said. "We've got plenty of hands here. And my new gentleman friend, Beau, should be here any moment with the artwork."

"Maybe I should hang around to meet him," Jackie teased.

"Maybe you shouldn't," Etah replied, being quite serious. "I think meeting Tally and Mitch and all the wedding planning team that's here will be quite enough, thank you very much."

Jackie laughed and said goodbye to Etah and then called out a greeting to Tally and her crew, before she buzzed away across the parking lot in her shiny golf cart.

"Where's Beau?" Tally asked when her aunt approached them.

"He'll be here any minute. Let's start unloading," Etah said in a tone that brooked no argument from her niece. Mitch, Pete, and the interns who were still in town – Liz and Katy – followed Etah to her vehicle and let her load up their arms with things to take into the building.

It only took them each two loads to get everything out of Etah's car, and to bring in the tables and tablecloths they'd need for their setup. Liz and Katy worked together to create the serving station for the Jekyll Juleps and donuts, and they spread out the pretty cookies in rows on one of the tables. Tribuzio's arrived with the donuts a few minutes early and the interns displayed them prettily on the big trays Tally had brought for just that purpose.

"Want to split one?" Katy asked Liz. "Purely for quality control purposes, of course."

"Of course," Liz giggled, picking up a donut and breaking it in half. She handed the smaller piece to Katy and took a bite of her own.

"Yummy," she declared. Then she poured herself a Jekyll Julep to wash it down. She took one sip and set the cup down. "What is this? This isn't what we had yesterday at Bonnie's," Liz said accusingly, as if she'd been tricked.

"That's the virgin version of it," Kelsi told Liz, laughing. "It's the exact same thing without the whiskey."

"Bummer," Liz said softly, looking at the punchbowl of cider in front of her. "I thought this was going to be a fun party when I saw the Jekyll Juleps."

Kelsi rolled her eyes at the intern and then continued on her way into the kitchen to find the tickets they were going to sell at the door.

"It's still going to be a fun event," Kelsi called over her shoulder.

"I agree with you," Etah sidled up to Liz. "And if you get desperate, there's a pint of Fireball in my purse. It's the black bag in the kitchen." The older woman winked at the confused intern and took her leave. "I don't know what's keeping Beau. He's probably waiting for us in the parking lot. I'm going to go check," she announced, and swept out of the room.

***

Etah stood in the parking lot behind Goodyear Cottage with her phone in her hand. She'd called Beau three times in a row, and all of her calls had gone directly to voicemail. This wasn't like him, even if he was driving. He wouldn't ignore her, and he wouldn't have turned his phone off. It didn't worry her initially, as the signals on the little road from the marina up to Riverview tended to be sketchy and unreliable. She'd have lost her mind if her iPhone didn't automatically connect with her wi-fi when she was at home. If Beau had just left her condo, his phone might go straight to voicemail.

But almost 10 minutes later, when he hadn't arrived and calls were still going to voicemail, Etah started to panic. She imagined that Beau might have had a heart attack or a brain aneurism while he was using the bathroom and died on the throne just like Elvis. Or maybe he'd tripped and fallen, and he couldn't get up, just like that damned commercial for an emergency button you could wear. Her mind was racing when she saw Mitch coming out to help her.

"Is he here?" Mitch asked, looking around.

"No, and I'm very worried, Mitch. This isn't like Beau. He said he needed to use the bathroom before he headed over, he should have been right behind me," she explained.

"I'm sure he's fine," Mitch said. "But why don't I drive over there and look for him. What kind of car does he have?"

"He borrowed his neighbor's SUV – it's grey – I'm not sure what make or model it is," Etah said.

"No problem, there won't be that many between here and there. Maybe he had car trouble," he suggested.

"Yes, maybe that's it." Etah hoped that was the problem. She had a sick feeling in the pit of her stomach that she couldn't identify. She was truly worried that something awful had happened to Beau. "Maybe I should go with you."

"No, you stay here and help them get ready for the gallery. Look, people are already arriving," he pointed to the front entrance of Goodyear Cottage, where a small group of people were milling around and chatting.

"Oh, good gracious," Etah exclaimed softly. "We don't have any Bill Hendrix artwork to show them."

"We will in a few minutes. The gallery isn't even supposed to open for another half hour. We have plenty of time," Mitch assured. "But let me get going now and I'll be back soon with your boyfriend and the artwork. Okay? Can I have your housekeys?"

Etah nodded in agreement and then fished in her purse until she found her key clump to hand him. Mitch jumped into his truck and pulled away before she could say anything else to him or ask why he needed the keys. She took a moment to collect herself before she started walking back over to the historic mansion where everyone was waiting.

Chapter 41

Mitch called Tally as soon as he was out of the parking lot.

"What's up? Where are you?" Tally looked around. Two minutes ago, she'd seen her husband in the kitchen behind her. Now it sounded like he was in a moving car.

"I'm on my way over to Etah's to look for Beau. He never arrived and Etah is starting to freak out. She wanted to come with me, but I figured that if he's dead on the floor of her condo, she didn't need to see that," Mitch replied, in a matter-of-fact tone. "She said he went up to the use the bathroom right before she left. But he should have caught up with her a while ago."

"That doesn't sound good," Tally agreed. "Thanks for going over to check. I'll go see what Etah's up to now."

"I left her in the parking lot. She's pretty shaken."

"I'd imagine so. I'll go check on her and get her to come inside. Can you let me know what's going on the minute you figure it out?"

Mitch promised he would and signed off. "I'm almost there."

Tally hung up the call and went to find her elderly aunt. She had a bad feeling in her gut. It was the same sensation Etah was experiencing as she watched her niece approaching the parking lot where she was still standing.

"Mitch called," Tally told her to explain that she already knew what was going on. "He'll call me back in a minute and tell me everything is just fine. You'll see." She sounded more optimistic than she felt. She realized she usually saved this voice for her clients. "But while we wait, why don't you come inside."

It was dark and wet in the parking lot, and Tally could feel a slight chill. She knew that her octogenarian aunt had to be cold. She put an arm around Etah and gently guided her back to the kitchen door of Goodyear Cottage. The group out front had grown – there were at least 20 people who had arrived to see the Hendrix artwork. Etah stared at them as they climbed the stairs to the kitchen door.

"What are we going to tell all these people?" she asked Tally in a soft voice.

"Nothing yet. Let's see what Mitch finds. Beau may roll up with him any minute," she told her aunt, but she didn't believe a word she was saying. That sick feeling in her stomach had only gotten worse the longer it took for Mitch to call her.

Finally, her phone rang. Mitch's name popped up on the display.

"Did you find him?" she asked when she answered.

"No. He's not here. Neither is a grey SUV. The condo looks fine. The front doorknob was locked, but not the deadbolt. But that makes sense if he didn't have the keys," he reported.

"Where could he be?" Tally asked, genuinely confused.

"You tell me," Mitch replied. "I'm going to call my dad. And then I'll head back over to you."

"We're not going to have this artwork for 5 o'clock, are we?" she asked.

"Nope. I think you'd better prepare yourself for whatever comes with cancelling this thing at the last minute. Tally, how valuable was the artwork that Beau was supposed to be bringing to Goodyear Cottage?"

"I honestly don't know. I think it's worth a lot," she said. "Bill Hendrix is pretty famous, and this stuff has never been shown in a gallery, to anybody's knowledge. I don't know if Etah had it appraised or anything because she was just showing it, not selling it."

"Are we talking hundreds of dollars or thousands of dollars?" he probed a little deeper.

"I'd guess thousands of dollars. But I wouldn't even guess how much really. I mean, if a painting was worth $5,000, but it's the only one in existence, isn't it really worth whatever somebody is willing to pay for it? How do you even put a value on something that has come from a family's private collection after so many years." Tally stopped talking because she realized she was ranting. And she needed to get off the phone and triage the situation that was slowly growing outside the front door of the arts association.

"Let me call my dad, and then I'll either see you or talk to you," Mitch promised. "This is getting weird."

"Tell me about it." Tally hung up and looked around for Kayla and Kelsi. She found them both at the donut table with mouths full. They looked guilty when they spotted her.

"We're just checking to see if they're good," Kelsi said with her mouth full.

"You can eat them all, the event is cancelled," Tally told them after looking around to make sure Etah wasn't within earshot. She quickly downloaded the latest information she'd gotten from Mitch to her trusted staff members, and Kayla and Kelsi's reactions were similar to her own.

"This doesn't sound good," Kayla said. "Is it terrible to say that I wish Mitch had found Beau knocked out and all the artwork right there?"

Tally chuckled. "You wouldn't be the first one of us to think that today."

Kelsi nodded in agreement, trying not to smile.

"Okay, so this is what we're going to do," Tally said, rallying her troops. "Obviously the show is cancelled. I need to talk to Etah first and see if she wants to make the announcement. Otherwise, I will. We'll tell all these folks that we'll refund their ticket money, and we'll send them away with a cup of Jekyll Julep, a donut, and some cookies to make up for their wasted time." She'd started putting cookies back into boxes as she talked. Kelsi followed her lead and started scooping up cookies from the table.

"Should we just take a whole table outside for the donuts and Juleps?" Kayla asked.

"That's probably the best idea. But take it out the kitchen door and around and set it up. Don't need to have a bunch of people watching us try to get it through the front door and down those steps," Tally said. Kayla nodded in understanding and went to get the interns to help her make it happen.

Tally found Etah standing in the entryway by the front door. She looked older than usual, and that made Tally sad. She looked up with a desperate expression when she saw her niece approaching.

"He wasn't there," Tally told Etah. "The doorknob was locked so Mitch let himself in. But he wasn't there. He didn't see a grey SUV anywhere in the parking lot or on the road on the way to the marina. It's like he just vanished." The last was out of her mouth before Tally thought about what she was saying. The look on Etah's face made her wish she'd been more careful.

"Vanished? What do you mean?"

"Well, he's not here, and he's not there, and Mitch didn't see him on the road between the two places..." Tally realized she was probably handling this in the most indelicate way possible. "He's calling his dad to see what we should do next. They'll want to get state troopers out looking for him all over the island in case something happened to him."

"What could have happened to him?" Etah asked, sounding like a lost child and not the bulldog reporter she was reputed to be. "He only had to go from there to here."

"I don't know, Etah. But right now, we need to figure out how to handle this crowd of Bill Hendrix art lovers on the front porch," she pointed to the people who were waiting at the bottom of the stairs.

"I have a plan," Tally continued, realizing that her aunt was in no mental state to make any tough decisions. "We're going to tell them the artwork didn't arrive due to an emergency – we won't classify the emergency – and we'll apologize and hand out goodies and drinks to them. I'll promise to have all their tickets refunded and notify them as soon as the Hendrix gallery show is rescheduled."

"Okay, whatever you think is best." Tally watched her aunt walk over to the desk that served as the checkout counter and take a seat behind it. She looked defeated.

Tally wanted to go comfort Etah, but she had business to attend to first. Etah would still be a hot mess 10 minutes from now when Tally finished telling the line of people out front that they'd wasted their time, and their money at the gate, to get onto the island on Black Friday for no reason.

Chapter 42

Tally and her girls all stood outside for the entire hour that the Hendrix gallery was supposed to have been shown, handing out cups of Jekyll Julep and Tribuzio's famous homemade donuts to the art lovers who arrived to see the pop-up gallery. Nobody was nasty about it – southerners weren't like that. The girls all stuck to the "emergency situation" line without elaborating, which prompted a number of people to inquire about Etah's health, since they didn't see her handing out donuts and cookies with the rest of them.

She assured everybody that her aunt was just fine and mentally crossed her fingers that it was the truth. She'd seen her father-in-law arrive at Goodyear Cottage a little while ago with another trooper she didn't recognize. They'd gone into the building through the kitchen door, and they hadn't come back out yet. Tally knew she should go check on what was happening inside, but she was dreading it. No matter what had happened, it wasn't anything good.

By the time she finally tromped up the front steps of the historic vacation home, Etah was headed toward the kitchen with Tom and the other trooper.

"Hey Tally," her father-in-law gave her a brief hug. "We're going to take Etah into the barracks to look at some pictures and help us try to figure out what happened to her friend."

Tom didn't mention the stolen artwork, but she was sure that it was at the top of his mind. He just didn't want to humiliate her aunt any more than she already had been. Etah looked small and old as her best friend's son guided her out the kitchen door and walked her to his patrol SUV in the parking lot.

***

When everything they'd set up for the gallery that didn't happen was cleaned up and put back into the vehicles it had arrived in, Tally thanked her team and sent them on their way. When she was alone in the parking lot, she pulled out her phone and called Mitch.

"What's going on?" she asked before he could say anything.

"Too much to tell you on the phone right now," he said, clearly letting Tally know that he couldn't talk openly in front of whomever was sitting with him.

"Should I come over to the barracks?" she asked.

"Probably a good idea," Mitch agreed.

"Okay, see you in a few," Tally said and signed off. She had Siri send a text to Bonnie alerting Mitch's grandmother that they were going to be home to relieve her from twin duty later than initially expected.

"No problem. Mitch already filled me in. Go take care of Etah," Bonnie texted back.

Chapter 43

Etah was a hot mess by the time she finished answering all the questions the troopers had for her. She'd been able to tentatively identify Beau's SUV leaving the island in videos from the gate, but she couldn't be 100-percent sure because she had only seen the vehicle for a few minutes, when they were loading the borrowed artwork into it.

Mitch's dad confirmed that they'd found footage of that SUV coming onto the island at about the time Etah said Beau arrived earlier in the day, and Tom said the cameras also caught what appeared to be the same battered, grey SUV leaving through the gates at 4:10 p.m.

"About the same time that he should have been arriving at Goodyear Cottage with the Hendrix artwork," Tally mumbled, mostly to herself.

"That's about it," the investigator she'd seen talking to Etah back at Goodyear Cottage told her. Tom had introduced him as Craig Hymowitz and said he was the best the Georgia Bureau of Investigation had to offer when it came to major crimes. "We stole him from NYPD."

"Major crimes?" Tally's heart sunk. This really was about the Hendrix artwork. "Has anybody called Emily to tell her what happened yet?"

"I don't believe so," Craig said. "But when you do, could you let her know I'll be in touch to find out what the insurance situation is for that artwork. We also need to know what it appraised for."

"I know Etah was doing some kind of insurance rider for this event – she mentioned it to me the first time we were planning," Tally told the GBI investigator.

"I've got that info from your aunt," he said. "I need to know what the pieces were valued at, and if there was any incentive for insurance fraud by anybody."

Tally started to protest but Craig held up a hand. "I'm not suggesting anything nefarious here. It's standard procedure to ask these questions and collect this information. It wouldn't be the first time that a crime was committed because of the insurance connected to it. But that's not what this is looking like right now," he assured her.

"What is it looking like?" Tally asked, looking around to make sure Etah wasn't close enough to overhear their conversation.

"It's looking like your aunt – who is a really sweet old lady, by the way – got bamboozled by a fraudster that she met on a cruise. It happens all the time," he said dismissively.

"My aunt is an award-winning journalist who only just retired last year," Tally corrected him, maybe a little too sharply. But it wouldn't do for the investigators looking into this mess to think Etah was a doddering old lady who wouldn't see a scam right in her face.

"Right now, she's a victim in a major case investigation," Craig corrected her. "I mean no offense, ma'am," he continued in a not-quite New York accent. "But it's better for people to believe your aunt got scammed than to think she had something to do with the art going missing."

"Nobody would think that!" Tally was appalled. Of all the scenarios that had run through her head while she was passing out donuts and apologizing to would-be gallery viewers, she hadn't considered that the authorities would think Etah had anything to do with what had happened. "That's just ridiculous to even say."

Mitch heard the pitch of Tally's voice rise across the room and went over to rescue the investigator who was the subject of her ire.

"Tell him that Etah would never be involved in stealing any artwork," Tally sputtered when Mitch got close enough to hear her.

"I seriously doubt her aunt's involved in this, man," Mitch told Craig, whom he'd met on several previous occasions.

"I don't think she is. But we have to clear her before we can follow other investigative routes. You know how it goes."

"He's right, Tally. They have to investigate Etah to clear her so they can go after the real thief. Or thieves. Do we have any idea who this guy is?" he asked.

"We know who he isn't," Craig said and sat down in front of his laptop and started clicking.

"What are you talking about?"

"There's no Beauregard Morris alive in Georgia, at least as far as we can tell," Craig said, pointing to something on his screen.

"There was a band director named Beauregard Morris at St. Stephens before that high school closed, but he died five years ago in Memphis. He'd moved there after retirement to be closer to his children, according to the obituary I found from the Atlanta Journal-Constitution," the investigator explained.

"So, who is this guy?" Tally asked.

"No clue yet. The crime scene investigation unit is over in your aunt's condo lifting prints right now. She said he's been spending a lot of time there, so unless he did a really good wipe down before he left, we should pick up something. It won't matter if his prints aren't in the system, but maybe we'll get lucky." He turned back to his computer and started typing away again, clearly finished with the conversation.

"What now?" Tally asked Mitch.

"Let's take Etah over to Bonnie's with us when they're finished with her here, and then we can go clean up the fingerprint dust at her place before we take her back home. I'm sure dad asked them to be careful, but that stuff is just a mess. And they don't clean it up after they brush it on all the surfaces," Mitch explained.

"Fabulous," Tally sighed. It was a good thing she didn't have any weddings scheduled this weekend because her to-do list had just gone to hell in a handbasket.

****

Etah wanted to go home directly from her interview at the barracks, and she was still pretty grumpy when they arrived at Bonnie's house a few minutes later. She hadn't talked to Tally for most of the ride, and her niece was starting to worry until they pulled up in front of Bonnie's house and saw Molly and Moody in the front window looking out at them. Etah's shell cracked and she couldn't help smiling.

"Look at those little nuts," she pointed to the window.

"Bonnie must have told them we were on our way. They love seeing you," Tally said, hoping to lighten the moment. "You hop out and I'm going to park in my own driveway. I need to run into the house and grab a phone charger."

She watched until her aunt made it inside Bonnie's house before she pulled away and around the corner, into her own driveway. Usually, she would have just parked here with Etah, but her aunt was looking more fragile tonight and Tally wanted to make her life a little easier.

She had just gotten into the house when her phone rang. It was Mitch.

"Hey babe," she greeted him. "What's up?"

"I'm over at Etah's condo. It's a pretty big mess here. On the plus side, they got a lot of fingerprints so hopefully something will hit when they run them through the computer," he told her.

"Should I come help you clean it up?" she asked.

"No, I think I've got it. My dad said he'd help me. He's got a bunch of paper towels and stuff in his cruiser," Mitch said. "We'll come over there when we're finished."

"Okay, good," Tally said, thinking ahead. "Then you can bring the twins home and put them to bed while I take Etah home and stay to hang out with her for a bit."

"That's probably a good idea," Mitch agreed.

Tally grabbed a charger brick from her bedside table and dropped it into a tote bag with her laptop. It might be a long night over at Etah's house, but at least she could try to get some work done if she had her computer with her.

$Chapter$ 44

Nothing else dramatic happened over the weekend. With Etah's permission, Tally called Emily Hendrix Slaughter from her aunt's condo late Friday night to tell her about what happened. Emily, to her credit, didn't get angry about the art theft – she just sounded stunned. Sort of like Tally felt when she first realized the Hendrix artwork had actually been stolen.

"Etah must be absolutely crushed," Emily said sympathetically. "And Beau seemed like such a nice gentleman. I had high hopes for them as a couple."

"I'd forgotten you met him," Tally said. "I didn't get to meet him yet. I guess I won't now, unless they catch him and I get to see him in court."

"I showed that man all around my house," Emily sounded horrified as the realization struck her. "I suppose I'd better start using that expensive security system I pay for. This is so weird. He was the last person I would have been suspicious of."

"That makes me feel a little better," Tally confessed. "The investigator was acting like Etah got scammed because she's old and incompetent, and we both know that's not the situation at all."

"Oh, good Lord, no," Emily cried. "Etah is, and always has been, one of the smartest women I know. If this Beau guy was a scammer, I didn't see it. And I'm skeptical as hell. Tell her I don't blame her for this at all. I'm mad about it, sure. But I'm not mad at Etah."

"I'm sure she'll appreciate that." Tally filled Emily in on what the GBI investigator, Craig Hymowitz, had told her about needing information about any insurance policies on the artwork.

"Okay, I'll start looking for all of that stuff. I know it's in my files. And I pay premiums for all of it annually, on top of my homeowners' policy. But I'm not sure what my coverage is when the art disappears under such strange circumstances," she worried. "Honestly, it's not about the value of the paintings. It's never been about the money for our family and our dad's artwork. I just wanted to see his paintings out there again for public viewing. Help remind people who Bill Hendrix was, and what he and my mom did for the whole art scene in this area."

"I know," Tally felt so badly for the woman on the other end of the phone. "I know they're doing their best to figure out what happened and get it all back. First, they have to figure out who this Beau guy is, though. Mitch said they got a lot of fingerprints at Etah's condo." She wasn't sure how much information about the investigation she was supposed to be sharing but figured it was okay since, at the end of the day, Emily was the actual victim here.

"Well, please let me know when you hear something about it, and I'll do the same for you," Emily promised before they hung up.

Tally went into Etah's room to check on her aunt. She'd said something about taking a shower, but Tally found her sitting in the armchair in the corner of her bedroom, still fully dressed and staring out the window into the dark night.

"You okay?" she asked, approaching her aunt slowly so as not to startle her.

"I'll be fine," Etah replied, sounding like herself for the first time in hours. "I'm just sitting here engaging in self-flagellation for having been so stupid as to believe that man had fallen for me."

"You're not stupid and why couldn't he have fallen for you?" Tally asked, taking a seat on the ottoman next to the chair. "You're a fun lady, Aunt Etah. You're well-educated, well-traveled, and you act like you're 25 years younger than you actually are. Not that I'm going to mention any specific numbers."

"You'd better not," Etah warned. "I raised you better than to bring up a lady's age."

"I know, I know," Tally groaned. "But I'm trying to tell you that you're a catch. Just because you never wanted to get caught before doesn't mean you can't get caught now, if you want to get caught..." She stopped because she realized she was starting to speak mumbo jumbo. "My point is that you could date almost any man you wanted, if you wanted to date."

"That's your opinion," Etah told her. "But I realize my best attributes are now located further south than they used to be, and if a man wanted to have sex with me with the lights on, I'd probably scream and run out of the room."

Tally burst out laughing at that admission, and Etah joined her in the giggle.

"I hate having sex with the lights on, too," she admitted, enjoying the shared moment of adultness with the woman who had raised her. "And that's a hard one in our master bedroom. It's never completely dark in there."

"I am familiar," Etah said with a chuckle.

Tally groaned. "I don't want to go down this road, do I?"

"Absolutely not. But speaking of roads, isn't it time for you to hit the road and go spend some time with your hottie husband? He should have the rugrats in their cribs by now."

"He'd better have them in bed by now, or they're going to be a holy nightmare to put down," Tally said with a threatening tone in her voice. "We've been trying so hard to keep them on a schedule – and that's not easy with the kind of life that Mitch and I live. But it's not the twins' fault that it's literally impossible for me to serve dinner at the same time every night. We've kind of given up on trying to eat with them most of the time. I just get them fed and ready for bed on time and then we eat later, after Mitch gets home."

"Do you eat when Mitch isn't home?" Etah asked with a little humor in her voice.

"Sure, I eat," Tally laughed. "But I don't cook. I eat leftovers from Bonnie's, random cookies that may be in the house, and sometimes I eat those little Welch's fruit things I buy for the kids at Sam's Club. I have also been known to spread peanut butter on graham crackers and call it dinner."

Etah rolled her eyes. "That's not real food and you know it. But I hear you. One of the things I liked most about you coming to live with me was having somebody to cook for. And even better, you were appreciative and willing to try new things," her aunt recalled. "I had your parents to thank for that because your mother had made you try absolutely everything by the time you got to me."

"Yes, but you were the one who taught me how to cook everything. My parents were never home long enough for that, unless they were recovering from a big election loss. That's when mom did a lot of baking for therapy. But we never cooked real food together. You're the one who taught me 10 things to make with shrimp in a pinch."

"Do you still remember all 10 things?" her aunt asked.

"Of course, I do. Peel-and-eat steamed shrimp, shrimp scampi, shrimp stir fry, shrimp kebabs, shrimp and grits, fried shrimp – although I never got good at frying things in oil – okay what else am I forgetting," Tally paused briefly. "Shrimp etouffee, jambalaya, shrimp diablo, and shrimp salad."

"Good girl!"

"But the only thing I ever do is steam them for peeling or grill them on skewers. Oh, and I make a kick-ass shrimp salad," Tally winked.

"That's my recipe, and I served it to Beau for lunch today here," her happy attitude vanished. "I feel like such a fool, Tally. And it's worse than just getting dumped by a guy, I let him steal some priceless artwork that belonged to a friend."

"You didn't let Beau do anything, Etah," Tally admonished her. "Stop talking that way. This isn't your fault, and I don't see how you could have seen it coming. He was just a nice man that you hit it off with on a cruise. I'd hope that if you go on another cruise, you might find another guy just as nice who piques your interest, and who isn't an art thief."

"I'm never going on another cruise," Etah vowed like she was swearing off alcohol the morning after a bender. "Never ever."

"You can't blame the entire cruise industry for meeting one shady guy. You'll miss out on too many good vacations with your friends," Tally laughed. "I understand how you feel. Hopefully, they'll catch him soon and get to the bottom of this. I think you'll feel better about everything once you know who this jerk is and why he targeted you."

Tally said goodnight to her aunt and then waited outside Etah's front door until she heard the deadbolt click. While it was unlikely that not-re-ally-Beau would be coming back to Etah's condo on Jekyll, it was better to be extra safe now than sorry later.

Chapter 45

The Monday morning after Thanksgiving weekend was quiet at Jekyll Weddings. Tally had given the interns an extra day off, to make up for having them work on Black Friday at the gallery that didn't end up happening. Kelsi and Kayla were both meeting with potential clients at venues somewhere on the island. She loved the fact that they were booking new clients without her having to be there. This was how it was supposed to happen at a growing company.

Tally had considered working from home, but Mitch was going to be there all day, and she knew she wouldn't get peace and quiet. Plus, it was a rare occasion that she and Yaya got to spend time together without the rest of the girls hanging around. Keeping that in mind, Tally stopped into Jekyll Market and picked up two breakfast sandwiches for them to eat while they got caught up.

"Why's it so quiet?" Yaya asked when Tally came in with their breakfast. "I'm so used to the noise now."

"This is what it was like in here before we hired interns," Tally reminded her and chuckled.

"It hasn't been this quiet since Kelsi joined the team," Yaya corrected her. "She and Kayla never shut up when they're working together." She didn't say it meanly, but rather, as if she were stating a fact. "They laugh so much, I don't know how they get anything done."

"You mean like you and I used to do, when we were making bouquets in Isabelle's kitchen late at night?" Tally asked with a grin on her face.

"Okay, maybe," Yaya allowed, smiling too. "But we were never as loud as them."

"That's Kelsi. Kayla only gets loud when she's trying to be heard over the rest of us. But you're wrong. I think you've been out of Puerto Rico too long if you think Kelsi is loud. Do you remember what your neighbors on Vieques sounded like when they were having a basic conversation?"

Yaya chuckled. "Yeah. If you don't understand Spanish, it probably sounds like they're about to kill each other."

"No probably about it," Tally laughed. "Do you miss it? You haven't gone home much since you got here."

"I miss my mom and dad, and my sister," she admitted. "But I don't miss wondering if the power is going to go out for no reason and if there will be any gas at the gas station. I don't miss having to take off an entire day for a doctor's appointment on another island or going into the grocery store for a list of items they probably don't have."

"You've gotten spoiled," Tally laughed at her friend.

"I haven't turned into a *gringa*, if that's what you're saying," Yaya corrected her. "I can certainly survive back on Vieques."

"But you don't miss it more than you do miss it?" Tally asked. Yaya gave her an "are you kidding me" look and Tally shrugged.

"I miss lots of things about it," Yaya sighed as she admitted she was a little homesick. "Vieques is my home, and it's the most beautiful place in the world to me. But it's not the same anymore.

"It's probably more like it was when I was a kid, but maybe not – because the Navy was there back then, and more locals had good jobs," she explained. "But now, after Hurricane Maria, so many businesses are gone. Important, big businesses like the W Hotel. I mean here we are, years later, and nobody has done anything about the wreckage from the storm over there. The wall is still laying on its side the entire way around the old hotel, except where people have stolen chunks for their own properties. They're supposed to be rebuilding the hospital but it's a long way from finished, and it's been six years now."

"Good point," Tally said. She'd only been back to Vieques once since the storm, and that trip had ended in a disaster of epic proportions when her ex-boyfriend died in a drunk-driving crash while she was there.

Although she'd never said it aloud, Tally doubted she'd ever return to Vieques after Eduardo's sister blamed her for his death publicly, to anyone who would listen. His sister had actually hunted Tally down on Jekyll Island with every intention of settling the score, but she'd targeted the wrong bride, and Mitch had intervened before anybody could get hurt. Vieques was a Pandora's Box for Tally, and she didn't want to even think about opening it ever again.

"What do you think about hiring all of the interns, full time, as wedding planners when their internships are finished?" Tally asked, switching the subject all of a sudden.

Yaya looked at her like she was crazy. She'd just taken a bite of her breakfast sandwich, and she gestured for Tally to wait for her to finish chewing. She definitely had an opinion.

"All three?" she asked after she'd swallowed. "Are you crazy? What do we need with three new wedding planners?" Yaya asked incredulously.

"We need them all if we let Kayla open up a St. Simons Weddings this spring," Tally explained, dropping yet another bombshell on her bestie.

"Oh, I see. She finally convinced you, eh?" Yaya gave Tally a knowing look.

"She's not wrong – it's a great business opportunity," Tally pointed out. "It's going to be good for your flower business, too."

"Don't remind me – those big weddings over on St. Simons Island a few weeks ago just about did me in. It's a pain in the ass running around over there and over here on the same weekend," Yaya complained.

"I know. And we'll have to bring more people on board to accommodate as we book more gigs over there. There's going to be a learning curve," Tally started to explain, but Yaya cut her off.

"A painful learning curve. Why do you always have to do things the hard way?" she asked.

"Because I'm good at it."

"No, you're not," Yaya laughed. "But whatever you decide to do, I've got your back – even if you've completely lost your mind." She started mumbling in Spanish what sounded like insults, but Tally let it go and laughed instead.

"You're going to be so happy once we have enough staff for you to order the girls around and then go home at a normal hour," Tally promised.

"*Mentiras!*" Yaya yelled, laughing. Tally recognized that word. Her bff was calling her a liar.

"I'm not lying. It will get better. Eventually," Tally started giggling, realizing the ridiculousness of the case she was trying to make. Wedding planning never slowed down or got any easier. Life just got busier and busier if she was successful. And the bigger the clients' budgets were, the bigger the pain in the ass the brides were likely to be. It was a fact of wedding life, and Tally was being silly to try to sell Yaya anything else.

"Okay fine, it's going to be nuts at first – especially if we also bring on some new interns," she dashed into the restroom and locked the door behind her as soon as that last bit was out of her mouth. She could hear Yaya yelling in the next room.

"Are you out of your mind? We just finished housebreaking these three, and you want to adopt more? There has to be a limit, Tally. There's no more room for them," she pointed to the crowded desks all over the room as Tally came out of the bathroom.

"There will be plenty of room when Kayla, one of the new planners, and one of the new interns all locate themselves in the St. Simons Weddings office, instead of in here," Tally argued, seeing Yaya's point as she looked at the office space. Up until now, she hadn't actually made the decision to rent office space for the St. Simons' operation. The overhead renting there was going to kill her, she thought. But Yaya was right, this plan wouldn't work if she tried to put three more people in this office space, all trying to work at the same time.

"I'm still figuring it all out," she conceded when Yaya continued to glare at her. "I promise that I won't add any more staff to this office. Is that fair? We won't bring on more bodies until we have someplace else to put them."

"Okay then," Yaya said, cleaning up the breakfast mess in front of her and dropping it in the trash can.

"Where are you going? I thought we were getting caught up?" Tally's feelings were hurt that Yaya seemed to be blowing her off.

"I'm going back into my office to run flower estimates while it's still quiet enough around here to get any work done. The way you're going, we're going to be stacking employees on top of each other out here soon."

"Oh, stop it," Tally laughed. "You're so dramatic. It won't be that bad."

"We'll see," Yaya replied in a tone that said she was not convinced. "I never know what you're going to come up with next." She started muttering in Spanglish again and went into her office. She left the door open, but her message was clear. She needed to work, and the conversation was over, at least for the time being. Yaya knew that Tally would ultimately do whatever was best for the company. She just wasn't sure that what was best for the wedding business was going to be good for her sanity.

***

Tally worked quietly in the office for a couple of hours, and then said goodbye to Yaya and went home to have lunch with Mitch and the kids. She felt guilty – like she was playing hooky – and she had to remind herself that it was okay. What was the point of owning her own business if she couldn't have lunch with her babies once in a while, right?

The twins were in their highchairs when Tally walked in. She got inside just in time to see Molly pick up a glob of whatever she was eating – *oh God, it was spaghetti* – and throw it at her brother. The noodles made a splat sound and Moody laughed. Then he picked up his own lunch and lobbed it at his sister. Unfortunately, Moody wasn't as coordinated as Molly, and the messy red blob flew over his sister's shoulder and hit the dining room floor with a splat that made both of Tally's toddlers giggle.

Molly was about to throw another handful of spaghetti when her mother intervened.

"No, no, no, young lady," Tally said as she rushed to her daughter. "We don't throw our food in this house. We put it in our tummy," she said as she carefully disarmed Molly. It looked like the food fight had been going on for a few minutes before she got home.

"Where is your father?" Tally asked the sauce-covered babies, shaking her head at the giant mess, and wondering if she could turn around and slide back out the front door before Mitch ever knew she'd been home. Molly just giggled at her, but Moody pointed down the hallway.

"Mitch!" Tally yelled from the kitchen sink where she was wetting a paper towel to begin cleaning up the kids.

It took a minute, but her better half came racing out of their bedroom. He stopped short when he saw the disaster area around the dining room table.

"What happened?" he asked, looking totally baffled.

"You left our almost-two year olds alone with spaghetti for lunch, and you're asking *me* what happened? Take a wild guess!" She tried not to sound pissed off, but it was hard. Really, the mess was funny if Mitch was going to clean it all up by himself. But he wasn't. This was definitely a two-parent disaster zone. It only took one parent to let the mess happen, but it would take both of them to clean up Molly and Moody and put the house back to rights.

Mitch kept swiveling his head around, looking at the scene, totally mystified. "I swear, I was only gone for a couple of minutes. I had to go to the bathroom."

"Based on this mess, I'd guess it was longer than a couple of minutes," Tally said, pointedly taking a seat at the kitchen bar, away from the destruction.

Mitch was still searching for something appropriate to say, and he gave up. "You're right. I'm sorry. That was dumb."

"Yes, it was," Tally agreed. "But I bet you'll never walk away while they're armed with food again, will you?" She was grinning now.

This was parenthood, and she enjoyed sharing it with Mitch. Too often, only one of them was around for the really ridiculous stuff. The little rats had done the same thing to her one day when she'd answered a client call while they were eating macaroni and cheese. She'd stepped out of their space for just a moment to answer a question for the bride without them making noise in the background, and when she came back... well, she preferred not to remember that mess. She'd gotten it all cleaned up before anybody else saw it. Now she was thinking that she should have waited until Mitch got home so he could be properly warned. *Too late now*, she thought.

"Okay, let's make a plan," she suggested. Mitch nodded at her, making it obvious that he didn't know where to begin. "You go hose them off on the back deck. I'll go get some nice clean towels and you can pass the kids to me one at a time. Do Molly first – she's your troublemaker and Moody won't fight you because he'll just want to catch up with his sister."

"I can do that," Mitch said. Tally started down the hall to get their towels when she heard the pitter patter of dirty little feet on her floor. She turned around and saw chaos. There were spaghetti footprints all the way from the kitchen to the back deck. *Had they been eating with their feet?* Mitch looked at her helplessly.

"I guess I should have told you to take them out of their highchairs one at a time and not set them down on the floor until *after* they were clean," she said much more calmly than she felt.

"That would have been good information to have," Mitch agreed. "A few minutes ago." He shook his head at her and followed his dirty toddlers outside. There was spaghetti sauce smeared all over the window in the door where Molly was trying to look through the glass to see if her daddy was coming.

Tally finished her mission and brought back towels that she set on a clean spot on the kitchen counter. Then she opened up the broom closet and pulled out her Swiffer. She looked at it, looked at the mess in the dining room, and then put the cleaning tool back, grabbing the mop in its rolling bucket instead.

"This is way too intense for a Swiffer," she told herself, and started to fill the mop bucket.

Chapter 46

Mitch took a shower after they were finished getting the kids and the kitchen cleaned up. Tally had made it pretty easy for him by tackling most of the kitchen while he hosed spaghetti off the twins. She'd washed the floors twice by the time he reappeared in fresh clothes.

"Go put your clothes and their clothes in the washing machine," she ordered him. Laundry was usually her job, but this was an exception. Mitch turned around to go back and get his dirty laundry and reappeared in the hallway a minute later. "Do you want me to put anything else in the load?"

"God no," Tally gave him a horrified look. "Let's not cover everything we own in spaghetti sauce today. Throw their clothes in with yours – use hot water, please. Then add two Tide tablets and three scoops of OxyClean. It's that box sitting on top of the dryer," she pointed to it. "That will get the spaghetti sauce out of the clothes."

Mitch loaded up the washer and peeked his head into the nursery to check on the twins.

"They look so angelic when they're asleep," he told Tally when he returned to the kitchen.

"Should we have taken pictures so you could remember what the little monsters did with their spaghetti today?" she asked, laughing. "If you've forgotten, I just spotted some sauce on the chair legs over there." She pointed and Mitch rolled his eyes. Then he grabbed the Windex and a couple of paper towels to wipe off the splattered furniture.

"I haven't forgotten," he assured her while he cleaned. "Wow, we should use toddlers as distraction devices during wars. Nobody would notice an enemy sneaking across the border if they were trying to feed two years olds."

"Valid point. Maybe you can find a way to use them with your task force," Tally suggested.

"Don't give me ideas. I'm so bored with the research we're doing that it's not even funny. This thing with Etah's friend's pictures is far more entertaining."

"Really? Did we find out anything new?" she asked.

"Yeah, that's how I got distracted when I was in the bathroom." Tally gave her husband an "are you kidding me" look and he laughed.

"No, seriously," he claimed. "Dad called while I was on the toilet and he was on speaker phone in his office, so I was waiting to flush."

Tally nodded at him like he was making perfect sense and resisted the urge to introduce him to the mute button on his phone. She knew her husband didn't multitask the same way that she did. He probably had felt stuck in the bathroom while his children were having a food fight in the kitchen.

"What did your dad say? Don't leave me hanging here," Tally had been trying hard not to think about the disaster her aunt's boyfriend had left in his wake while she was working this morning, but she couldn't stay focused. She needed an update if she was going to accomplish anything this afternoon.

"They've identified Beau," Mitch said. "Or rather, they have fingerprints from Etah's condo that match a suspect nobody even realized was back in the area. The last time this guy was on anybody's radar screen was in the early 2000s."

"Why did they have his prints on file? Has he been arrested before?" she asked, afraid of the answer. "And what's his real name?"

"His real name is Archibald Murdaugh, and he doesn't live in Atlanta. He's from South Carolina," Mitch was reading the information from a text on his phone.

"Wait, Murdaugh in South Carolina? Any relation to the Alex Murdaugh who murdered his own family?" Tally had been following a podcast about it.

"Don't know yet."

"And why did you have his prints on file?" Tally didn't give her husband a chance to finish his thought. "Does he have a criminal record? Is he a known art thief?"

"Yes, he has a record. He's been arrested - numerous times, actually. But the charges have never stuck, according to what the files say," Mitch continued. "It's interesting because this sort of ties into the stolen art investigation I'm working on with the task force. But we don't investigate random art heists – just specific ones with potential international consequences." He said it like his task force had more important things to do than look for the Hendrix artwork.

"Art like the stolen Chagall?" Tally asked.

"Right."

"But isn't the theft of Bill Hendrix just as big of a deal in this area?" she asked.

"I guess. Sort of," Mitch allowed. "But there's nothing to indicate they're going to try to move the pieces out of the United States, at least not yet. And that's the stuff we investigate. It's not federal until it leaves the state or the country."

"Oh." Something about her tone made Mitch look back at his wife and see the sad expression on her face.

"Tally, they're still investigating the theft – it's just not assigned to my task force. I have more access to information about what they're doing because of the Cultural Antiquities Task Force I'm working with, but my task force isn't working on this particular art theft," he explained.

"I wish you were," she said, frowning.

"No, you don't. Because if that artwork was on our target list, the chances of it ever being recovered would be significantly lower. For all we know, this Beau, er, Archibald guy is a just a shyster who saw an opportunity and took it. It probably wasn't some big pre-planned art heist by professionals."

"But you don't know that," she sounded like she was accusing him of something. She wasn't sure why she was trying to pick a fight with her husband, but that was definitely where this was going.

"You're right – I don't know that for a fact. But my gut tells me this is a local thing. Dad said the same thing," he told her. "Bill Hendrix artwork is going to be more valuable in the Golden Isles than anywhere else."

"And suddenly I'm married to an art expert," Tally muttered under her breath as she worked her way around the kitchen, pulling out items to toss in the crock pot for a dinner she was going to call "stew."

"Tally, I'm taking this seriously," Mitch told her, realizing his wife was actually annoyed with him. "I just can't do anything more than what I've done. Now we have to let the GBI investigators do their jobs." The Georgia Bureau of Investigation handled all of the state patrol investigations beyond traffic-related incidents.

Tally turned and looked at him. She realized she'd sounded like a brat. Too much time around toddlers, perhaps. "I'm sorry. I know you've done everything you can. I just hate this."

"I don't blame you."

"Susan McLemore told me that there are all sorts of nasty rumors going around the island about me and Aunt Etah," she told him.

"Seriously? What kind of rumors? Bonnie didn't mention it when I talked to her." Mitch's grandmother knew everything happening on Jekyll Island. And she was Etah's best friend.

"Yeah, well apparently Cinnamon Lurch and her husband have been telling people that this is all a big scam to make money off the insurance policy on Goodyear Cottage," Tally explained. "It's ridiculous, of course, because the artwork was insured by the Hendrix family and Aunt Etah's umbrella policy. No one has even suggested making a claim against the art association's policy. But you know how rumors are. Half the island probably believes it's true by now."

"Maybe you should put in a call to *The Brunswick News* and tell them the real story," her husband suggested, naming their local newspaper. "They reported there had been a theft, but there was absolutely no detail. I don't think GSP has released anything about it. Maybe it would be a good idea for you to call the newspaper and tell them what really happened."

"Aunt Etah would be humiliated," Tally protested.

"Don't tell them about her relationship with Beau. Just call him an acquaintance. The story is about the stolen Hendrix art, not your aunt," Mitch said.

"Maybe."

"You know, Tally. If my dad's right, this guy stole that artwork to sell for a quick profit. That means he's going to sell it to somebody in this area. I think getting *The Brunswick News* to report on the stolen artwork might shake loose some information on where it is."

"Or at least discourage somebody local from buying it from him," Tally agreed. "Okay, I'll make the call. But I better give Etah a heads up first."

"Good idea."

Chapter 47

Tally sent an email to her friend that worked at their local newspaper after she'd talked to Etah later that afternoon. Then she put the entire Hendrix art fiasco on the back burner, at least in her head, because she had more important things to focus on.

Jekyll Weddings' last four weddings of the year were taking place over the next two weeks. She printed out a calendar page for December and got out her colored pens – time to figure out how to make everything work and celebrate the holidays with her twins. She began by using a red pen to mark all the Holly Jolly Jekyll events that she couldn't miss. This was the first year the twins were old enough to enjoy them. She made a note on the side of the page to ask Mitch if he wanted to decorate Etah's golf cart for the Christmas parade this year or just be enthusiastic spectators.

Next, she added all the wedding events in blue – with the name of the clients first and then an arrow across all the days that group would be on the island. *Oof,* she thought. The calendar was filling up quickly. The guests for the Pickering/Doyle wedding at Faith Chapel on Saturday would start arriving in two days. The Mossbach/Walsh elopement on Driftwood Beach was Friday, but the bride and groom weren't arriving on the island until Thursday evening, according to the schedule Kelsi had left in her box.

Cameron/Breslow was a smallish-wedding – only about 35 guests according to the file – on Glory Beach the next Wednesday. *Why on a Wednesday,* she wondered. A quick troll through the file answered her question. Both the bride and groom's parents had gotten married on December 13th some 25 and 30 years ago, respectively. *That was cool,* she thought. But ugh, they were arriving on Sunday and had planned a lot of activities for their group. There was a sunset dolphin cruise to welcome everybody on Monday, a trolley tour of St. Simons Island and the spirit trees on Tuesday that would ultimately take them to the rehearsal dinner in the speakeasy backroom of Reid's Apothecary in Brunswick. The kicker was the fact that the wedding ceremony was taking place at sunrise the next morning. Sunrise, not sunset. Tally groaned when she thought about it.

Stephanie Cameron was a runner. She'd been on the track team at Georgia, and she still ran before work every day. It was too hot to go running in Georgia when she got home most days. As a result, she'd fallen in love with sunrise. The groom, U.S. Army Captain Aaron Breslow, was also a morning person. He'd proposed to Stephanie at sunrise on a beach in Hawaii a year ago. So, they wanted to seal the deal at sunrise, too. On the plus side, a sunrise wedding meant everything would be finished and cleaned up by noon. Just in time to take a quick break before greeting the couple who would be Jekyll Weddings' last wedding of 2023.

The Slater/Hightower wedding was going to be their last nightmare of the year, Tally concluded after she reviewed the wedding plan. The brides were arriving on the island next Wednesday with their entourage, and the rest of their 300 guests would arrive on Thursday. The good news was that they had taken over Crane Cottage for the entire four days and almost all of their wedding events would be held on that property. That made coordinating things significantly easier.

Tally closed the file when she got to Kelsi's notes about the brides wanting to put up a teepee in the front yard of the historic home. She'd read enough. If the gossips on Jekyll hadn't already crucified her and Etah over the stolen artwork, the Slater/Hightower wedding décor was going to put Jekyll Weddings on everybody's hit list. There couldn't be some weird-looking neon display set up on the lawn of Crane Cottage, within view of other houses and Faith Chapel, during the holiday festival of lights. She made a note to tell Kelsi that if she was planning to put up a teepee in the historic district during Holly Jolly Jekyll, she'd better be covering it completely in Christmas lights.

Once her paper calendar was all marked up with events, she made a few more notes for the staff meeting tomorrow morning. It would be the last big one for the year and they had a lot to go over. They also needed to talk about having an office Christmas party before the interns went home for the holidays and Kayla disappeared on her vacation with Jake.

Party planners were the worst about scheduling their own events. Tally figured that out when she had to plan her own wedding. It was sort of like the old saying about how the roofer's house always has the biggest holes in it or the painter's house always needs to be painted. Regardless, she valued her team, and she wanted to make sure they got together to celebrate before everybody scattered to the four winds. She'd already bought their Christmas gifts on her last excursion to the outlets up by Savannah.

Chapter 48

The staff meeting the next morning ran much longer than it should have because everybody was feeling a little goofy. There's was a bit of holiday fever in the air. Knowing they were in the final run-up to a few weeks off had everybody in an excellent mood.

Everyone except Kelsi.

"I really, really like Suzy and Jessica but they're driving me nuts with all the last-minute décor additions. I'm sick of calling JIA to ask what's permissible and what's not. I'm pretty sure their receptionist thinks I'm an idiot," she complained.

"Why would you say that? You're supposed to check with them about things we're not sure about," Tally said.

"Because she thinks I should be smart enough to figure it out without calling her again. I should know that the answer to my question is going to be 'no.' As in no giant spotlight for beside the red carpet because it could confuse the turtles. No bubble machine in the courtyard during cocktails because it would make the stones slippery. And absolutely no pop-up petting zoo in the sunken garden the day before the wedding."

"Seriously?" Kayla looked at her.

"Oh Mylanta – I am so serious! We haven't even gotten to the damned teepee," she cried, sounding desperate.

"You're putting up a teepee?" the interns started laughing but Kayla looked horrified. "At the most expensive home ever built by the millionaires on Jekyll Island? Please tell me that one of the brides is Native American."

"Um," Kelsi looked at her file. "I don't think so. It's never come up. Jessica saw it on another bride's inspiration page and just had to have it. I couldn't even find one to rent in this area – at least not one big enough for this wedding. Jess wants to be able to get at least 25 people in it at a time."

"Why?" Tori asked, looking intrigued.

"I didn't ask. But if you want to go check it out that night, be my guest. Somebody should go look. We all want to know why we had to put up a freakin' teepee at Christmastime in Georgia for brides from New York City," Kelsi said dramatically.

"Take it down a notch," Tally told Kelsi gently. "How's their budget? Have they paid all their balances?"

"Their budget was a nightmare and yes, they have paid all of their final balances," Kelsi announced with a smile. "It was supposed to be a $25,000 wedding," she paused and rolled her eyes for effect. "But it ended up being an $80,000 wedding. Of course, the guest list literally doubled and they're serving top-shelf open bar at everything for four days. But it's all paid up. And Yaya said it was the biggest floral budget of the year for any of our weddings."

Everybody at the table hooted and clapped. Usually, the bigger budget clients were harder to collect from when they hit the 30-day-out mark and it was time to pay up. The more money the couple had, the more ridiculous upgrades they'd add, and the harder they'd argue about the numbers on their final spreadsheet in an effort to renegotiate things they'd agreed to pay for months earlier. Brides and grooms with tighter budgets knew what they'd spent and usually signed off on the final budgets without any complaints or surprises. The fact that Kelsi had gotten the Slater/Hightower balance sheet cleared to zero two weeks before the wedding was fantastic.

"And they've given me a credit card to pay whomever we can bribe to set up and take down that damned teepee," Kelsi added, with a sly smile.

"Add in the cost of covering that sucker with lights," Tally told her, crossing that item off the list in front of her. "Regular holiday light colors. All white or multicolored – I don't care which – maybe get some of those nets of lights and just cover the entire thing. That way, at least it will look pretty after dark."

"Wishful thinking," Yaya said, laughing at her friend. "This is the first time I've ever had to order in neon-dyed flowers. And girl, we have got a ton of them coming. Literally hundreds in a variety of neon colors. Gerbera daisies, hydrangeas, roses, and at least one of everything else Potomac Floral Wholesale carries that could be turned into neon. Pretty sure my sales guy there thinks I've lost my mind."

Yaya turned to face more of the ladies at the table. "That reminds me - bring old clothes to do flowers this week, if you're going to be helping with arrangements and bouquets for Slater/Hightower. You guys remember what a mess that floral dye can be from the St. Patrick's Day wedding last year?" she directed her question to Kelsi and Kayla, both of whom nodded. "I don't even want to think about neon dye," she groaned and shook her head. "Our hands are going to be weird colors for a week."

"Is it worth it for what they spent on flowers?" Tally asked.

"Oh, hell yes. Absolutely. But that doesn't mean I'm not going to bitch about it."

"I'm happy for you guys," Kayla interrupted. "But we're still missing the final payment for the Mossbach/Walsh wedding this weekend. Can we talk about that?"

"That's a straight elopement package?" Tally asked, shuffling through the papers in front of her until she found the right one.

"Yes, but they had a few add-ons, like a wedding video and ceremony music."

A wedding video was an extra $350, and the ceremony music was $150 because they'd chosen to have one acoustic guitarist for an hour. Under the elopement package, they hadn't needed to put deposits down for those specially-requested items, but they did have to pay for them in full when they settled up the remainder of their planning fee, 30 days before their wedding date. That meant that if an elopement client cancelled at the last minute, Jekyll Weddings had to eat the deposit to the vendor. Most vendors required cancellation 30 days out for a full refund, and the Mossbach/Walsh wedding was already way past that.

Kayla watched Tally scan through the slim file – elopements weren't usually problem clients – and volunteered additional information.

"I emailed them the final balance owed two weeks before it was due. It was easy because it was just the second half of the elopement fee, plus the video and music add-ons. I didn't hear anything back, so I emailed again a few days later and asked the bride to confirm she'd gotten it. It took a couple of days, but the groom finally replied and said he would get the credit card number to me by the following Monday. Which would have put them right on time," Kayla said.

"But of course that was too good to be true," she continued. "Because I haven't heard from them since. I've emailed three more times to follow up, and nobody has responded. I'm going to have to try to call her today."

"Let's call her together after this meeting," Tally suggested. "We'll call from my phone number, and I'll leave the message if she doesn't pick up. It's time to shit or get off the pot, as they say. If she doesn't settle up with us today, we're cancelling the wedding this weekend."

"Would you really do that?" Katy asked, somewhat aghast at her boss's suggestion. "I mean, I hear you threaten that all the time, but never so close to a wedding day and never with somebody who has actually broken our contract. Have you ever cancelled a wedding on a couple because they didn't settle their bill?"

"Yes, I have. And it was a horrible experience. But it wasn't as bad as the sweet couple that I got friendly with my first year in business, because I was new and they visited Jekyll a lot," Tally recalled.

"What happened?" Kelsi asked. "I don't think I've heard this one."

"Probably not. It's one that makes me bitter to talk about, but it's an important planning lesson to share with all of you," Tally took a breath and continued. "That sweet couple did a small wedding package and added on every conceivable bell and whistle they could think of. I tried to stop them because I knew they were blowing their budget, but they were on a mission to have the best of everything, even if they were doing it on a smaller scale."

"Nothing wrong with that," Liz commented.

"There's nothing wrong with it if you can afford what you've planned," Tally corrected her. "And this sweet couple – I'm still Facebook friends with them, but we don't get together when they're on Jekyll anymore – there was no way they could pay their final balance when I handed the bill to them a month before their wedding."

"What did you do?" Liz asked.

"I didn't realize how dire the situation was. The bride sent me a payment for about half of what was owed as soon as she got the bill. And promised another payment the following week. I was okay with that because I thought we had become friends and it never occurred to me that they couldn't afford what they had asked for. It's not like the cost was a surprise," Tally sounded a little defensive as she explained. The girls at the table nodded with understanding.

"She sent me another payment before they got here for their wedding weekend, but it wasn't the full amount. They still owed me something like $1,500 when they got married."

"Wow, that's against the rules," Kelsi said.

"Not back then. That wedding is why I made that rule. And I've only had to enforce it once – I cancelled on a gay couple who tried to play games with me two weeks after their final balance was due," Tally's face turned serious. "Fool me once, shame on you. Fool me twice, shame on me. I will never again execute a wedding for a couple with an outstanding balance. Anybody who is more than two weeks late should consider their wedding plans in jeopardy. It pretty much says that in our client guide," she added.

"What did the clients do when you cancelled their wedding? Did they totally flip out?" Katy wanted to know.

"They probably did, but I didn't have to listen to it. I'd gotten a couple of nasty voicemails from the one I thought of as the bride," Tally winked. "And so, I sent them all to my girlfriend Stacey Mazin – she's an attorney – and Stacey wrote them a scary letter informing them that they had violated the terms of our contract by failing to pay their balance when it was due. And they'd further violated the agreement by leaving inappropriate and threatening voicemails for a member of our team. The letter told them the wedding was cancelled, and they were not to contact us again in person, on the phone, or via the Internet." She looked around. All of the girls' jaws were dropped.

"And I got the point across by having one of Mitch's brothers hand-deliver the letter to the clients' home in Atlanta. In uniform." Tally had a wicked grin on her face. "I never heard from them again."

"Can you do that?" Tori looked skeptical. "I mean, can you have something delivered by a cop to a client?"

"It wasn't official," Tally replied simply. "I just asked my brother-in-law to deliver the letter and confirm they received it."

"It's a police family thing," Yaya added and gave Tally a knowing look. That made Tally smile. Her bestie was getting the hang of being married to a law enforcement officer.

She wondered if Matt had gotten Yaya a "Deputy's Wife" credential case for her driver's license yet. More than once, Tally's "brass pass" had gotten her off the hook when she was stopped her for speeding. When an officer asked for her license, she'd hand it to them in the credential folder with a miniature of her husband's Georgia State Patrol badge. In gold print, under the badge, were the words "Trooper's Wife."

The officer usually took a good look at it and then handed it back to her and told her to slow down and be safe. She'd giggle and beg him not to tell Mitch. It worked pretty much every time. And Tally got stopped for speeding a lot.

Yaya was still learning how to take advantage of the few life perks afforded to the wives of law enforcement officers. She'd put up with an obnoxious neighbor's loud music for a week before Matt had heard it when he was home and done something about it. He'd been baffled and slightly annoyed that she hadn't mentioned it to him and she'd been confused at his reaction. On Vieques, you didn't call the police on your neighbors for music or they might feed antifreeze to your pets. Seriously.

Tally had told Yaya not to hesitate to throw Matt's name around, once they were married, if she found herself in a pickle. Being a Durham wife had gotten Tally through countless festival roadblocks on Jekyll Island. Yaya should be able to get courtesy-waved through stopped traffic due to a wreck on the Torras Causeway on a busy wedding Saturday.

It was called "police courtesy" when a cop made another cop's wife's life easier. They'd usually let an officer's spouse off the hook, same as when they didn't give a ticket to an off-duty officer that they stopped for some traffic violation. Most law enforcement agencies across the country extended police courtesy when they pulled over fellow officers and blue line family members. Pretty much everyone except the Virginia State Police. Those troopers would write a ticket on their mothers if they caught them speeding.

But Virginia was the exception to the rule. Most of the blue line family looked out for each other and treated each other's family members the way they hoped other officers would treat their own wives and mothers.

The crew around the table was getting restless, so Tally called an end to the meeting and sent everybody on their way except Kayla.

"Let's go call your clients together and beat the balance out of them," she said in a joking tone.

She borrowed Yaya's office and shut the door to block out the chit-ter-chatter, then she sat down and passed her phone to the other wedding planner. "You dial. Put it on speaker," she told her.

The call went to voicemail after the first ring, but a text popped up just as Tally was getting ready to leave a message.

"Tied up on a call. Will get back to you later," the message read.

Tally left a message anyway. "Hi there, this is Tally Davis from Jekyll Weddings. I'm Kayla's supervisor. I'm reaching out to you to see if you can settle up your final balance before end of business today. Otherwise, we'll have to start cancelling the vendors who have been scheduled for your wedding. Please call me back directly." She left her cell phone number.

"If they try to get around me by calling you, just let it go to voicemail and I'll call her back," Tally said.

"I'm sorry to bring this to you," Kayla began, but Tally held a hand up to stop her.

"Your job is to help book clients and execute beautiful weddings. You are not a bill collector. And I won't treat you like one," she said sternly. "If somebody misses the deadline to pay for their wedding, it becomes my problem."

Kayla started to argue that she could handle most of it herself, but Tally cut her off.

"That's fine, but you don't have to. When you are running St. Simons Weddings, you'll have to be more aggressive than you are right now. But here, I'm willing to take one for the team if it means they'll pay up and not treat you like crap when they're here. I'd rather they have a grudge against me," she explained.

"I guess that makes sense," Kayla said. "But you're going to have to let me listen in on a couple of the calls you make to delinquent Jekyll Island clients so I can learn from the master."

"Absolutely. I am happy to teach you how to make brides pay their bills without bloodshed."

Chapter 49

Mitch and Joe were sitting in an unmarked car parked as close to the St. Simons Island Pier as they could get, watching a conversation take place on a bench between two older-looking gentlemen. At least one of the men was suspected to be negotiating the transport of stolen artwork out of the United States. They weren't sure if the guy who'd sat down next to him a few minutes ago was his co-conspirator or a just an acquaintance. They'd figure that out.

Mitch was taking his turn at watching their target while Joe paged through a thick hand-out they'd both found in their task force mail-boxes that morning.

"Holy moly!" Joe exclaimed. "Italy has upwards of 20,000 art thefts a year, and they still say that many of them go unreported. How many would that be a day?" he asked, looking up.

"A lot," Mitch said, keeping his focus on the bench. He was holding a camera, and he looked through the viewfinder and snapped a bunch of very clear pictures of the men he was watching.

"And the vast majority of antiquities thefts track back in some way to terrorist organizations – did you know the 9/11 terrorists funded that attack with looted antiquities?"

"I did not know that." The other man had turned sideways to say something to the target and Mitch snapped a few good pictures of his profile.

"DOJ says that art theft is the third highest-grossing criminal enterprise in the United States now. Drugs are number one, and guns are number two. But the FBI's art squad has only existed since 2004. That's interesting," Joe commented.

"Fascinating," Mitch agreed, never taking his eyes off the men on the bench.

"The Art Crime Team has recovered thousands of stolen items valued at $150 million. Jesus!"

"What?" Joe's tone got Mitch to look at him, finally.

"We should have been art thieves instead of going into law enforcement," Joe said with a straight face.

Mitch shook his head and looked back at their target, who appeared to be wrapping up his conversation.

"Heads up," he told Joe. "I wonder where we're going now." The gentleman they were watching rose from the bench and shook the other man's hand. Then he turned and started walking up the sidewalk directly towards Mitch and Joe.

Without pausing, Mitch popped the hood on the car and opened the door to get out. "Go look in the trunk and see if we have jumper cables," he called back in to Joe, much louder than was necessary, with his back to the approaching target.

"Uh, yeah, sure," Joe replied, a little slow to catch on. He opened the passenger door and was starting to get out when Mitch waved him off. He pointed to the man walking with his back to them.

"He didn't even notice us," Mitch said. "Get in the car and we'll follow him."

Their target walked a block before he stepped into a barber shop and took a seat in the waiting area by the window. Mitch and Joe parked across the street to watch him.

"Isn't that the guy he was talking to on the bench?" Joe asked, pointing at a dapper-looking man who was making his way down the sidewalk.

"It sure is," Mitch nodded, and snapped a picture of him.

"That's interesting," Joe said, pointing as the man turned into the parking lot of an apartment building.

Mitch looked over at the barber shop and saw their target being escorted to a chair. "We have a few minutes – let's see where this guy is going." He put the car in drive and slid out of the parking space.

They coasted past the entrance to the parking lot where the man had turned in time to see him climbing the staircase to the second floor. Mitch pulled the car into a space clearly marked as "No Stopping, Standing, or Parking" and pulled out the camera. He snapped a few pictures of the man letting himself into what they presumed was his apartment. Mitch zoomed in after the door to the apartment closed and got a clear shot of the address number on the door.

Once that was done, he pulled a quick illegal U-turn and drove down the block until he found another empty space near the barber shop.

"I can't see the window from here," Joe said.

"I can't see anything," Mitch complained. "But there's no place else to park around here right now."

"I'll go sit on that bench across the street and keep an eye on him," Joe volunteered. "Go ahead and move the car to a better spot if one opens up." He jumped out of the car and walked quickly across the street. Mitch watched as his partner pulled a St. Simons Island map out of his pocket and consulted it. Then Joe sat down on the bench to look at the map more closely, like any normal tourist would.

Mitch updated the log sheet while he waited. They were required to keep track of where they were and what they were photographing throughout the surveillance. The bosses wanted clear and accurate answers when they asked where the suspect was when a certain photo was taken. His progress was interrupted by a text from Joe.

"He's done. He'll be leaving in a sec. I'll stay here in case he goes the other way."

Mitch looked across the street, made eye contact with Joe and nodded.

Fortunately, their target turned right and headed down the block in the same direction their unmarked car was already facing. Mitch stayed put and Joe hopped back into his seat a couple of minutes later.

"Where'd he go?" Joe asked, looking worried when he couldn't spot the man on the sidewalk.

"He went into Iguana's. Probably to have lunch."

"We could watch him better from inside the restaurant," Joe suggested with a smile.

"Absolutely," Mitch agreed with a grin, and turned off the car.

Chapter 50

Both weddings that weekend went smoothly. Sarah Mossbach had called Tally back with a credit card number for the full balance of her wedding bill so that was no longer a problem. Kayla was in the office when Tally got the call, and her boss put the phone on speaker when she answered so it could be a teachable moment. But nothing dramatic happened. Tally's voicemail must have had the desired effect because the bride apologized and wanted to pay what she owed before she didn't have a wedding.

Nothing had slowed down for the wedding planners as a reward for finishing the first two weddings. The couple getting married on Wednesday – Stephanie Cameron and Aaron Breslow – arrived on Jekyll before the guests from the Pickering/Doyle wedding on Saturday left. There had been no down time for anybody on the Jekyll Weddings team. But that was okay because they only had two more to do, and then they had almost three weeks off.

"Why would anybody ever want to get married at sunrise?" Katy asked Kayla, as they double-checked the contents of the tubs for the couple's events one more time.

"I have no idea. You'd have to get up at 2 a.m. to do hair and makeup," Kayla answered. "It's stupid. But the pictures will be amazing."

"How did I get to be the lucky intern working the sunrise wedding?" Katy joked. "This should count as two weddings."

"It really should," Kayla agreed. "They have over-planned the hell out of this week for their guests."

"Do you think that's bad?"

"It's not bad – it's good for us because it means they spent more money on wedding events. But I'm not sure the guests all appreciate the effort and expense because most of them were just hoping to have a little downtime while they were here. And that's not happening for Stephanie and Aaron's guests," she picked up their schedule to make a point.

"Yeah, I guess it would suck to be overscheduled at a destination wedding," Katy said, thinking out loud.

"Look, the bride and groom put a lot of time and money into everything, and our goal is make sure the guests have a fabulous time. The only thing that has me nervous is that rehearsal dinner at Reid's Apothecary," Kayla said.

"Why?" Katy didn't recall Kayla having mentioned a problem when they were planning.

"I'm just worried that it's a rather alcohol-heavy event the night before a sunrise wedding."

"Oh jeesh, I hadn't thought about that. Probably because we're never allowed to drink," Katy said, making a face.

"I'd be willing to bet that we're missing a few guests at sunrise on Wednesday. But that's okay," she was quick to add. "The bride and groom won't even notice if everything else is perfect."

***

Kelsi's last wedding of the year was going to be a lot more complicated than Kayla's sunrise service, but she wouldn't have traded her for anything. She'd seen that day-of schedule at their meeting and just laughed. Liz and Tori had been very glad to be working with Kelsi that week and they'd teased Katy about not waking them when she left for the Cameron/Breslow wedding before morning.

Despite all the joking, Kelsi had a feeling that Liz and Tori had gotten the short end of the stick for their last wedding of the year. Katy might have to get up really early one morning, but the other two were going to run their butts off keeping Suzy and Jessica and their high-maintenance, big-city friends happy.

Suzy Slater and Jessica Hightower had invited 300 guests from New York City to help celebrate their wedding on Jekyll Island. Suzy's grandmother owned a house on Jekyll when she was small, and she still had fond memories of spending time there. When Jessica proposed to her, Suzy said yes with the caveat that they would get married in Georgia at the Jekyll Island Club Hotel. She'd always pictured taking wedding pictures on the croquet lawn out front while holding a parasol. Jessica quickly agreed to getting married on Jekyll Island, but she hadn't been able to resist pointing out, more than once, that it was "a shame" her bride hadn't fallen in love with a wedding destination a little closer to a major airport.

The brides had a big budget and huge imaginations. Everything was going to be decorated in neon. That didn't seem awful until they chose Crane Cottage, on the historic side of the hotel, for their venue. Crane was one of the most beautiful homes on Millionaire's Row, and all of the planners loved doing events there. It was recently-renovated, and it had several large spaces available for entertaining, plus multiple outside options. The courtyard in the middle was the perfect spot for cocktails and wedding pictures, and Kelsi told the brides she didn't think they really needed to spend much money on extra décor. Her clients disagreed.

"Are we allowed to dye the water in the fountain?" Jessica asked.

Kelsi laughed in reply, and when the brides fell silent, she realized they weren't kidding.

"I have no idea, I've never asked," she said, trying to save the moment. "I'll find out for you. What color were you thinking?"

"Either neon pink or green," Suzy told the wedding planner.

"Orange is still in the mix, too," Jessica added, and Suzy rolled her eyes at her. Even so, Kelsi had a feeling the water would end up being neon orange if they colored it. Jessica didn't seem like a bride who would do much compromising with her soon-to-be spouse if she had her mind set on something.

Fortunately, the hotel had given them a resounding "no" on adding anything to the fountain in the Crane Cottage courtyard. It was one of many pieces of bad news that Kelsi had to give Suzy and Jessica as they kept coming up with new and even wilder décor ideas.

"Have we found anybody to set up the damned teepee yet?" Tally asked as she stepped over the ginormous box that had been occupying the office floor for a few days.

"Still working on it. I'm trying to see if I can hire some of the JIA guys to do it after hours. That way, we'll know that we've done everything possible to make it as Christmasy as possible," Kelsi told her.

"Great idea, but we need them to confirm on that today. Mitch will kill me if he and Pete have to decorate that thing for us at the last minute."

"I'll get Jake to help them," Kelsi offered. "It's only fair since he's my brother and it's my wedding problem."

"And I'm sure they'd appreciate his help. But that still isn't going to get me out of trouble with my husband. Let's just find somebody who can definitely take care of it for us. Have you called Jamie Sanders?"

Jamie's business, the Jekyll Island Errand Girl, had saved the wedding planners' butts more than once. Her company motto was, "If it's not illegal, we can probably do it." And that was the truth most of the time.

"I know they hang Christmas lights for several residents. We might be too late to get them now – we really need to get that teepee up tomorrow – but give her a call and see what she says. Maybe we'll get lucky."

Chapter 51

"Oh my God," Tally couldn't stop laughing. At first, Kayla and Katy just glared at her. But then their boss's laughter became contagious, and they both smiled as they watched her.

"That has to be the wedding blooper of the year," Tally said when she caught her breath.

"What happened?" Yaya asked. She'd come out of her office to see what the commotion was. "You okay?" she asked Tally, looking concerned.

Tally wiped away the tears streaming down her cheeks and nodded. "I'm fine. I just laughed so hard I cried," she started laughing again and couldn't finish her thought.

"What are we laughing at?" Yaya asked.

Tally started to speak, but she giggled instead. And then she started laughing all over again.

"What?" Yaya's voice rose a little bit with annoyance. "What happened with your sunrise wedding?" she directed her question at Kayla.

"Nothing," the younger woman replied. "Right?" she asked her intern.

"Nothing," Katy agreed.

"What does that mean?" Yaya was getting irritated that she wasn't in on the joke.

"It means what we said it means – nothing happened because the bride and groom didn't show up."

It took a moment for Yaya to absorb that news and then she started laughing with Tally.

"You've got to be kidding me," she gasped. "Did anybody show up?"

"Yeah," Katy said. "There were like 15 guests there by the end."

"The end?"

"We gave them an hour – and neither Stephanie nor Aaron answered their phones or responded to texts – and after an hour, we had to let the photographer and minister go home. I wasn't going to commit to paying them double if the bride and groom never showed up," Kayla explained.

"That was probably a good call," Tally had calmed down enough to participate in the conversation, but she was still fighting the giggles. "Have you heard from them since?"

"I got a text from Stephanie about an hour ago. Just said 'omg so sorry, will explain later,'" Kayla reported, holding up her phone to show them the message.

"That was it? No other explanation? I could understand one of them oversleeping, but both of them? For hours?" Yaya was horrified. Even a Puerto Rican wouldn't be that late to their own wedding. She went back into her office, muttering in Spanish and shaking her head.

"Were their parents there on the beach waiting for them or were they M.I.A. too?" Tally wanted to know.

"His parents were there but hers were not. Her aunt was there, and she made several loud remarks about how she wasn't surprised because her sister had never arrived on time to anything in her life," Kayla reported.

"Oh ouch," Tally cringed a little.

"Yeah. The whole thing was awful. I had second-hand embarrassment for the bride and groom because everybody who was there before sunrise seemed kinda pissed when there wasn't a wedding," Katy said.

"I can imagine," Tally nodded. "What did you do about the brunch?"

"What could I do?" Kayla asked. "I called Tribuzio's and told them to feed it to the regular customers."

"Did you really?" Tally asked, impressed with Kayla's chutzpah.

"I did. I mean, what were they supposed to do? They had everything ready to go in chafing dishes – it was a massive buffet. And we didn't have a wedding. I know some of the guests were planning to get in their cars and leave when they got back to their hotels. It was no longer a joyous occasion at that point."

"Well at least Tribuzio's had already been paid for that catering, whatever they ended up using it for," Tally shook her head. "What if you had a wedding and the bride and groom didn't show up?" she joked. "Oh wait, now we know the answer to that." She shook her head. She couldn't make up the stories her clients provided for dinnertime fodder with her friends. No wonder her blog was so popular when brides skipped weddings they'd paid for.

"On the plus side, everybody had a fantastic time at the rehearsal dinner. They were in that private area in the back at Reid's Apothecary. It's decorated like a speakeasy – you have to enter through a hidden door in the wall, and everybody always loves that. Anyway, the groom started ordering up flights of fancy bourbon and I saw the bride doing shots with her girlfriends. They probably had a little too much fun to get up this morning," Kayla explained. "I tried to slow them down. I knew it was going to be ugly when they spent a fortune to have the trolley do a second roundtrip so the wedding party could stay to shut down the bar. But I didn't consider that they might not show up at all." She shut her eyes and shook her head. "You cannot make this stuff up."

"Oh wow," Tally replied, eyes wide. "Well, that explains this morning. Make sure they know we're happy to schedule a do-over, but it would come with a fee attached. Everybody who was standing on Glory Beach this morning had to get paid, even though they didn't end up having a wedding."

"I'm just waiting to see what she has to say when she finally calls me. I had to cancel her wedding reception for God's sake. And we haven't even discussed it. It makes me nervous," Kayla confessed.

"There's nothing for you to be nervous about. I think you handled it all as gracefully as possible. What were you supposed to do when the bride and groom stood everybody up? Do you think the guests would have wanted to go have breakfast?" Tally asked.

"Definitely not," Katy jumped in. "His parents were not happy. I heard his dad say the groom's behavior was 'conduct unbecoming an officer.'"

"Yowsers, he was really mad," Tally frowned. "But I still say that Kayla did everything in her power to make things right. And telling Tribuzio's to do whatever they wanted to do with all that food was a good decision. They were ready to serve breakfast to the Cameron/Breslow wedding party at 8. I bet the whole team had been up for hours prepping. That's what annoys me about this. *Everybody else* got up for Stephanie and Aaron's wedding."

Chapter 52

Once the mess was cleaned up from the wedding that wasn't, Kayla was technically finished with her wedding responsibilities for the year. She had finally heard back from Stephanie and Aaron, who were apologetic about missing their own wedding ceremony. Fortunately, they didn't have the gall to ask for a refund.

"Really Kayla, it was just a huge goof up," Stephanie claimed. "I set my alarm for p.m. instead of a.m., and Aaron usually wakes up on his own before my alarm goes off. I don't know what happened but we both slept later than we have in years."

"We know it wouldn't be fair to ask you to do it all over again tomorrow, or to ask our guests to stay another night because of our mistake, so we're going to have this whole thing be a funny story, and we'll get married by a judge back home after our honeymoon," Aaron told the wedding planner.

I'd be happy to do it all over again if you pay us all over again, Kayla thought, but did not say.

"As long as you had a great time at all of your events that you did attend, we're happy if you're happy," Kayla told them and then got off the phone as quickly as she could. She didn't want them to change their minds about getting married by the judge.

Kelsi had told Kayla she wouldn't need her help at Crane Cottage for the teepee wedding, but she wasn't going to make any plans just in case things changed. Suzy and Jessica were going to be a handful. They were beautiful brides who knew what they wanted and Kelsi was probably going to lose her mind making sure they got it. But her friend had things under control with the help of two interns, so Kayla was planning to pack for her wedding that night.

She was still struggling over their decision to keep Kelsi in the dark about their plan to elope. The logic behind the decision had been sound when she and Jake made it, but now it was feeling like maybe keeping the big news a secret from her best friend, who also happened to be her fiancé's older sister, was a very bad idea that could have long-term consequences. Kayla desperately wanted to ask her mom or her sister for advice, but they weren't in on the secret, either. It was a Catch-22.

Kayla was cleaning up her desk and putting away all the items that hadn't been used from the Cameron/Breslow wedding. When the prep tubs were empty, she peeled off the labels and stacked the empty containers on the proper shelf. By the time the week was finished, the office was going to be clean enough to be functional again. At least they'd finally gotten that giant teepee box out of here.

***

If Kelsi had been expecting the wedding weekend to be as exotic as Suzy and Jessica's décor, she would have been disappointed. As dramatic and colorful as the brides were, most of their friends in attendance were pretty normal and didn't make the kind of weird and whacky requests that the wedding planners had been dreading.

Even without neon dye in the courtyard fountain or a spotlight on the neon red carpet the guests walked from the driveway into Crane Cottage, Suzy and Jessica's wedding was spectacular. Their welcome party and rehearsal dinner had gone off without a hitch. The wedding ceremony and reception had gone almost as perfectly, if you didn't count some drama that unfolded when a bridesmaid was caught flagrante delicto with a husband that belonged to another bridesmaid.

Kayla had been worried the brides would freak out when they found out that one of the wedding guests had been arrested for drunk-driving his rented golf cart over the Jekyll bridge. But it turned out he was the date of a friend, and the brides didn't know him, so it ended up being the kind of funny story they'd tell at dinner parties for years to come. Tally asked if anybody had gone to bail the guy out and Kayla had replied, quite honestly, that she had no idea. But he hadn't been at the wedding or reception.

Chapter 53

"Tell me about the teepee," Kayla begged when Tori arrived at the Jekyll Weddings Christmas party at Tally's house. "Did you go inside and see what they were up to?"

"Yes, and they were up to nothing. It smelled like somebody might have been smoking a joint in there, but they were burning some sage and other weird stuff so my nose could have been wrong," Tori explained.

"Really? Nothing?" Kayla asked. "All that hubbub about getting permission for a teepee and they didn't do anything special in it."

"I didn't see Suzy and Jessica doing anything special, but I think it saw action later that night. Rumor at the farewell brunch was that a certain morally-questionable bridesmaid spent the night in the teepee with a certain husband of another bridesmaid," Tori reported.

"Oh my!" Tally had caught the last part of the intern's story. "That certainly wasn't a boring wedding, was it? It'll give you girls some good stories while you're home for the holidays. Would anybody like a Jekyll Julep?"

"Are they real Jekyll Juleps, or the Goodyear version?" Kelsi asked.

"Etah made them," Tally pointed to where her aunt was stirring something in the kitchen. "They're probably dangerous. Good thing none of you has to drive home."

Mitch and Jake had volunteered to be the designated drivers for the night so the wedding planning team could celebrate and get a little sloppy together. Matt dropped Yaya off at Tally's house and popped in to say hi to everybody, but he was on duty so he couldn't stay. Jake promised to return Yaya home safely after the party.

"Any news on the art theft?" Matt asked Mitch before he left.

"Not really. They know who the guy is, but nobody's seen him around here or along the coast in South Carolina where he's supposedly from, since he stole the artwork from Etah," Mitch said, as he walked Yaya's husband to the door. They stepped out onto the front porch to continue the conversation.

"It's a sore subject around here right now because I'm working on a federal task force that's investigating stolen art, but not *this* stolen art," Mitch explained.

"I get that," Matt nodded in understanding. "Look, I know it's a party tonight and I hate to bring up work for the girls... But can you do me one favor if you get a chance?"

"Sure, man, what do you need?"

"Can you ask your wife to tell her clients that their wedding guest is being arraigned tomorrow morning, and somebody needs to bring his wallet to the jail?"

Mitch started laughing. "Nobody tried to bail him out?"

"Nobody's even checked to see if he's alive," Matt laughed. "But he's obnoxious and we'd like to see him released tomorrow, so he's going to need his ID and some money."

"I will be happy to pass along the message," Mitch promised. "But no guarantees that anybody from that wedding is going to rush over there with his wallet. Especially if they didn't try to bail him out today." He started laughing. "Thanks, man. This is the perfect Christmas present for Tally," he said, and then he went back into the house chuckling.

***

It was time for the party to end, but Kelsi and Kayla were having way too much fun to call it quits yet. Kayla rarely drank, but she'd indulged in some of the Jekyll Juleps after the interns made fun of her. Now she had the giggles.

The Christmas party had been the perfect end-of-year celebration for their little wedding planning team. In keeping with tradition, Tally had given designer purses to all of the girls who worked for her. She'd shopped Michael Kors, Coach, and Kate Spade this year, and griped about having to shop in more stores now because they had so many more women on the team and she didn't want to duplicate. She'd gotten purses for the interns, too. Big ones that could hold wedding files.

"Oh my God, Tally, it's cerulean blue!" Tori squealed when she pulled a Coach purse out of her gift bag.

"That's why I got it for you," Tally said. Liz and Katy made faces and rolled their eyes when Tori wasn't looking, but their bosses let it go. Everybody was having too much fun to worry about a little snark.

At the end of the night, Kelsi and Kayla made their way out on the deck to look at the moon and stars over the Atlantic Ocean, and they ended up hanging out there while the others started cleaning up inside.

"Should we go help?" Kayla asked.

"Nope," Kelsi replied. "Not unless they ask for help. Let's pretend we don't see them."

Kayla giggled her agreement and the friends sat there in companionable silence for a little while. Until Kayla's conscience got to her.

"Hey Kelsi, I need to tell you something about our trip," Kayla began.

"Oh Mylanta – are you putting more on my to-do list?" Kelsi asked. She'd had quite a bit of Aunt Etah's famous punch and was feeling dramatic. "I'm already taking care of Howie and the other animals and checking messages and returning calls for Jake's vet practice."

Kayla could tell her bestie was winding up for a rant and she cut her off. "It's not something you have to do. It's what we're going to do. But you have to promise that you'll keep this a secret, even from Jake – he'd be so mad at me for telling you," Kayla said with a very serious expression on her face.

"What's wrong?"

"Nothing is wrong. We're fine. But we're going to get married while we're away and I don't want you to be mad at me when you find out about it. And I knew if you found out we got married when we got back, at the same time that everybody else found out, you'd be really, really mad. Because you are the most important person to both of us. So, I'm telling you. Even though your brother would be furious with me for doing so," she said the last like she making a confession.

Kelsi opened her eyes wide in surprise, then she grinned and threw her arms around Kayla.

"That's awesome. I'm so happy for you!"

"You can't tell anybody about it until we get home. We're going to tell my parents when we get to Iowa, and I'd imagine we'll probably call your parents then, too," Kayla shared.

"Can I plan a big-ass reception for you when you get home? You know it's totally not fair to deny me the right to help plan my brother's wedding to my bestie, right? You can make it up to me if you let me plan your reception. No wait, we won't call it a reception. It'll be a party for you guys."

Kayla was so relieved that Kelsi wasn't angry that she would have agreed to just about anything her future sister-in-law asked for right then.

"You can definitely plan something after we get back. We'll have a great party, and you can be in charge of everything. I'll just pretend I'm a bride."

"You will be a bride," Kelsi corrected her.

"That sounds so weird," Kayla said.

"Yeah, it does," Kelsi agreed. "But you'll get used to it. Just like we'll get used to telling our clients that we're actually sisters."

Chapter 54

The entire wedding planning team was on vacation for the next two weeks, but Yaya didn't take the same time off. She'd worked hard to get lots of hotels and businesses to hire Jekyll Flowers to provide their table arrangements and lobby décor, and that didn't take a break over the holidays – it got busier and more demanding. But Yaya loved what she did and so Tally had given up on trying to stop her friend from working. She did make a point to reward Yaya's efforts on December 31st with a bonus equal to half of the profits they'd earned on her holiday flowers.

Tally and the twins popped into the office to visit Yaya a few mornings into what should have been vacation. She locked up the shop and walked around the corner with them to Sunrise Grille, where she and Tally ordered shrimp and the toddlers gobbled their favorite chicken tenders. She told Yaya the spaghetti food fight story – *how had she not told her about it already*, she wondered. They really needed to make a point to get together alone more often, outside of the office. They'd gotten out of the habit because they worked together so much. But now, with the company growing, they needed to get away to catch up on each other's lives without an audience.

"Tally, I need to tell you that we've had some cancellations because of that mess at Goodyear Cottage," Yaya's tone was dark.

"Seriously? Who, and what did they say?" Tally asked, suddenly concerned.

"The Minterns cancelled their holiday flower orders for the church. Said that they were going to get them someplace else while you're under investigation for that art theft," Yaya reported.

"Did they actually say that? That I'm under investigation?"

"Afraid so. And it was the mister who called it in. He's a crusty old goat," Yaya said.

"Who else?" Tally asked, a sinking feeling growing in her stomach.

Yaya dug through the papers on her desk and pulled out a sticky note. "The Bassets cancelled their Christmas party flowers for this weekend. Same reason. That one's annoying because the flowers are already on their way. The Christophers cancelled the arrangements they usually send to all their VIPs on Christmas Eve, but they didn't give a reason. That one was a message left on my voicemail."

"That's all super weird. I got a message this morning from a resident wanting to cancel her granddaughter's upcoming wedding consultation with us," Tally told Yaya. "I didn't think anything of it at the time, but she's good friends with all of those people you just named."

"I think we have a little public relations problems, Tally."

"I think you're right," Tally agreed. "But it's a *big problem*, not a little problem, if we're already losing clients because of some ridiculous gossip."

"What are you going to do about it?" Yaya asked.

"I'd like to find out who is spreading that BS story about us trying to get insurance money for the Hendrix artwork," Tally said angrily. "But more importantly, I need to do some triage on my company's reputation and make sure the community knows we were just volunteering at the event and Jekyll Weddings had nothing to do with the theft, or any insurance related to it."

"Is Etah going to feel like you're throwing her under the bus?" Yaya sounded concerned.

"Absolutely not. I'll be sure to tell everybody how this is truly a case of no-good-deed-goes-unpunished for her. She was trying to raise money and show a late friend's artwork. Now she feels terrible the art was stolen and she's being accused of being involved in the crime. How does volunteering for a good cause go so horribly wrong?"

"She's related to you, isn't she?" Yaya chuckled. "When was the last time you did a good deed and got bitten in the ass for it? Do you remember? Cuz I do."

Tally groaned and put her hand over her face. She wasn't sure which particular incident Yaya was referring to because it could have been any number of things. Her record on this particular track was not stellar.

"I'm just saying that you don't have to be so nice to everybody all of the time. We'd all probably get yelled at a lot less if you started saying no when you're asked to do things. Call it self-preservation or whatever you want – continuing to do the same thing over and over expecting a different result is the definition of insanity," Yaya reminded her.

"Thank you, Einstein."

***

Tally took Molly and Moody home for naps after lunch and found Mitch working at the dining room table.

"I didn't realize you were going to be home today," she said and kissed him. "What a nice surprise!"

"I'm not really home. I just stopped by to get my crap organized ahead of this big meeting we have at 6 tonight. This whole stolen arts and antiquities thing is complicated. I feel like I'm taking a 600-level class on it, but I missed the prerequisites," he complained.

"Etah was going to come over and babysit while I go do some Christmas shopping. Should I call her and cancel?" Tally asked.

"No, don't do that. I can't stay. I just wanted to use our printer to print out a bunch of stuff for my meeting, so I came home for lunch," he explained. "The one at my office doesn't print in color."

Molly had climbed up into Mitch's lap at the table and was starting to play with the colorful pages he'd printed out. He gently removed her fingers from the pictures and stood up with her.

"How about if I read my favorite bedtime story to you guys?" he asked the twins. "Would you like that?"

Molly and Moody squealed with excitement and then ran down the hall to their bedroom to find the book. Mitch followed them with a grin on his face that made Tally's heart melt.

Chapter 55

"Tally!" Etah's shout echoed through the beach house. "Tallulah Davis, you get out here right now!"

Tally was in the bathroom when she heard her aunt's scream, and it terrified her. Etah occasionally raised her voice, but she never yelled like that.

"What's wrong?" Tally asked as soon as she got to the kitchen.

Etah was standing beside the dining room table, and her face was white as a ghost.

"This!" her aunt replied in a sharp tone, pointing her index finger at the pictures on the table.

Tally looked at the pages her husband had left on the table. About half of them were color photos.

"You guys want to hold it down?" Mitch said as he joined them. "The twins can sleep through a lot but there's a limit," he joked.

"Why do you have pictures of *that man* on your table?" Etah asked Mitch, giving him a very stern look.

"Which man?" Mitch leaned over the table to see what she was pointing at. He extracted the picture of two men sitting on a bench. "This one?" he held the picture closer to Etah so she could inspect it.

"Yes, that one. Why do you have pictures of Beau?" Etah asked in an accusing tone.

"I didn't know I did," Mitch told her honestly. "That guy is Beau?" He pointed to the acquaintance who had met up with the target of his investigation on St. Simons.

Etah nodded, her lips pursed. She was trembling.

"Huh," was all Mitch said, but Tally could see that his mind was spinning. "Are you sure?"

"Absolutely. He's shaved off his mustache but that's him. I bought him the handkerchief he's got in his breast pocket at a cute little shop in France." Etah tapped the picture where a yellow pocket square appeared.

Mitch was already gathering up all of his papers, shoving them together to make a stack. "You are amazing, Etah. I need to go tell my boss we've identified him. We crossed paths the other day when Joe and I were doing surveillance for another art investigation."

"Nobody even considered that the theft of the Hendrix artwork could be related," he continued. "Dammit, Tally tried to get me to go down this path a week ago and I blew her off. This guy could be the key to solving both investigations."

"Go find that artwork, Mitch," Etah ordered him.

"Yes, ma'am. I'm surely going to try," he promised with a grin.

Mitch put everything into his canvas briefcase, planted a kiss on Tally's lips, and headed for the door.

"I'll call you girls when we have some good news," he called as he raced out the front door.

Chapter 56

Mitch jumped into his truck and started the engine, but before he put the truck in gear, he took a moment to text Agent Butler and Joe with the new development. He told them what Etah had said about the mustache and handkerchief and that he was on his way into the office.

Lots of things happened quickly after that.

By the time Mitch got to the makeshift office the task force was using on the bottom of the federal building in Brunswick, Agent Butler had collected everybody else in their group, and officers from multiple law enforcement agencies were already seated around the conference table.

"Our tech guys confirmed that it's Archibald Murdaugh on the bench with the target in that photo," Agent Butler told Mitch when he arrived. "We weren't even looking at him in connection with this. If Ms. Davis hadn't recognized him in that picture, we'd likely have missed him entirely."

"By the way, his name isn't Archibald Murdaugh, either. Although it turns out the dead guy he's impersonating now was, in fact, related to *that* Murdaugh family in Camden County, South Carolina." He gave them an amused look as he said it. All of the cops at the table cringed a little bit when they heard the Murdaugh name because it was currently on the front page of every newspaper in the southeast. "That would have been interesting if he was actually a Murdaugh," the agent in charge laughed.

"Who is he? Do we know?" Mitch asked. He was frustrated.

"Nope. But at least now we know who he is not, which is more than we had yesterday, thanks to your wife's aunt," Agent Butler replied.

"We've got guys sitting on the apartment where we think the un-sub is staying," a stiff-looking young Homeland Security agent Mitch had only met once told them. Mitch resisted the urge to roll his eyes. They didn't actually call unidentified suspects "un-subs." Agent Flannery must watch too much CSI.

"We're watching the apartment about two blocks from the pier where you and Joe watched him go after his meet-up on the bench," Agent Butler explained. "We don't know if he lives there or if he was just stopping to visit a friend. We need to figure that out before we go crashing in there. If we think there could be a stash of stolen art in the apartment, we'll want to enter gently."

Some of the group around the table chuckled at that. Law enforcement officers regularly used flashbangs and other distraction devices to make entry to buildings where a suspect was hiding. Those methods were very effective, but they were not gentle. There was a good chance that anything too near by the flashbang would get ruined. And the bosses in DC got salty when insurance claims named federal law enforcement agencies as the entity that had destroyed valuable property.

"We're going to watch him while we get warrants to search the place," Agent Flannery continued. "We're hoping he'll leave at some point, and we can scoop him up on the street. Makes it all a lot easier to explain later. We can't legitimately claim exigent circumstances on this unless the building is on fire."

Mitch's partner, Joe, joined them shortly before the meeting ended. He had a much longer drive to Brunswick from Camden County. Mitch filled him in on what he missed.

"No way. That's crazy," Joe said. "But thank God you went home to print out those pictures."

"Right?"

"Now we've got to figure out how Beau is connected to the international smuggling ring we've been sitting on, right?" Joe asked.

"That's the plan. They're going to interrogate him as soon as they have him in custody and hopefully, he'll give up the other guys to save himself. He's too old to go to prison for a long time," Mitch said.

"Oh man, Tally and Etah are going to be pissed off if he gets a deal with no time after stealing the Hendrix art and making their lives miserable," Joe said.

"No kidding. I may have to come stay at your place for a while. Or sleep with one eye open at mine," Mitch joked.

***

Eighteen hours later, there were four cars, with two agents each, detailed to watch the apartment where they thought Beau/Archibald/whoever was hiding. Mitch and Joe were back in the unmarked car, sitting in the parking lot of the building. All of the spaces were numbered and there were lots of signs threatening to tow if you didn't have a permit, but so far, nobody had said anything about the 2020 black Jeep Liberty sitting in spot number 12.

"Butler just texted that we have the warrants," Joe told Mitch. "He's on his way – wants us to hold in place until he's here."

"I'm not sure we're going to be able to do that," Mitch said, staring at something over Joe's shoulder. Joe turned around to see what his partner was looking at.

"Holy moly. That's him alright, Let's go," he started to open his car door, but Mitch put a hand on his arm to stop him.

"Let's wait a minute. Let him get halfway down that staircase and then we'll appear to take him. I don't want to give him any chance to get away, but I also don't want to get blamed for causing the old guy to take a header down those metal stairs," Mitch said. "If he breaks his neck, he won't be able to tell us what his connection is to the smuggling."

"Fair enough."

Mitch used his radio to make sure the other watchers had seen the action at the front door of the suspect's apartment. Everybody agreed to wait until they saw Mitch and Joe with hands on the suspect before they showed themselves.

The older gentleman took his time. It was late morning, and he stopped outside his door to take in the scene around him. Then he slowly walked to the top of the staircase, and started making his way down, pausing more than once to look at something that had caught his attention.

"He's looking for us," Mitch said in a low voice. "That behavior is suspicious as hell."

"You ready?" Joe asked as the old man reached the landing that was the halfway point on the staircase.

"Let's do this thing," Mitch agreed, and they both jumped out of the car.

Chapter 57

Tally called Etah when Mitch said he was on his way home with good news. Etah was having lunch with Emily Hendrix Slaughter at Golden Isles Olive OIl on St. Simons when her phone rang, so she and Emily jumped in Emily's SUV and drove straight over to the oceanfront house to find out what was going on.

"I don't know anything yet," Tally said when they walked into her house about 30 minutes later. "Mitch should be here any minute."

"Did they find my dad's artwork?" Emily asked.

"I don't know. He said he had 'good news' on Etah's investigation and that was it. He said he couldn't talk – which I took to mean he had an audience – and said he'd explain everything when he got here," Tally told them. "Does anybody want coffee while we wait?"

"I don't need any more caffeine than I've already had," Etah laughed. "But I wouldn't say no to a large glass of wine."

"Me either," Emily agreed, and patted Etah's hand. "I need to be mentally prepared if he isn't coming to tell us they found it."

"There is no way to prepare for that," Etah said. "They have to find those pictures. Otherwise, Tally and I are going to have to find another place to live." She filled in Emily on the gossip going around about the insurance policy.

"Well, that's just ridiculous," Emily agreed. "I'm sorry that doing a nice thing turned into such a dumpster fire."

"Bored people will always come up with something to keep life entertaining after retirement," Etah said. Then she chuckled. "Take me, for example. I got bored with retirement after a few months, so I dated an art thief to make life more interesting."

Tally and Emily laughed with her about that one.

Molly and Moody had lost interest in the cartoon that Tally put on the living room television set for them and they joined the ladies at the table because it looked more interesting.

"Well, hello there," Emily said when Molly, who had never met her before, climbed right up into her lap.

"Hello to you," Molly replied with a drooly grin.

"Sorry about that," Tally reached over with a fabric diaper she had draped over her shoulder and wiped her daughter's mouth. "They're both teething. You've been warned."

Moody took a flirtier approach to getting attention by wrapping his arms around Etah's leg and grinning up at her.

"You want to sit on my lap?" she asked her great-great-nephew. She reached a hand out to the little boy, and he climbed up onto her like she was a jungle gym.

Tally's phone rang just then, and it was a local, 912-area code number that she didn't recognize, so she picked it up, in case it was Mitch calling from somewhere other than his cell.

"This is Tally," she said when she answered.

"Tally, you don't know me," a woman said. "But I have something of yours that I need to return."

"What's that?" Tally put the phone on speaker and made a face at Etah and Emily to indicate something strange was happening.

"I have Snoopy," the woman said.

It took Tally a few seconds to connect the dots but suddenly it clicked.

"The inflatable Snoopy that was taken from my interns' yard?" she asked, sounding confused.

"Yes. I have it. I'll return it tomorrow," the woman said. "And I'll explain it all to you then. We weren't trying to be malicious."

"Why don't you just bring it over right now?" Tally suggested. Now that she knew what they were talking about, she was getting irritated. Liz had been devastated when Snoopy was taken, and she'd been sad about it for the rest of football season. It probably sounded dumb to some people, but Tally understood how she felt. She knew that having her Ohio State Snoopy decoration stolen out of their front yard had made Liz feel violated in a place she had believed was completely safe.

"I can't."

"Why not?" Tally was not amused.

"Because he's in Atlanta."

Tally was silent. She looked at Emily and Etah to see what they thought. Emily had to look away because she was about to burst out laughing. Etah was smiling and when she saw her niece looking at her, she winked.

"Alrighty then. Please bring Snoopy over when he gets back."

The woman on the other end of the phone – she never did identify herself – promised Snoopy would be returned by noon and hung up.

"I'm not sure this day can get any weirder," she told the others, shaking her head. "But Liz will be so happy to hear he's been returned. I tried to replace that stupid inflatable for her, but it's backordered."

"You know," Emily said slowly, as if she was thinking. "Jekyll Island has gotten a lot weirder than it was 40 years ago when I had a summer job driving the trolley."

Chapter 58

When Mitch finally got to his house, he wasn't alone. Joe and another man Tally had never met walked in behind her husband and followed him into the kitchen.

"Tally, this is my new boss," he said. "Agent Butler, this is my wife, Tally. And these are our twins, Molly and Moody."

"Hi to you!" Molly chirped. And Moody waved one chubby hand in the air in greeting.

"Hello to you, too," Agent Butler said, smiling at the toddlers.

"And these ladies here," Mitch gestured to the other side of the dining room table, "are Etah Davis and Emily Hendrix Slaughter. I think it's fair to call them our guests of honor, don't you?"

"Oh absolutely," Agent Butler agreed. "I guess that means you're the people I'm here to see." He pulled out the empty chair next to Emily. "May I?"

"Yes, of course," Tally said, jumping up from her own seat. "Mitch and Joe – please sit down. Can I bring anybody some sweet tea?"

"Forget the tea, Tally. Did you find the stolen artwork?" Etah asked, sounding rather perturbed.

"We did, Ms. Davis. We found the stolen Hendrix pictures and a whole bunch of other stuff, too. Everything was stashed in a warehouse down by the port. Your boyfriend led us right to it, once we had him in handcuffs," the federal agent explained, speaking slowly and frequently making eye contact with Etah and Emily as he spoke.

"He's not my boyfriend," Etah said, frowning. "I don't even know his real name."

"His real name is John Roy Smith," Agent Butler revealed. "Once we got ahold of him and could print all of his fingers, we figured it out. He's got a long, complicated rap sheet if you put together everything he's been fingered for as Archibald Murdaugh, Beauregard Morris, or John Roy Smith."

Tally was shaking her head. "He has the most boring real name in the world. I wonder why he chose such whacky AKAs."

"Probably because they were so dramatically different from his own name," the agent suggested. He lifted a little notebook up so he could read from it. "John Smith has served time in South Carolina and Georgia. He's a career thief. And not a particularly good one.

"His last conviction was for scamming an elderly woman out of all of her money," Agent Butler continued. Mitch watched Etah's already pale face go two shades whiter.

"Did she get her money back?" Etah asked in a whisper.

"That I don't know, ma'am. But I know he ended up pleading guilty to get a lighter sentence because the evidence had him dead to rights," he explained. "He was granted a compassionate early release in late 2020, when the courts were trying to clear as many old convicts out of the prisons as possible because of the pandemic."

Everybody nodded in understanding and he continued.

"Smith checked in with his parole officer once, right after he got out. But he never went back again. There should have been warrants out for his arrest – and eventually there were – but he fell off the Georgia Department of Community Supervision's radar about six months after his release. By the time anybody realized it, he'd left the area. And because he was old, and all of his convictions had been for nonviolent crimes, nobody put him on the Most Wanted list. They just hoped he'd never get caught breaking the law again because then they would have to explain how it was that he wasn't in prison."

"Well, we all know how that turned out," Tally joked. Etah cut her eyes at her niece. She wasn't seeing anything humorous about this situation. Tally looked away, chastened.

"We're still investigating all of this, so I expect that we'll learn even more soon, but it seems that your boyfriend," Agent Butler began.

"He's not my boyfriend!" Etah said, a little too loudly.

"My mistake, Ms. Davis. It seems that Mr. Smith was on that cruise when you met him because he needed to get out of Miami quickly and there was a ship leaving the next day," Agent Butler explained.

"Why did he need to get out of Miami?" Tally asked.

"Because the adult children of his latest scam target were on their way to see their mother and meet the man who had convinced her to liquidate her biggest assets. They told their mom they were bringing the police. She told John and he was out of there."

"Oh jeez," Emily groaned. "That's horrible."

"So, he went from fleecing her to using me. That's just lovely," Etah drawled, a disgusted look on her face.

"Don't be so hard on yourself, ma'am," the agent told her, reaching out to pat her hand. "John Smith is a professional scam artist. He's lived his life on the backs of other people. Really, you should be glad that all he did was steal your friend's artwork," he said, gesturing to Emily. "Usually, he takes all of the woman's money and disappears. If he hadn't given himself away by stealing the art, he might have convinced you to let him move in. And then you would have been his next victim."

Etah stood up suddenly. She was shaking. "Tally, may I excuse myself to your bedroom to collect myself?" she asked, always the southern lady.

"Of course," Mitch replied before Tally could answer. He took the elderly woman by the arm and walked her the 15 feet to the door of the master bedroom. "Do you need anything?" he asked.

"Just a moment to find my dignity," Etah whispered and then pulled the door shut.

Everybody at the table was quiet for a moment, but then Emily broke the silence.

"When can I have the pictures back?" she asked.

"I'd imagine it will take a couple of weeks to sort out the paperwork for that. But we really need you to testify at the trials, and so I'm sure we'll be as accommodating as possible about returning your property," Agent Butler explained.

"It usually takes a lot longer than that," Joe commented and Mitch nodded in agreement.

"As long as I get it back eventually, it'll be fine," Emily told them. "But you said trials? Is there more than one person in custody for stealing my dad's art?"

"There are three men in custody right now, and there will probably be more before the day is over," the agent replied. "John Smith was storing everything in a freeport controlled by the other gentleman in the picture with him."

"Freeports are areas, or zones, at every major international port where cargo can be stored for short periods of time without being taxed for

actually entering the country," Joe volunteered. "The stuff in a freeport –
freeports are actually called 'Foreign Trade Zones' - is considered 'in transit'
while it's in that space."

"But freeports are not closely monitored," Mitch jumped in to explain.
"And that's how lots of wealthy people get away with using freeports to
store high-value items like artwork, cars, and other luxury goods to avoid
paying import duties, sales tax, and capital gains. If they made the purchase
as an investment, the owners can leave the items in the freeport for decades,
appreciating in value without having to pay taxes on any of it."

"That sounds shady," Tally said.

"It can be. There's a lot of stolen artwork stored in private freeports all
over the world. Most of it will never be recovered," Agent Butler said. "But
we got lucky this time. John Smith knew he was the smallest fish in this
deal, and he rolled over on the other guys right away. He doesn't want to
go back to prison."

"When we raided the freeport – it took forever to get those search
warrants because of the international implications – we found the Hendrix
artwork, the Chagall stolen from the gallery in Manhattan, and several
other paintings that were on our 'watch' list," Mitch told them.

"They also found a bunch of those glass thingy-dos from here that
hadn't even been reported stolen yet," Joe added, looking smug.

"Glass thingy-dos?" Emily asked, a confused look on her face.

"For the treasure hunt," Joe added.

"Ohhh," Tally sighed. "You found the treasure balls. Oh my God, so
they were stolen after all?" She connected the dots quickly when she remembered all the posts on the residents' Facebook page making fun of the
island's administration for losing the hand-blown glass fishing floats.

"Apparently so," Mitch told her. "We might not have recovered them
if John Smith hadn't specifically mentioned them. He was somehow in-

volved in that heist, too. But we're not sure how yet. He'll probably get immunity from most of the charges because the information he provided resulted in the recovery of so many stolen items."

"That's really burns me," Emily said. "He shouldn't get off scot-free."

"He may not," Agent Butler reassured her. "He'll be off the hook on any charges related to the stolen treasure balls, but that won't save his butt on all the other crimes he's committed. He'll get some consideration for having cooperated but it's likely that he's going to do some time. Just probably not as much as you'd like to see him get."

Emily shrugged. "I'm just glad that I'll get those pictures back. It was the first time I ever loaned them to anybody, and I just felt awful that they'd been lost."

"Does that mean you're not going to let Etah reschedule the pop-up gallery?" Tally asked, only half joking. They'd refunded everybody's ticket money, but Tally had promised that the people who'd bought tickets to the cancelled show would be notified first when tickets were available for the redo.

"Not right away. Maybe eventually. I need to think about it," Emily told her honestly.

"Fair enough," Tally agreed.

"Maybe life will start getting back to normal now," Etah said from the doorway of the bedroom. She rejoined the group at the dining room table, looking better than she had when she left. "What did I miss?"

"We were just talking about all the other artwork that was recovered because of the investigation into the stolen Hendrix stuff," Tally told her, then her eyes lit up. Her aunt was going to love this next bit. "They even found the missing treasure balls."

"You're kidding!" Etah gasped. "So they weren't misplaced after all? They were actually stolen? Fascinating."

"Dougie got back from his cruise a few weeks ago and said the boxes of balls weren't where he'd left them," Mitch updated them. "Lucy has been going crazy making emergency rush orders with every glass artist in their stable. Mark Ellinger had a few balls that he held back to sell at Glass Quest, and he's going to ship those to her, too. But until the hundreds of Ellinger balls were found today, they weren't sure if they were going to have to cancel the treasure hunt."

"Well, that's not right," Etah perked up. "Everybody loves the treasure hunt tradition. And it's a great tourist draw for the hotels in the off season. I'd hate to think that rat I brought to Jekyll was responsible for ruining such a special event."

"End of day, no damage was done, Etah," Joe told the older woman. "The guys who stole the artwork and the treasure balls are in custody – at least some of them – and I'd bet we'll arrest more of them before the investigation is completed."

"We will definitely be making more arrests in connection with this operation," Agent Butler confirmed. "And Mitch will keep you all updated on our progress. We really appreciate all the help you gave us, Ms. Davis. We'd still be looking for the artwork if you hadn't identified John Smith." He looked over at her and smiled. Etah smiled back for the first time that evening.

"Thank you for all that you did for us," she said sincerely.

"It was our pleasure," he assured her.

"You know, Etah, next time you want to date somebody, you should have me and Mitch background check him first," Joe joked.

Etah gave him a dirty look.

"Too soon?" Joe asked with an innocent look.

"Way too soon," Mitch told his partner.

Chapter 59

Mitch and Joe went back to work with Agent Butler after they'd filled the women in on everything. Molly and Moody had behaved amazingly well during the serious conversation, but they went wild once everybody got up from the table.

"I need to get going, too," Emily said as she watched Tally disarm Molly, who was about to whack her brother over the head with toy dump truck. "You certainly have your hands full here, don't you?"

"We sure do," Tally agreed. "I don't know why Etah wants to keep them for me so often," she joked. "If our situation was reversed, I'd be sitting in my condo laughing at the chaos over here."

***

Tally didn't see Mitch again that night. They exchanged a few text messages, and he told her to go to bed without him because he had no idea when he'd be home. She didn't hear him come in shortly after 4 a.m., but she felt it when he snuggled up next to her in bed. When her alarm went off the next morning, she turned it off and rolled over to look at the handsome man sleeping next to her. She reached out and ran her finger down the side of his face, scraping on the rough stubble of his beard, and it woke Mitch up.

"Go back to sleep," Tally whispered, snuggling up tight against him. She decided that she would stay in bed this morning until the twins woke her up. Usually, she tried to get up and have coffee and do something productive before the little Tasmanian devils erupted from their nursery. But there weren't many mornings where she and Mitch found themselves in bed together with nothing urgent pulling them apart. She'd take advantage of the moment.

It really was only a moment before Molly started screaming, "Mommy, Mommy, Mommy" at the top of her lungs. Moody joined in and the racket coming down the hall and through the baby monitor was obnoxious. Mitch opened his eyes and looked at her.

"I know," Tally said, climbing out from underneath the covers. "Do you have an alarm set?"

Mitch grunted something that sounded like "yes."

"Okay good. Go back to sleep. I love you," Tally told him and pulled the door to their bedroom closed behind her.

***

After a breakfast of French toast sticks and strawberry slices, Tally took the twins down to the beach to run off some energy. Mitch had gotten in really late, and she didn't want their toddlers to blow him out of bed before he got some decent rest. Law enforcement was dangerous work and her husband needed to be well-rested to be safe at his job. She knew that he'd get up and help her with the twins if she asked him to, but she wouldn't do that. Her sister-in-law, Robin, had warned her about Mitch's brother, Pete, doing the same thing when their boys were small.

"They love us and they worry about us, and they don't like to see us trying to do everything at home on our own," Robin explained when Tally was pregnant. "But they're already working crazy hours at a dangerous job. Sleep deprivation can kill a cop faster than anything else. So, we can only let them help us with the babies as much as they can contribute without become as exhausted as we are."

"I get it," Tally replied. But she hadn't known what she was claiming to understand at the time. Now, almost two years later, it all made perfect sense. Sure, she was totally wiped out most of the time. But the chances she'd get shot at work were significantly lower than Mitch's. It was more important for him to be well-rested and on top of his game. She had Kelsi and Kayla to get her back at work when things became too overwhelming.

The twins ran and tumbled all over the windy beach. Tally raced around with them and then found a rock to sit on while she watched their antics. When she'd had enough – Molly and Moody would stay on the sand forever if she let them – Tally helped the toddlers back up the wooden staircase over the dune and then followed them on the sandy path back to their house.

She was surprised to see an unfamiliar car parked in the driveway and a woman standing on their front porch holding a big black trash bag. Mitch had gotten up to answer the door, and he stood in the threshold talking to the woman, but he didn't appear to be inviting her inside. He waved to Tally when he saw her.

"I'll be right there," she yelled, and pointed to the children who were already hosing themselves off at the bottom of the staircase up to the waterfront deck. She let them do the job themselves until Molly started tormenting her brother with the hose.

"Okay, that's enough," she said and turned off the water. "Let's go see Daddy."

Molly and Moody beat her to the front door. The woman stood back to let them race past her, and Mitch excused himself to get them settled inside.

"Hi Tally," the woman greeted her when they were alone. "I called you last night."

"Snoopy!" Tally blurted as she realized what was in the bag the woman had set down by the door.

"I'm so sorry about this. I'm truly mortified."

Tally took a step back and assessed the situation. She recognized the woman – she'd met her several times at various island events. She and her husband had lived on Jekyll for as long as Tally could remember, although they didn't run with Etah's social circle.

"Come inside and have some coffee and tell me what happened," Tally said, opening the front door.

The woman reluctantly followed Tally past the sofa where the twins were bouncing while Mitch fought to put cartoons on the TV for them.

"Would you like a coffee? Or maybe sweet tea?" Tally asked the woman. She shook her head no. "You're Ellen, right? We've crossed paths before." She kept a friendly tone but the vibe in the room was seriously awkward.

Mitch had gotten the twins settled and he joined the women in the kitchen.

"Ellen is returning Liz's Ohio State Snoopy," she told her husband. "I assume that's what's in the trash bag on the porch?" The woman nodded. "Ellen called yesterday and said she had it. But with all the other stuff happening, I forgot to tell you."

"How did you get Snoopy?" Mitch asked, his warm smile changing to what Tally called his cop-face. He folded his arms across his chest and looked at the older woman.

"It's so embarrassing. I'm so terribly sorry. It was a mistake."

"How is trespassing on somebody else's property to unplug and remove an inflatable yard ornament a mistake? There's nothing accidental about that," Mitch's voice was stern but not mean.

"I just don't know how it happened," Ellen cried. "I didn't even remember doing it until after I saw Snoopy's picture on a milk carton on Facebook."

Tally and Mitch looked at her but said nothing.

"You see, we had our annual meeting of the Pink Flamingo Universe just down the street, and I think I had too much to drink," the woman looked so flushed that Tally wanted to cut her a break before she keeled over in her kitchen.

"The pink flamingo what?" Mitch asked.

"Universe. It's a lady's club – well, more of a secret society actually – and once a month, we all dress up in flamingo costumes and have a party." It sounded harmless enough.

"Is the club all Jekyll women," Tally asked, amazed by what she was hearing. She knew about Sand Dollar and the Paupers, two members-only clubs that had existed on Jekyll since forever. But she'd never heard of these flamingo ladies.

Ellen ignored the question and continued her story. "I should have stuck to wine – I'm 85 years old and I guess I can't hold my liquor anymore. I didn't drink that much, or at least, I don't remember anything after my second glass of pink punch. That may not have been my last though," she allowed. "It's all a little fuzzy."

"But how did you end up stealing an Ohio State decoration?" Mitch asked. He wasn't as fascinated by the details of the pink flamingo party as his wife was.

"And how did it end up in Atlanta?" Tally asked.

Mitch's head whipped around. "Atlanta?"

"My sister took him home to Atlanta with her," Ellen told him.

"Unbelievable," Mitch said.

"But I still don't understand how you got from a cocktail party to grand theft Snoopy," Tally said. "Why did you take it? You had to know you were stealing." She took a sip from her water bottle.

"Well, it was my night to wear the inflatable flamingo suit," Ellen began but she stopped talking when Tally started choking. She'd just taken another big gulp of water when the image of the woman standing in front of her dressed in a flamingo costume caused her drink to go down the wrong pipe.

Ellen and Mitch waited while Tally coughed. Then she walked to the counter and pulled a paper towel off the roll on the starfish dispenser. She blew her nose and then turned her attention back to their guest.

"Okay, sorry about that. Let's go back to where you were wearing a flamingo costume when this all occurred," Tally tried to say without laughing. She made eye contact with Mitch and then quickly looked away because she wasn't going to be able to control herself.

"It was my turn to wear it," Ellen said again, as if that made an inebriated elderly woman running around in an inflatable bird suit perfectly normal.

"Of course it was," Tally nodded. "But how did Snoopy get involved?"

"I guess my girlfriends and I were on our way home when we saw the Snoopy in the yard. My sister has always been obsessed with Snoopy," she told them. "She stopped the car and told me that my flamingo suit made me the apex predator, and it was my duty to clear all the other animals from the yard. I guess I'd had enough of that magic pink punch to believe her."

"You're kidding," Mitch said.

"I wish I were. But there's video of me, in that stupid inflatable pink costume, circling the Snoopy like I'm about to attack it," she admitted. "No, I won't show it to you. Admitting all of this has been humiliating enough."

Neither Mitch nor Tally said a word. The woman had gotten drunk and committed a crime. It wasn't funny. Or rather, it shouldn't be funny. They should be angry to learn there was a pack of octogenarians dressed as pink flamingos drunk driving around the island in the middle of the night stealing other people's property.

"Well, um, thank you for returning it," Tally tried to keep the laughter out of her voice. "I'll mail it to Liz at home tomorrow – Ohio State is going to the playoffs, of course, and I know she'll want to have it."

"Please don't tell anybody that I was the one who took Snoopy," Ellen begged them. She looked absolutely tragic, her hands clasped in front of her. "Everybody would be furious with me, and I'd have to leave the island because I would never be invited to anything ever again."

"I won't tell anybody," Tally said, feeling very sorry for the woman all of a sudden. Ellen was seriously worried about her reputation on Jekyll Island. As funny as the whole thing was, she wasn't wrong. A lot of the island's residents would judge the hell out of her if they heard what had really happened.

Ellen looked at Mitch to see if he was in agreement with his wife.

"I don't see any reason to publicize your late-night shenanigans and misdemeanors," he told her gently. "But it had better never happen again."

"Oh, it won't," Ellen promised. "Next time it's my turn to wear the inflatable flamingo suit, I just won't drink."

Chapter 60

Kelsi was waiting at the Jacksonville airport to pick up Kayla and Jake. They'd set up a ride through Jekyll Island Errand Girl, but Kelsi called Jamie and cancelled it. She explained that it was Jake's birthday, and she was throwing him a surprise party. And in order to pull it off, she said she had to be the one to pick them up at the airport. Kelsi invited Jamie and her husband, Adam, to the party at Jake and Kayla's house in Brunswick, and they enthusiastically accepted.

The day after Kayla told her about their plan to elope, Kelsi had been really bummed out. She'd been happy when Kayla first confided in her. But when she woke up hungover the next morning and realized that she wouldn't be there to see them get married, she dissolved into tears that lasted, on and off, for most of the day.

Unfortunately, she knew that Jake and Kayla had a super-early flight and so she'd need to get over to their house by noon to let Jake's dog, Howie, outside to pee. Instead of putting a pillow over her head and hiding all day, she pulled up her big girl panties and got her act together. She'd already packed for her stay over at Jake's house. All she really had to do was put on shoes with her pajamas and leave. It wasn't like there was anybody left in town to see her.

Kelsi moved back into her old room at her little brother's house for an extended stay and made herself comfortable. Kayla had left the fridge and freezer well stocked and Kelsi took full advantage. She let herself pout in her pajamas for two more days, and then on the third day, she showered and got things cleaned up.

She had been invited to Christmas dinner at Bonnie's house the next day, and she'd volunteered to bring a dessert. A quick search of Kayla and Jake's pantry told her that she'd need to run to Winn Dixie to grab a few ingredients if she didn't want to bring lime Jello. She threw a load of laundry in the wash after she'd made her grocery list. Then she popped out to the grocery store to get what she needed to make a Hershey bar pie.

Kelsi had expected to feel lonely on Christmas Day, but that was impossible surrounded by the Durham family. She'd been with people she loved all afternoon, and she had a fantastic time. Celebrating the holidays with the twins had made it even better. Something about being around children enjoying the magic of Christmas restored her faith in humanity. And she'd been seriously questioning the world she lived in lately.

She'd stepped outside to talk to Kayla and Jake when they called to wish her a Merry Christmas.

"Guess what, big sis?" Jake teased her.

"What?" Kelsi asked.

"I got married before you did," he told her in that annoying sing-song voice he'd used to aggravate her since they were kids.

"What?" Kelsi acted surprised. Apparently, she and Kayla were going to keep it their own little secret that she knew they were getting married.

"Kayla and I got married on a beach in Puerto Rico a couple of days ago. Don't be mad – I wouldn't let her tell you. She was just so stressed out about the whole planning thing – mostly how to find two weeks she could take off from work – we decided that this was a much better idea for everybody. We really wanted to get married. If we'd done the whole big church thing, it would have meant waiting at least another year to do the deed." Jake was talking fast, like he wanted to tell her all the reasons for what he'd done before she could challenge him.

"It's okay, I'm happy for you," she told him and meant it. "We'll have a party to celebrate it later. Right now, just have fun with your new bride. This is technically your honeymoon, right?"

"We are staying with her parents right now," he laughed. "I think we can get away with calling this a family vacation and still plan a real honeymoon later on. I mean I like her family, but I don't want to bring them on my honeymoon."

"Fair point," Kelsi agreed.

He passed the phone to Kayla, who pretended that Kelsi was surprised by the news and apologized for leaving her out.

"No apologies for getting married," Kelsi told her. "But I'm holding you to that promise that you'll let me plan your reception."

"I won't forget," Kayla swore.

Kelsi said goodbye to her new sister-in-law and went back inside the house, where everybody asked about Kayla and her brother. She was about to tell them the good news when she had a better idea. Without giving it a second thought, and before she could change her mind, Kelsi invited everybody to a surprise birthday party for Jake on the night he and Kayla returned from their trip. It wasn't Jake's birthday but that was okay. Everybody would be blown away when they learned the real reason they'd been summoned for a celebration.

***

"You really didn't need to come pick us up," Kayla told Kelsi for the umpteenth time since she'd surprised them in the pick-up line at arrivals.

"Stop saying that – I wanted to. I missed you both. You're not allowed to go away without me for so long again. It knocked my chakras out of whack of something," Kelsi said.

Kayla rolled her eyes. "Your chakras?" she laughed and didn't wait for a response. "Tell us everything that has happened since we left."

"There's been all kinds of crazy going on," Kelsi said. "I guess the most important news is that they found the Hendrix artwork that was stolen."

"That's amazing. Did they find Beau?"

"Beau is actually John Smith, a career criminal who took the cruise where he met Etah to escape the wrath of the adult children of an elderly woman he'd just scammed," Kelsi reported dramatically.

"No!" Kayla cried.

"Wow," Jake said.

"And when they found the stolen Hendrix pictures, they also found some other stolen artwork, including that famous piece Mitch went up to New York City about," Kelsi told them. "And guess what else they found hidden in that warehouse."

"What?" Kayla asked.

"All the treasure balls that JIA has been trying to track down in their storage units for the past month."

"You're kidding! They'd been stolen?" Kayla was getting confused.

"Yep, by somebody in the same art theft ring as Beau, er, I mean John Smith. They were just sitting there on a shelf in the warehouse where they found all the other stuff," Kelsi explained.

"You did have an exciting holiday," Kayla said with a chuckle.

"But wait, there's more," Kelsi announced, like a late-night infomercial host.

"What?" Kayla wanted to know. Her eyes were wide.

"Snoopy came home," Kelsi announced.

"Who?" Jake was totally confused.

"No way. Where was he? Who took him?" Kayla asked.

"Tally won't tell anybody who the actual thief was – she says it's a nice lady who made a mistake and she's mortified," Kelsi said. "All I know is that she was dressed up in a pink flamingo costume and pretending to be an apex predator with Snoopy as her prey."

"She was what?" Kayla was sure she'd misheard.

"Did you know there's a secret society of old ladies on Jekyll who dress up like flamingos and get up to drunken shenanigans? I kind of admire that. I mean I know how upset Liz was, so it's absolutely not okay. But where else in the world would you find a secret flamingo club but Jekyll Island," Kelsi mused.

"Is it like the other clubs on Jekyll where somebody has to die for a new member to be accepted?" Kayla asked.

"I have no idea. But I can tell you for sure, right now, I'm not joining even if I get an invitation," Kelsi declared.

They pulled into the crushed oyster shell parking lot next to the entrance of Jake's veterinary clinic and the vibe in the SUV changed instantly.

"Whose cars are these?" Jake asked.

"Kelsi, what's going on?" Kayla asked, sounding very nervous.

"Remember how you told me that I could plan your wedding reception when you got back?"

"Yes," Kayla shut her eyes. She knew what was coming.

"Well, I didn't want to steal your thunder and tell everybody that you guys got married. So instead, I invited all of your favorite people over for Jake's surprise birthday party. We'll tell them it's actually your wedding reception when you get inside."

"Please tell me you're kidding," Kayla said, but she knew it was pointless. She'd told Kelsi she could plan a party for them after they got back. They were back. She needed to remember to be more specific with her sister-in-law in the future.

***

"This is pretty incredible," Kayla admitted to Tally an hour later, after everybody had been surprised by their news. And literally everybody that she and Jake knew in Glynn County was there.

"Kayla honey," Rozell tugged her arm to get her attention. "Where's the white sundress I sold you that I'm pretty sure was your wedding gown?"

"Oops, busted," Kayla admitted. "I did wear it for our wedding. And it's in the hanging bag that's still out in the car."

"Blu," Rozell turned to her husband. "Will you run out to Kelsi's SUV and bring in the hanging bag that's in the back for me, sweetheart?"

"Sure thing," he said with a smile and disappeared from the room.

"I want you to go put on your dress," Rozell told Kayla.

"No, I'll look silly," Kayla protested. She felt a flush creeping up her neck.

"You'll look like a bride, which is what you are. I love you too much to let everybody keep taking wedding pictures of you in your traveling clothes,"

Rozell said, gesturing to the black leggings and Walleye Weekend sweatshirt that Kayla had flown home in.

Blu brought the garment bag in, and Rozell grabbed it and dragged it and Kayla into another room. Before Kayla could protest, she'd opened the bag and fished out the white sundress.

"Good girl," Rozell said when she held it up to the light. "No stains or spots. I bet it won't look this good in a few hours."

Kayla laughed at her friend. "You win. Give me the dress."

***

The celebration lasted until late into the night. Tally and Mitch were two of the last guests to leave. The twins were spending the night at Mitch's parents' house, so they didn't have a curfew for a change.

Tally wandered out onto the back deck looking for Kelsi and Kayla to say goodbye and found them sitting in lounge chairs by the pool.

"Mitch and I are about to leave," she told them. "We had a really great time – Kelsi, I cannot believe you lied to all of us about a birthday party when you really had this all up your sleeve. And you didn't even ask any of us for help! You're fantastic."

Kelsi blushed. "I'm glad you had a good time."

"Kayla, I have something for you. It's not a wedding gift – it was supposed to be a surprise when we all got back to the office. But I have a feeling that tonight is the perfect night to tell you the news, and let Kelsi in on our little secret," Tally said. She looked at Kelsi. "I hear you're good at keeping secrets."

"She made me!" Kelsi protested.

"Whatever," Tally said and rolled her eyes.

"What's the surprise, Tally?" Kayla tried to get them back on track.

"I signed a lease on an office building on St. Simons Island yesterday," Tally told them. "It's occupied right now, and it's not going to be available for us to move in until May. The current lease is up on April 30. But we're official." She paused to give Kayla a chance to react but the woman in front of her was speechless. So, she continued.

"I even went over to the Superior Court and filed the DBA paperwork for St. Simons Weddings so you can start advertising and marketing to those clients immediately," she told them proudly. They understood her point. Tally hated to deal with business paperwork.

"Let's keep this to ourselves right now, until after everybody is settled back into the groove. We need to make offers to the interns so we know how many more weddings we can handle come summer. Jekyll Weddings already has a packed schedule, and you'll all be covering it through May. But if everything goes off the way I'm planning it, you and your team will be running a new branch of this company on another island by spring."

Epilogue

Memorial Day Weekend

Kayla and Kelsi stood across the street, watching as Mitch and Jake attempted to hang the new sign above the office door. They were both up on ladders, and Tally stood beneath them giving instructions.

The office space Tally rented for St. Simons Weddings was in a building three blocks from the pier and the major tourist shopping area on the island. The building had signage requirements, so Tally had ordered the sign several months ahead of time. They wouldn't be allowed to open their doors without it, per her rental agreement.

It had been a close call – the sign finally arrived that morning and their opening reception began at 5 p.m. Kayla had hand-delivered some invitations, but the event was open to anybody who wanted to stop in, and Tally had been advertising the "Open House" all over social media for the last three weeks.

When the sign was up, they took pictures underneath it to memorialize the moment. And then Tally posted them on a bunch of social media platforms with a reminder about the opening that night.

Mitch and Jake cleaned up the packaging from the sign and put the ladders away while Tally, Kayla, and Kelsi rejoined the girls in the office. Liz, Katy, and Tori were sitting at a table stuffing swag bags to give to the people who stopped in to check out the new operation. Kayla stopped to watch them and smiled. They weren't interns anymore.

Liz and Tori had helped Katy move into the little apartment above the new office a few days earlier. Long-term rentals on St. Simons weren't cheap, and a compensation package that included housing was a real incentive for the New Yorker to stay in the Golden Isles after her internship was completed. Liz and Tori had accepted the offers Tally gave them to stay on Jekyll Island as full-time wedding planners. Their package didn't include housing because Kelsi needed the space in the cottage for three new interns who would be joining the team to replace Katy, Liz, and Tori.

Aunt Etah had been called into action, once again, to help find housing for the new wedding planners, and she didn't disappoint. She'd found them a housesitting gig for a friend who was going to be in Europe for a year, and who would prefer not to leave her house empty or rented out to strangers.

By the time Etah got off the phone, she'd negotiated a fantastic deal for Liz and Tori. The girls would pay the electric and water bills while they lived there and keep up with regular house maintenance. They also had to gather up the homeowner's mail once a month and put it in a pre-addressed package to drop at the post office. In exchange, they would live rent-free for a year in a beautiful three-bedroom ranch-style home on the south end of the island, walking distance from St. Andrews Beach.

"What's left to do?" Tally asked Kayla from the doorway.

Kayla picked up her clipboard and started to check her list when a thumping sound at the door distracted everyone. Tally pulled the door open and found Etah juggling a big construction-sized cooler.

"Oh, good Lord," Tally cried as she reached to take the heavy jug out of her great-aunt's hands. "Etah, don't carry things like this. Just text me from the car when you arrive. I'd rather come carry things in for you than have to take care of you after you break a hip."

Etah straightened her jacket and gave Tally a chastened smile. "I'll admit it wasn't my best decision. But I think I would have been fine if I'd just worn flats today."

"Uh huh," Tally resisted the urge to argue. They were setting up a party and nagging the woman who'd raised her in front of her entire team wasn't the best way to set the vibe. She decided to let it go.

Her aunt had struggled to hold her head up in the community for a few months in the wake of the scandal that surrounded John Smith, the gentleman formerly known as Beauregard Morris or Archibald Murdaugh. *The Brunswick News* wrote a lengthy article on it, and published several follow up stories, that made it clear neither of the Davis women on Jekyll Island had anything to do with the criminal enterprise that had been exposed. But neighbors were still gossiping about it in late January, and Jekyll Weddings hadn't had any new client consultation requests from the local area lately.

So, Tally came up with a plan to publicly restore both her company's reputation and Aunt Etah's dignity. She convinced Emily to loan them her father's pictures for a one-night-only showing at Goodyear Cottage on Valentine's Day weekend.

"I promise Mitch won't let them out of his sight," Tally told Emily. "He'll be the one who picks them up from your house, and he'll personally return them afterwards, unless you want us to just load them straight into your car when it's over." Emily and her daughter, Jenna, were planning to attend the second attempt at a pop-up gallery.

Jekyll Weddings gave free tickets to the show to everybody who had been refunded for the Black Friday event. They also set up ticket sales for others who had heard about the art heist and now wanted to see what all the hoopla was about. Tally wrote a check to cover the donation for the initial tickets and combined with the funds raised for the second ticket sale, they were able to launch an art scholarship in Bill Hendrix's name.

After that, Etah had slowly returned to her normal social activities with her head held high, and she'd also thrown herself into helping Kayla get the new office space ready. The conference table they were going to use to meet with clients was the kitchen table Etah had bought for her new condo and never liked. Giving it to the girls for the office gave her an excuse to get something she had her eye on for her kitchen.

"We're setting up the bar out on the back patio. Why don't you let us take everything out there and you can arrange it for service," she suggested.

"I'll help you take stuff out," Kelsi said and began loading up a basket with cocktail napkins, cups, and other things that were stacked on another table. "We already put up the table, but the linens are sitting on top of it. We should put those on the tables now and get started."

"Where do you want us to put the swag bags?" Katy asked, holding one of the bags they'd ordered especially for the occasion in the air. A wedding gown was on one side of the bag, and a tuxedo on the other. They used pink tissue paper and stuffed the bags with a brochure about St. Simons Weddings, a free-delivery coupon for Jekyll Flowers, and a bunch of tchotchkes printed with both the St. Simons Weddings and Jekyll Weddings logos.

Kayla and Katy had chosen all the items they'd had printed with the logos, and everybody thought the stress ball, pens, and sticky notepads turned out great. But the pièces de résistance were the bride and groom rubber duckies with the wedding companies' names printed on them. Tally had asked them to order an extra 150 duckies so they could give them to potential clients.

"They're so much more fun than a pen and planning notebook," Tally said. "We should sell them in the shop, too. I bet a lot of our clients would get a kick out customized wedding duckies for welcome bags or reception favors."

"Totally," Kelsi agreed. "I might do those for my wedding if I ever find a groom." She made the remark in a joking tone, but the problem was real. She hadn't dated anyone since that sleazeball totally bamboozled her a year ago. The trust issues she felt were keeping her from checking out dating apps, and there were no eligible bachelors under the age of 75 on Jekyll Island.

"Does anybody want a Jekyll Julep?" Etah called from the doorway, where she held two paper cups printed with both wedding company logos.

"Aren't we calling them St. Simons Juleps tonight?" Katy asked.

"Absolutely not! That's blasphemy," Etah looked at the young wedding planner with a shocked and horrified face. "One does not just rename the Jekyll Julep because it's more geographically convenient," she announced like she was teaching an etiquette class.

"Don't get your back up, Aunt Etah. You're right. We can't call your fantastic Jekyll Juleps – famous for tasting just as good warm or over ice – St. Simons Juleps," Tally agreed. "That would just be wrong." She pulled out a cute plastic stand-up sign that she'd made for the beverage table. It read "Jekyll Juleps" and had a pretty map of Jekyll Island under the name.

"However," Tally continued dramatically, "we can certainly call the *boring* virgin version of your drink a St. Simons Julep, can't we?" Tally continued, chuckling. "Everybody knows that Jekyll Island is better," she said, looking at Kayla, daring her to disagree.

Kayla just laughed. "Oh Tally, are we starting this already? We aren't going to make t-shirts that say, 'My island is better than your island,' are we?"

"Maybe," Tally laughed. Then she reached into a box on the table and pulled out another sign. She set it in front of her aunt.

It read "St. Simons Juleps" and featured a map of that island under the name. But the graphics were smaller and not nearly as interesting as the elaborate signage for the Jekyll Juleps with Fireball in them. Everybody started laughing.

"So, this is how it's going to be," Kayla asked, looking from Tally to Kelsi. All she could do was shake her head. It was funny that, even within their own team, the rivalry between St. Simons and Jekyll would ruffle some feathers. It wasn't quite at the level of the Ohio State vs. Xichigan rivalry she'd lived through last fall, when Jake crossed out every "M" in their home with red tape for a week before what turned out to be a tragic game. But it would be ignorant to pretend the rivalry between St. Simons and Jekyll didn't exist. Even in their office, apparently.

"Oh Kayla, don't pay any attention to us," Kelsi said, throwing an arm around her sister-in-law. "We're just giving you a hard time. It's got to be difficult to know that no matter how successful you are over here, we'll always be the original over there." Her tone was sweet and she was smiling, but the message was definitely snarky.

"Out with the old, and in with the new," Kayla shot back with a grin. "At least I won't have to explain which island when I refer to 'the island' with my clients." That was a low blow because it annoyed everybody on Jekyll when folks from SSI referred to "the island" as if everybody should know they meant St. Simons.

"Ouch," Tally said, stepping in to redirect everybody. "Careful how snarky you get with each other, all of you," she directed her comment to all of the women in the room. "We're still all one company, just working in different divisions. And everybody, except me, is probably going to spend half their lives going back and forth on the Sidney Lanier Bridge for the first year of this transition. We're still a team."

"Oh absolutely," Kayla replied, nodding in agreement.

"We're an excellent team," Kelsi added. Liz, Katy, and Tori were nodding too, but wisely held their tongues.

"Exactly, that's what I'm saying," Tally said with a sly smile, looking at Kelsi. "We shouldn't be arguing amongst ourselves anyway, because we all know that Jekyll Island is the best."

Aunt Etah's Recipe for Jekyll Juleps

Ingredients:

4 oz muscadine grape cider

1 1/2 oz of Fireball

1/2 oz fresh lemon juice

1/4 oz honey or spiced simple syrup

Dash of orange bitters (optional)

Splash of ginger beer or sparkling wine (optional)

Combine all of the ingredients, except the Fireball, in a pot on the stove over a medium heat. Stir until fully mixed. Lower the heat to simmer, add the desired amount of Fireball and stir for another minute. Serve warm or over ice. Garnish with cinnamon sticks or candy canes.

Acknowledgements

Thank you to Kayla Seeger Blunk, Kelsi Welch, and Kate Boyer, my editing team. You ladies are all amazing and your expertise in weddings and/or law enforcement has kept me from embarrassing myself more than once. I couldn't have published *Christmas on Jekyll* this year without you.

Thank you to talented local photographer Carol Ann Wages, who kindly allowed me to use one of her beautiful pictures as the cover of *Christmas on Jekyll*. Not only is she an award-winning, talented photographer, she is also the only woman I know who is on a first-name basis with every alligator on the island.

About the Author

Author Sandy Malone is best known for starring in TLC's reality TV show "Wedding Island" and writing hundreds of wedding advice columns that were published in BRIDES, WeddingWire, and HuffPost. She wrote a DIY wedding planning book in 2016 that was traditionally published, and she released her new fiction series - Gem of the Golden Isles - in April 2024. She has also ghostwritten books for well-known reality TV stars (including a Real Housewife). Most recently, she was editor of The Police Tribune.

Sandy got her journalism degree at The Ohio State University and was a reporter and editor for major news publications before she returned to her hometown of Washington, DC, for a career in public relations and government affairs. She began planning destination weddings professionally after her own was nearly a disaster, and ended up planning more than 500 weddings in the Caribbean in 11 years with her retired SWAT-commander husband.

Sandy and her husband, Bill, live on Jekyll Island, Georgia, with their coonhound Sherlock. *Christmas on Jekyll* is the fifth book in her Gem of the Golden Isles series. Learn more about her at www.SandyMalone.com.

Also by Sandy Malone

Escape to Jekyll Island – Gem of the Golden Isles Series Book One
Twenty-nine-year-old destination wedding planner Tally Davis lost her home, her job, and her boyfriend in one fell swoop when Hurricane Maria hit Vieques Island, Puerto Rico. After she's finally evacuated, she goes home to Jekyll Island, Georgia, to start over. There's no wedding planning company on the island, so Tally launches Jekyll Weddings. But not everyone is happy that Tally is home or wants her to succeed. She's unknowingly kicked a hornet's nest by reconnecting with a childhood friend. Will a 10-year-old grudge ruin her first big wedding on Jekyll Island?

In Bloom on Jekyll – Gem of the Golden Isles Series Book Two
Tally Davis reinvented herself after a hurricane left her homeless and jobless in Puerto Rico, and now she has survived her first year in the wedding planning on Jekyll Island. Bonus - she's in love with a hot state trooper she's known since childhood. She's ready to grow her business by opening a flower shop in Georgia when a former client turns up with an outrageous demand. Will Tally figure out how to rise above the chaos or will her past burn her future to the ground?

Treasure on Jekyll – Gem of the Golden Isles Series Book Three
*Winner of a 2025 International Impact Book Award for Women's Fiction
– Mystery/Suspense*
Tally Davis is struggling to act like a bride and plan her own wedding to her childhood crush while her event planning and floral company is going gangbusters on Jekyll Island, Georgia. She takes her state trooper fiance back to Vieques Island with her on an errand and opens a Pandora's box while they're there. Will her past in Puerto Rico ruin her future on another island, or will Tally live happily ever after with Mitch?

In the Shadows on Jekyll – Gem of the Golden Isles Series Book Four
Tally Davis is a victim of her own success. Her wedding and flower businesses on Jekyll Island are going gangbusters when she's doubly-blessed with motherhood. But she can't keep so many balls in the air for her clients without more help. The only solution is to hire and train more staff to help manage her brides and grooms. But Tally doesn't have the same kind of time to train and get to know the new staff the way that she did with Kayla. And as her team grows, so do her problems.
Not everyone is who they appear to be when she hired them – some just wanted unfettered access to Jekyll Island. Tally's starting to think she has a black cloud following her. Will her state trooper husband be able to save the day again?

How To Plan Your Own Destination Wedding: Do-It-Yourself Tips From An Experienced Professional, Skyhorse Publishing 2016
Ten years ago, when Sandy was planning her own destination wedding in the Caribbean, she learned everything the hard way. After 11 years in business and more than 500 successfully executed weddings, she wrote

a DIY guide that any wedding couple can follow to create a fabulous
destination wedding for themselves anywhere.

Coming Soon!!!

Sandy Malone's new *Under the Oaks on St. Simons* series, featuring some
of the same characters you fell in love with on Jekyll Island, is already in
the works and expected to be released in 2026.

Check out Sandy's blog and sign up for her newsletter to find out about
upcoming novels and book signings.

www.SandyMalone.com